John D. MacDonald and The Murder Room

>>> This title is part of The Murder Room, our series dedicated to making available out-of-print or hard-to-find titles by classic crime writers.

Crime fiction has always held up a mirror to society. The Victorians were fascinated by sensational murder and the emerging science of detection; now we are obsessed with the forensic detail of violent death. And no other genre has so captivated and enthralled readers.

Vast troves of classic crime writing have for a long time been unavailable to all but the most dedicated frequenters of second-hand bookshops. The advent of digital publishing means that we are now able to bring you the backlists of a huge range of titles by classic and contemporary crime writers, some of which have been out of print for decades.

From the genteel amateur private eyes of the Golden Age and the femmes fatales of pulp fiction, to the morally ambiguous hard-boiled detectives of mid twentieth-century America and their descendants who walk our twenty-first century streets, The Murder Room has it all. >>>

The Murder Room
Where Criminal Minds Meet

themurderroom.com

John D. MacDonald (1916–1986)

John D. MacDonald was born in Pennsylvania and married Dorothy Prentiss in 1937, graduating from Syracuse University the following year and receiving an MBA from Harvard in 1939. It was Dorothy who was responsible for the publication of his first work, when she submitted a short story that he had sent home while on military service. It was initially rejected by *Esquire* but went on to be published by *Story* magazine – and so began MacDonald's writing career. One of the best-loved and most successful of all the masters of hard-boiled crime and suspense, John D. Macdonald was producing brilliant fiction long after many of his contemporaries had been forgotten, and is still highly regarded today. *The Executioners*, possibly the best known of his non-series novels, was filmed as *Cape Fear* in 1962 and 1991, but many of the crime thrillers he produced between 1953 and 1964 are considered masterpieces, and he drew praise from such literary luminaries as Kurt Vonnegut and Stephen King, who declared him to be '*the* great entertainer of our age, and a mesmerizing storyteller'. His novels are often set in his adopted home of Florida, including those featuring his famous series character Travis McGee, which appeared between 1964 and 1985. He served as president of the Mystery Writers of America and in 1972 was elected a Grand Master, an honour granted only to the greatest crime writers of their generation, including Ross MacDonald, John Le Carré and P. D. James. He won many awards throughout his long career, and was the only mystery writer ever to win the National Book Award, for *The Green Ripper*.

By John D. MacDonald
(published in The Murder Room)

The Brass Cupcake (1950)
Murder for the Bride (1951)
The Neon Jungle (1953)
Cancel All Our Vows (1953)
Area of Suspicion (1954)
Contrary Pleasure (1954)
A Bullet for Cinderella (1955)
    (aka On the Make)
Cry Hard, Cry Fast (1956)
April Evil (1956)
Border Town Girl (1956)
    (aka Five Star Fugitive)
Hurricane (1956)
    (aka Murder in the Wind)
You Live Once (1956)
    (aka You Kill Me)
Death Trap (1957)
The Price of Murder (1957)
A Man of Affairs (1957)
The Deceivers (1958)
Soft Touch (1958)
Deadly Welcome (1959)
The Beach Girls (1959)
Please Write for Details
    (1959)

The Crossroads (1959)
Slam the Big Door (1960)
The Only Girl in the Game
    (1960)
The End of the Night (1960)
Where is Janice Gantry? (1961)
One Monday We Killed Them
    All (1961)
A Key to the Suite (1962)
A Flash of Green (1962)
I Could Go On Singing
    (screenplay novelisation)
    (1963)
On the Run (1963)
The Drowner (1963)
The Last One Left (1966)
No Deadly Drug (1968)
One More Sunday (1984)
Barrier Island (1986)

Collections

The Good Old Stuff (1961)
Seven (1971)
More Good Old Stuff (1984)

Hurricane

John D. MacDonald

An Orion book

Copyright © Maynard MacDonald 1956

The right of John D. MacDonald to be identified as the author of this work has been asserted in accordance with the Copyright, Designs and Patents Act 1988.

This edition published by
The Orion Publishing Group Ltd
Orion House
5 Upper St Martin's Lane
London WC2H 9EA

An Hachette UK company
A CIP catalogue record for this book is available from the British Library

ISBN 978 1 4719 1140 8

www.orionbooks.co.uk

AUTHOR'S NOTE

Certain minor liberties have been taken with the geography of the Florida West Coast. There is a Waccasassa River and a bridge over it on Route 19. However, there is no bypass road nor wooden bridges. And, of course, the old house does not exist.

To anyone who might be skeptical of the possibility of Route 19 being inundated during a hurricane, it can be pointed out that this highway was under water in the vicinity of Yankeetown and Withlacoochee Bay during the 1950 hurricane known in the area as the Cedar Key Hurricane. Residents of Yankeetown were evacuated because of fear that the Florida Power and Light Company dam might burst. By the time it became apparent that it would have been a far better idea to evacuate the residents of Cedar Key, Route 24 was under water and impassable.

Though the chance is statistically remote, there need only be the unfortunate conjunction of hurricane path and high Gulf tide to create coastal death and damage surpassing the fictional account in this book.

1

Except for a slow oily swell, the Caribbean Sea was flat and quiet and eerily still on the morning of Sunday, October fourth. Sarrensen, Captain of the Swedish motor vessel *Altagarde*, had a late solitary breakfast in his cabin. He had slept poorly and his digestion, never reliable, was bothering more than usual on this trip.

He was a small quiet remote man with a soured expression and a reputation for reliability. It was after nine when he climbed to the bridge, nodded to the Third, checked the log and the heading, and walked out onto the port wing of the bridge. He put short blunt fingers inside his belt and pressed against the area of a stomach cramp and looked at the sea world around him. He did not like the look of the day. The sky, though cloudless, was too pale. The sun was fierce and white. The flat sea had the look of a blue mirror on which warm breath has been blown, misting it. It was impossible to see where the sea ended and the sky began.

The immediate destination of the *Altagarde* was Havana, about five hundred nautical miles away. He looked at his gold watch and looked at the sky and estimated their time of arrival at nine on Monday evening. But he did not like the look of the day.

He walked in and stood by the Third and looked at the barometer. Low. Not dangerously low, but significantly low.

"Still slipping," he said.

"Not much. It's pretty steady. Been about where it is since six. I told Sparks to pick up all the weather he can."

"Good."

Sarrensen walked out onto the starboard wing. He leaned his arms on the rail and gave a small grunt of pain at an especially sharp stomach twinge. There was no sense of motion in the *Altagarde*. It moved smoothly across the featureless sea, rocking but slightly to the long slow swells. The wake was a ruled line behind her. Through the soles of his shoes, and in the tremor of the rail, Sarrensen felt the deep

1

and comforting *cha-gah, cha-gah, cha-gah* of the turning shaft.

He took out his watch and timed the swells. Somewhere between five and six a minute. In these tropical waters the norm was eight. A hurricane reduces the incidence of the swells, and sends them radiating out in all directions from the center of the storm, moving sometimes as fast as eighty miles an hour, moving far ahead of the storm, carrying a sure warning to primitive peoples of the islands. He carefully noted the direction from which the swells were coming in relation to the compass direction of the ship. Then he went below.

At three o'clock in the afternoon on Sunday, October fourth, the wind began. It came out of the east. It was a fitful, elusive, teasing wind. It riffled the misted blue of the sea. Infrequent gusts, almost as sturdy as a squall, pressed against the steel flank of the *Altagarde,* and she would roll in response. Sarrensen went out onto the starboard wing. Streamers of high cirrus cloud radiated from a point on the southeast horizon. Sarrensen faced directly into the wind. It was a rule of thumb, as old as the half-rule of man over the sea, that in the counter-clockwise winds of hurricanes in the northern hemisphere, when you face into the wind your right hand points at the storm center. It gave new confirmation of the direction the swells had told him. It was far from him, behind him. Knowing the location of it stilled some of the uneasiness he had felt all day.

The *Altagarde* radioed her position and reported the estimated position of a tropical disturbance. The report was relayed to Miami where it became a partial confirmation of previous reports. At the time the report was received the tropical disturbance was termed an area of suspicion. By five-twenty on Monday evening the first search aircraft entered the area and radioed back sufficient information so that by the time of the six o'clock news broadcasts the disturbance had been dignified by awarding it the name of Hilda. It was the eighth storm of the season.

But it did not begin, as though on signal, with the designation of a name. It began earlier, and in a timeless way. Flat sea baking under a tropic sun. Water temperature raised by the long summer. The still air, heated by sun and sea, rising endlessly, creating an area of low pressure to be filled by air moving in from all sides to rise in turn.

But these factors alone could not create *hurakan*. There must be added the thousand miles an hour spinning of the earth itself. The warm currents rose high, and there was the effect of drag, the way a speeding car can raise dust devils along the dry shoulder of a highway. The spin began slowly at first, very slowly. At times it died out and then began again. It covered a great area, and the winds spun slowly at the rim of the wheel, but more quickly toward the hub. It gathered momentum. It began to gain in force and speed and it seemed to feed upon itself, to gain greater life force as it began to move slowly from the area where it began, began to move in the long curved path that would carry it in a northwesterly direction until, on some unknown day in the future it would at last die completely away.

As it moved it pushed the hot moist air ahead of it, and the moisture of that air, cooled by height, fell as heavy drenching rain.

Man spoke across the empty air above the sea. The location, direction, velocity were charted. Man warned man. Prepare for this violence that is now aimed at you.

But the other living creatures were warned in other ways. They were affected by the barometric changes. Birds turned away from the path of the storm. On small keys legions of fiddler crabs marched inland, ponderous claws raised. The fish ceased feeding and moved at lower levels.

By eight o'clock on Monday night the wind velocities near the center of the disturbance were measured at eighty miles an hour. The hurricane had begun its lateral movement. At from fifteen to eighteen miles an hour it moved north-north-west toward the long island of Cuba. It was carefully watched and plotted.

In Miami, a city wise in the ways of hurricanes, sucker disks were fastened to the big shopwindows and thumb screws tightened the disks to rigid metal uprights that would keep the windows from picking up the vibration that would shatter them. Men climbed on roofs and put additional guy wires on television aerials. The sale of radio batteries was brisk. Drinking water was stored. Gasoline stoves were taken out of storage. There was a flavor of excitement in the city, even of amiability, as man accepted this immediate and understandable tension in fair exchange for the tiresome tensions of his everyday life.

3

2

At some time during the middle of Tuesday, October sixth, Hilda changed direction. She picked up her great gray skirts and moved west. Ten billion tons of warm rain had fallen heavily on Cuba and, at two in the afternoon, the gusts which struck Havana reached a measured peak of fifty miles an hour. They began to fade in intensity and the rain stopped.

Key West got the rain too. And winds no more serious. Hilda skirted them and moved on into the Gulf of Mexico. Precautions were relaxed in Miami. The cities of the Florida West Coast began to prepare as Miami had prepared.

By midnight the sky over Cuba was still and the stars were clear and bright. It was then that the sky over Key West began to clear. In Naples it was raining torrents. And in Fort Myers. The rain had just begun in Boca Grande. The rain did not begin in Clearwater until three in the morning....

Jean Dorn had been awakened by the rain at three o'clock. When the alarm awakened her again at seven it was still raining. She turned off the alarm before it awakened Hal. He should get as much sleep as possible. He would be driving all day. She pushed the single sheet back and got quietly out of bed, a tall blond woman with a sturdy body, which was just beginning to show the heaviness of pregnancy. Before she went to the bathroom she looked in at the children. Five-year-old Stevie slept on his back, arms outflung. Three-year-old Jan, still in a crib, slept curled in a warm ball. In the gray light of the drab morning both children looked very brown from the long summer of the Gulf beaches.

They were healthy little animals, full of energy. Three days in the car was going to be very wearing indeed. She decided to wake them at the last possible moment.

Jean walked from the children's room to the living room.

Rain was drenching the patio, a hard thick rain that looked as though it would never end. She looked at the room she had loved, at the furniture so carefully selected, and she felt a grayness in her heart that matched the rain. Now there was nothing personal left in the room. They had disposed of some things. They had packed the things they couldn't bear to part with. The rest went with the house. Cold phrase. It goes with the house. *And my heart goes with the house,* she thought.

If they had only known. If they had only been just a little wiser. Bought a less pretentious place. Then they might have been able to stay longer, might have been able to hang on until the turning point came and they would be able to stay on in this place they both loved.

Defeat was a very bitter thing. They had never suspected that it would happen to them. They were the golden ones. The undefeated. Accustomed to the warm bright smile of good fortune.

Two years ago Hal Dorn had been an Intermediate Consultant with Jason and Rawls, Industrial Engineers, in New York. He was well-paid, well-thought-of. They had been married six years and, after Stevie was born, they moved out of their uptown apartment to a small house in Pleasantville. They had met in college, and theirs was a good marriage. Hal, dark, lean-faced, tense, was a perfect foil for her blond calm, her sense of fun.

Though Hal often complained that his work was a rat race, Jean knew that he enjoyed responding to the challenge of it. The future seemed certain. Were Hal to stay with Jason and Rawls he would become a Senior Consultant, and perhaps later a junior partner.

Change began two years ago in a doctor's office. Stevie's attack of asthma had been so bad this time that she had been in panic. She could remember the doctor's words. "I don't think we're going to be able to do much good with medication with Stevie. He may eventually grow out of it. What he really needs is a different climate. A warmer place. These winters are criminal. But I guess it would be impossible for you people to pull up stakes and get out."

At first it had seemed impossible. But it was Hal who said, "Good Lord, Jean, it's just a job. It isn't a dedication. Suppose I have to start something new. I'm thirty-one. And how in hell could we ever forgive ourselves if . . ." He did not have to finish the sentence.

It had taken a lot of thought and a lot of planning. They got less for the Pleasantville house than they had hoped. It had been sold furnished. It was Hal who had seen the opportunities on the Florida West Coast. The firm had been sorry to lose him, but Mr. Rawls had been very understanding when they told him about Stevie.

They had sold themselves the idea of change, and they had begun this new life with optimism and excitement. Hal had specialized in accounting procedures, and so, in downtown Clearwater he had opened a small office. Harold Dorn, Consultant. Jean had found the house for them. A little more than they had expected to pay. A nice home in Belleaire in a neighborhood where there were other small children.

They had been so certain that they could make it, that they would never fail. Hal, with all his tireless energy, could not be defeated. But he had been. Soundly whipped. He had picked up some small accounts. Some bars, a few neighborhood stores, a small boat company. But not enough. He had given up the office to cut expenses. He worked at home. It did not help enough. She cut every possible penny from their expenses, but it was not enough. The meager reserve dwindled as their fear grew. There was no one to turn to, no one in all the world.

And she had to watch Hal tearing himself apart. That was perhaps the worst part. He found a full-time job in a warehouse and he would work on his accounts at night, often falling asleep at his desk. He became thinner and more silent and he became irritable with the children.

A month ago they came to the end of the line. Hal said, "We can't do it. We can't make it. We're licked. We've got to go back while we can still afford to go back, or I don't know what's going to become of us. We've got to get our money out of this house and go back. I'm . . . sorry, Jean. I'm so damn sorry." And, shockingly, he had wept and she knew they were tears of exhaustion.

He had gone up on a day coach. He was gone four days. He came back with a smile she knew was too cheerful. "I start October fifteenth with Brainerd."

"But what about . . ."

"Jason and Rawls? So sorry. Full staff right now. They don't like their people to take off and then try to come back.

It won't be the same kind of money with Brainerd. But it will be ... enough. Thank God, it will be enough."

"The next time we come back here, we come to stay," she said.

"Sure," he said. "Sure. The next time."

"Stevie's had two years here, Hal. He's never been so healthy. We had to give him those two years. We can't be sorry about that."

She looked through the side windows of the kitchen and saw the station wagon in the car port. It was the same car they had driven to Florida. It was packed to the roof. The luggage carrier on top was heavily laden. There was a small nest for Stevie and Jan just behind the front seat.

With all my worldly goods I thee endow.

She wondered why she should think of that phrase. She sighed and reviewed what there was to do. Pack the few remaining items. Have Hal dismantle the crib and stow it in the wagon. Lock up and leave the keys in the mail slot in the front door of the real estate agent who had sold it for them. Have breakfast in the diner and head north up Route Nineteen. End of episode.

She remembered how it had been when they had left Pleasantville. Farewell parties. Silly parting gifts. Gaiety. Confidence. "Going to live in Florida, hah? Wish I had it so good."

But even though they had friends here, good friends, they were leaving furtively. The good friends knew the score. It happened so often in Florida. *The Dorns? Oh, they had to go back north. Couldn't quite make it. Damn shame, too. Nice people. But you know how it is. Everybody thinks they can come down here and make a living. One of the toughest places in the world to make a living unless you can come in with enough money to set up a real tourist trap.*

There would be no pleasure in saying good-by. Better to write them after getting settled in the north. Maybe, one day, there'd be a chance to visit them. She knew that they would not try again. Not ever. It had taken too much out of Hal. It had taken something away from him. It had taken some of his spirit. She knew that his confidence in himself would never be the same again, and thus it was possible that others would never have the same confidence in him. It could be that the bright future was forever lost. That was too bad, for his sake. But it could not change her love. Nothing could change that.

She woke Hal and then went in to get the kids and dressed. Stevie woke up in a sour mood. He had been a real beast about leaving. He did not want to leave. He liked it here. He did not see why they had to leave. He didn't want to be anywhere else in the world but right here, forever. Jan sang her placid little morning song and ignored the querulousness of her brother.

When she went back to the bedroom, Hal sat on the side of the bed staring out at the morning. "Great day for a trip, eh?"

"It can't rain this hard very long. Up and at 'em. I've got to fold these sheets."

He stood up slowly. "Very efficient, aren't you?" The way he said it made it unpleasant.

"I'm a demon packer-upper," she said lightly.

He looked at her and then looked away. It was not often lately that he looked directly into her eyes. When he did she saw the lost look in his eyes, the uncertainty. "At least that bucket won't overheat on us. It's damn sticky feeling, though."

"I guess it's the tail end of that hurricane."

"We'll be out of the way of it soon enough."

"Hal, I'm sort of anxious to see autumn in the north. People raking leaves. Football weather. All that."

"How obliging of you."

"Please, darling. Don't."

"Then stop being pollyanna and trying to make everything come out cozy and perfect. It isn't coming out cozy and perfect, so why not admit it."

"And go around wringing my hands and moaning?"

"Like I do?"

"I didn't mean that and you know it. Hal, let's try to be a little bit cheery, even if it hurts."

He clapped his hands sourly. "Goody, goody. We're going on a trip." He trudged to the bathroom, head bowed, pyjamas too baggy on his body. She looked at the closed door and sighed again and finished folding the bedding. She put on her Dacron skirt and a light-weight blouse. She took the bedding into the kitchen and put it on the counter near the carport door.

They left at eight o'clock. Before they left she went in and took one last look around. The house was bare and impersonal. It was as though they had never lived there. They dropped off the keys. They ate at the diner. Hal seemed to be making an effort to be pleasant. Stevie was naughty enough to merit the threat of a spanking. They drove out toward the Courtney Campbell Causeway and turned north on Route Nineteen. The heavy rain cut visibility. The quality of the light seemed more like dusk than morning. All cars had their lights on. The wipers swept solid water off the windshield. She touched Hal's arm lightly and was relieved when he smiled over at her.

A few miles from Clearwater they turned on the car radio. "... to give you the latest word on Hurricane Hilda. Hilda is now reported to be in the Gulf about a hundred miles west and a little north of the Tampa Bay area. The central West Coast is experiencing heavy rains as far north as Cedar Key. Though the experts predicted that Hilda would begin to lose force during the night, it is reported that wind velocities near the center have actually increased and are now as high as a hundred and fifteen miles an hour. After moving on a steady course for many hours, the northward movement has slowed and it is less easy to predict the direction the storm will take. The Louisiana and Texas coasts have been alerted. We now return you to the program already in progress."

Hal turned the radio off after two bars of hillbilly anguish.

"Could it come back in to land ahead of us?" Jean asked.

"Could what come?" Stevie demanded, leaning over the front seat. "Could what come?"

"The hurricane, dear," Jean said, knowing that it might take his mind off the woes of leaving Clearwater.

"Wow!" Stevie said, awed.

"This rain, Stevie," Hal said, "always comes ahead of a hurricane, but we're sort of on the edge of it. It's going up the Gulf and I don't think it will cut back this way."

"I hope it does," Stevie said firmly.

"And I most fervently hope it doesn't," Jean said.

"It would be pretty improbable," Hal said. Ahead of the car, in the gloom, he saw the running lights of a truck. He eased up behind it, moved out, accelerated, dropped back into his lane in front of the truck.

I can do this, he thought. *I can drive just fine. I can boil right along in the old wagon without endangering my three hostages to fortune. What else can I do? Shave neatly and tie*

9

*my shoes and make standard small talk. And make a living
in a very narrow and specialized profession.*

*We went down there with over seven thousand dollars and
now we have twenty-one hundred left, and the car, and what
we've got with us. Clothing that has seen better days.*

If it was only that. A loss like on a crap table, or taken by
somebody who forced a window. But there's the other loss.
Esteem. Husband who couldn't make it. Father who dropped
the ball.

And he knew that was the area of greatest soreness.
Father:

... sitting there in the dark front room on a winter afternoon. A room seldom used. Front room in a mill town
house, one of a row of houses all rubbed gray as with a dirty
eraser. Down across the viaduct were the slag piles, with skin
frozen harsh in winter so that they could be the great dead
lizards that Miss Purse told the class about—nobody knew
why they'd all died. She said some men thought that a small
rodent-like animal had multiplied and it was that animal that
ate their eggs.

Slag heaps, and down beyond the town the silent red night
fire of the furnaces—silent in the distance but when you went
down there they huffed and roared like dragons that were
alive.

Jerry's dad comes home at night black as licorice. And
startling white around his eyes. Comes home walking, trud-
ging up the hill, loose Thermos in the black tin bucket going
clink as he steps. But your father is at the mill, not in the
mines, and he comes home clean because foremen have a
place where they can wash up. His nails are black but he
smells of hard yellow soap and when you are little you run
down the hill and he picks you up and his great arm is like a
bar of iron, holding you once too tightly so your leg went to
sleep but you didn't tell him, and fell when he put you down
on the porch.

Now he is home on a winter afternoon when you get out
of school and it is like the world has fallen apart. Things have
been strange at school this winter. The town has been strange
this winter. But a strangeness that has not touched you.
Except in little ways. The end of the piano lessons. Maybe
you can start again later, dear. And a disappointing Christmas, but you did not let them know how badly you had
wanted the Elgin Bicycle, and how certain you had been that

you would get it, so certain that you got up in gray dawn and went down to look at it and touch it there under the tree, and if it was up on its stand perhaps turn the rear wheel and watch the spokes go around in silver pattern. Maybe they would bring the bike in later, but they did not.

Then he was home when he should be at work.

—*Don't go in there and bother your father.*

—*But why is he home?*

—*Go on out and play. Don't think about it. Don't worry about it. Go on out and play. Or go to your room and read.*

Laid off. When you found out that those were the words they had a funny sound. Not laid down. Or laid away. Laid off. Off in a far place.

Home every day. Mend the porch. Paint the fence. Fix the roof. Fix the chair. Then nothing. Sit. Then be gone all day and come back and sit. No smile. Never again the laugh that made the walls spread out to make the room and the house and the world bigger.

And the funny time at supper that night. Later, when it was warm and the doors open. He held his hands out and he looked at them and curled the fingers and looked at his hands and his face was funny and he made a strange sound. Sam! mother said. Sam! But he went away. Bang of the chair falling. Bang of the front door. Clump of feet on steps and gone then.

—*Eat your food, Harold.*

The god did not die quickly. He died little by little. There were other jobs. Some of them were little jobs, very little jobs. They did not last long. They all worked. He remembered the exact moment when the god was finally dead. It was the summer before his senior year of high school. He had a road job. The first few weeks had nearly killed him, but he had lasted and the work became easier and he felt his body growing wider and tougher. He got paid and rode back into town and had some beers, home-brewed beers, and then walked home feeling bigger than the night, walked home thinking about Krisnak's sister and the way she walked.

The old man sat at the kitchen table drinking coffee. The old man hadn't worked in a couple of weeks. He sat there and he looked shrunken. He sat there in his pants and underwear, with cords on his neck and wattles under his chin, hair wispy on the naked skull, eyes dulled and chest hollow. Hal stood at the sink and pumped a glass of water and then turned around, sipping it, looking at the old man with a cold objective eye. The only thing big about the old man was his hands. They grew tough from the end of white wrists, tough and curled, horny and thickened. So this was what had been the laughing giant, strong enough to carry him all the way up the hill.

Old bum. Too damn dumb to hold a job. Stinking house in a stinking mill town. No car, no clothes, no future.

Not for me, he thought. *Not for me. Not this crappy life. All A's and one B last year. All A's next year, I swear, because that's the only way out. And I want out. I want out so bad I can taste it.*

He drove the wagon through the heavy rain and he said to himself, "Old man, forgive me. I stood at your grave on that bright warm day. I felt affection, and regret, and contempt. Forgive me for the contempt."

A sudden burst of rain slapped hard against the left side of the station wagon. The gust of wind swayed the wagon. Pine tops dipped and swayed.

"It's getting windier," Jean said.

[*Windier. A cross wind pushing the flat side of the station wagon, so that the driver has to make quick little compensating twists of the wheel.*

North, in the wind, in the rain, in the great anonymity of the highway. Even in the best of weather the roads of the land are curiously impersonal. In a day of heavy travel you see forty thousand cars, but you do not look at them as cushioned compartments in which ride humans as vulnerable as yourself. You see them as obstacles, as force and danger . . . a flash of chrome and roar of engine. But rarely you see the other person. Something fixes your attention. The fool who blocks your way. The top-down blonde at the light. The old crate full of kids and pots and pans, with crated chickens on top.

The man in the station wagon drives through the rain and the wind. A low sleek car passes him at high speed, startling him. The boy asks what it is. The man tells the child it is a Mercedes, and even as he says it he feels the dull burn of envy, and for no other reason he hates the driver.

Later he sees the car again. It is parked by a small

restaurant. A young couple hurry through the rain to the restaurant door. He wonders if he will see the car again. Sometimes it happens that way on a long trip. The faster driver makes longer stops, and two cars leapfrog north.

He increases his speed. He wants to be as far north as he can get before the sleek car comes up behind him again.]

13

3

Bunny Hollis awoke before nine in a motel on Route 19 and he lay there listening to the hard roar of the rain. It was a rain so intense that when you listened to it carefully it seemed to be increasing in force from minute to minute. It was a muggy gray morning. He wondered what morning it was. He counted back and decided that it had to be Wednesday, October seventh. He stretched until his shoulders creaked, knuckled his eyes and sat up. There was a faint pulse of liquor behind his eyes, a sleazy taste in his mouth. He sat naked on the edge of the bed and took his pulse. Seventy-six. And no suggestion of a premature beat. Lately when he smoked too much and drank too much the premature beat would start. He had been told by a very good man that it was nothing to worry about. Just ease off when it started.

He turned and looked at his bride in the other bed. She lay sprawled as if dropped from a height, a sheaf of brown hair across her eyes. She had kicked off the single sheet in her sleep. The narrow band of white across her buttocks was ludicrous against the dark tan of her.

Betty did look better with a tan, he decided. And he had chided her into losing ten pounds. Another fifteen off her and she'd look even better. But not tan nor weight loss was going to do very much for pale eyes that were set a little too close together, for teeth too prominent and chin too indistinct. But she was young and she could be amusing and at twenty-one she was worth close to three million dollars, and when she became thirty there would be another chunk coming in that should bring it damn near up to ten million.

He went quietly into the bathroom, closed the door and turned on the light. He examined his face in the mirror with great care, as he did every morning. He thought the face looked about twenty-six, nine years younger than his actual age. And, as always, he wondered if he was kidding himself. It was a face in the almost traditional mold of the American

14

athlete. Brown and blunt, with broad brow, square jaw, nose slightly flat at the bridge, gray wide-set eyes with weather wrinkles at the corners. A very short brush cut helped mask the encroaching baldness. It was a face made for grinning, for victory, for locker room gags, for Olympic posters.

He cupped cold water in his hands and drenched his face and rubbed it vigorously, massaging it with strong fingers, paying special attention to the area under the eyes, at the corners of the mouth and under the chin. He massaged his scalp and dried his face and head and then turned and studied his body in the full-length mirror on the inside of the bathroom door. Athlete's body to match the face. Waist still reasonably lean, though not what it once had been. Deep chest and slanting shoulders. Brown body with the crisp body hair on the legs and arms burned white by the sun. Long slim legs with the slant of power. Muscle knots in the shoulders, square strong wrists.

At least the product she was getting was adequate, he thought. *Cared for. Slightly rotted, but not enough to show. Years of wear left in it. Enough virility to be able to fake adequately the intensities of honeymoon.*

Three zero zero zero zero zero zero.

And heah, ladies and gentlemen, we have a little girl who represents thu-ree million dollars. Who will be the lucky man?

Bunny Hollis, of course.

Bunny, who always ran out of luck every time but the last time. Like the good old Limeys. Never win a battle and never lose a war.

A long, long way from the skinny, sullen kid out in southern California, practically living at the public courts with a secondhand racket and one hell of a forehand drive for a twelve year old. No net game. No backhand. No lobs. No cuts. Just that base line drive that had heaviness to it, had power and authority.

Cutler had come down from his personal Olympus to look at a girl on the public courts. He hadn't thought much of the girl, but he had seen Bunny Hollis. Life changed then.

"Do you want to learn the game, kid?" He looked at Cutler, heard the harsh voice, saw the red face, the round belly, the small unfriendly blue eyes.

"I know how to play."

15

"All you know so far is which end of the bat to hold. You want to learn the game?"

"I got no money for lessons."

"Where do you live?" Bunny told him. "Come on. My car's over there. We'll go out and see your folks."

He learned the most important thing the first week. Cutler had him swinging the racket. No ball. No court. Foot work and swing on the count. One two THREE. One two THREE. "Too much break on the wrist on the backswing, kid. Elbow down." One two THREE.

He tossed the racket onto the grass. "Nuts," he said.

The meaty hand cracked against his face and split his lip, knocked him down. He cried, more from anger than pain. Cutler leaned over him, eyes cool, voice low. "A wise kid. You come from nothing. You are nothing. You ever try that again and I'll throw you out and you'll stay nothing. Maybe you think this is a game. Pat ball. If you want to be something, do as you're told. Who told you it would be easy? Get on your feet and pick up that bat. You're going to do what I say, eat what I say, think what I say, live what I say. Every damn minute of every damn day of your stinking little life. Okay now. One two THREE. Better. But keep that handle parallel to the ground all the way through the imaginary ball. One two THREE. Brace that right leg. Put something in it, kid. I want to hear that bat whistle."

When he was fifteen, the first year he really started winning, Cutler got him a job and a room at his own club, the Carranak Club. He had lost a lot of the sullenness. He was beginning to be treated as someone of importance. It felt good to be treated that way. He seldom went home. He'd never gotten along with his stepfather. His mother was having one kid after another, regular as a machine.

He was skinny and brown and tireless. He had the fundamentals of what could grow to be a big game. He won junior tournaments up and down the coast. Cutler would go along when he could, but Cutler had other players who were nearer their peak, who were on the national circuit.

He had learned to smile at the people, take adverse decisions with grace, enjoy the look of his name in the papers. They were good years, fifteen, sixteen and seventeen. Cutler insisted that the schooling continue. The right sort of strings were pulled and at eighteen he went into U.C.L.A. on an athletic scholarship. Cutler had good friends. He achieved the last of his growth at eighteen. He was six-one, one hundred and sixty-two pounds, rangy and fast, with power in every stroke. Under Cutler's guidance, under his orders, Bunny led a monastic life, with every free hour subject to the discipline of constant practice. He no longer minded. He had learned to enjoy winning. If you had to live like this to win—it was little enough to have to do.

Bunny often wondered what the years would have been like if Cutler had been able to accompany him on that first big trip out of the state to the tournament in New Jersey. Cutler had planned to go. But an ulcer started to bleed and there had to be an operation. Cutler had given him his instructions in the hospital.

"It's big time. Don't get sucked into the social routine. You've got money enough to get your own place to stay. Eat right and sleep a lot. You'll have three days to practice. The ball floats different there. Your timing will be off. Don't get into the high society deal. A lot of them are sharks who want to feed on you. Play your game. I don't expect a win. I'll expect a win next year. I expect a good showing this year. Good enough so they'll think about you for the cup."

He went out by train. He felt scared of what was ahead. The letter told him where to report. It was a bigger place than he expected. He saw some people he knew because he had seen their pictures. They told him where to find the man with the list.

"Yes? Bunny Hollis. Let me see, F.G.H. Hollis. Singles. Let me check the schedule. Today is Tuesday. Here you are. Saturday, one-fifteen. Court number seven. Against Bill Tilley."

Bunny felt enormous relief. He had beaten Tilley once in Sacramento and once in Los Angeles. "How about practice?"

"Find Mr. Glendinning. I think he's down in the locker room. He's assigning the practice courts and hours. Wait a minute. Don't rush off. You're billeted with the Lorrings."

"I was going to a hotel."

"Don't be silly, Hollis. They've got a nice place and they're nice people. Tennis fans. Great supporters of the tournament. They've got private courts just as well surfaced as these. You'll live well there, better than you will in a hotel, and

17

they're glad to do it. If I remember, Mrs. Lorring asked for you particularly. She's been following your career. Wait until I give her a ring."

He waited out in front with racket case and suitcase. It was warm and he was sweating and he wondered if he should take his jacket off. A green convertible came in and swung around across the gravel with a certain flair and stopped so close to him that he stepped back. "Bunny? Of course it is. I know you from your pictures. I'm Regina Lorring. Sorry if I kept you waiting. I was in the tub when George phoned me. Put your stuff in back and get in. Now remember which way we go, so you can find your way back."

She was a smallish woman. He could not guess her age. She could have been thirty or forty. She had a tanned pretty face, but so heavily lined it made him think of a small brown monkey. She wore a low-necked blouse and her breasts were large and it made him feel uncomfortable to look at the front of her. She drove very briskly and competently. Finally they went up a ridge road and turned through big iron gates and up a private road to a house that looked like a president had lived there. A polite man came and took the racket case and suitcase. She said he might as well look the place over and then she would show him where his room was. The keys would be in the little green convertible and he could use it as his own. He saw that she had a nice figure.

She showed him the courts and the stables. His room was big and the bed was vast. That night at dinner he met Mr. Lorring, a man who looked about eighty. His head shook all the time and he had white hair. Things kept dropping off his fork and he didn't seem to be able to follow the conversation very well.

He went to bed early, following Cutler's wishes. It took him a long time to get to sleep. He was awakened in the middle of the night and he was so confused and startled and dazed by sleep that it took him a long time before he understood that it was Mrs. Lorring who was in bed beside him in the dark room, holding him in her arms and smelling of liquor and laughing in a low funny way deep in her throat. He was a virgin. It shocked him and terrified him and yet at the same time it made him feel deliciously guilty. He was frightened and then it was all right and when he awakened in the morning she was gone, but she had left one of

18

her slippers beside the bed. He hid it in the back of the bureau.

He had breakfast alone and got lost twice driving down to practice. He got home at five and she was having cocktails with some people he didn't know. To look at her you would never know anything like that had happened. He began to wonder if it really had. But there was the slipper. He knew the slipper was real. She introduced him to the people and said they were going out to dinner, but she had arranged for him to have a nice dinner alone here. He went to bed early and he was still awake and waiting when he heard the car and later footsteps in the hall, and much later the sound of the door opening and closing, softer footsteps, then felt the edge of the bed sag under her weight, felt the softness of her under something sheer as she came into his arms.

He fought hard for the first set. Three times he got it to set point, but Tilley was very brave and very determined and he was playing over his head. Tilley took it eleven and nine. Bunny was stung and came back strong to take the first four games of the second set, breaking Tilley's service twice. Tilley took the next game. Bunny took the next to make it five and one. The first point of the next game was a very long point. It went on and on. Bunny began to feel oddly leaden. He could not float across the court. His feet came down heavily, jarring him. Tilley's returns seemed to be where he could barely reach them. Tilley took the next two games, and then another one, to make it five and four. Bunny summoned up every ounce of energy and took the final game and the second set, six to four.

Bill Tilley, almost without opposition, took the final and deciding set by a score of six love.

As the train pulled out of the station he unwrapped the gift she had pressed into his hand on the station platform. There was gray heavy paper around a small flat box. It was tied with pale blue ribbon. Inside the flat box was tissue paper. When he opened it he saw a plain gold money clip. The engraving on it was very tiny. R.L. to B.H. There were five one-hundred-dollar bills in the clip, twice folded. It was the newest and crispest money he had ever seen.

He sat with the money in his hand. He thought of her and

of her wrinkled simian face and her heavy breasts. He
thought of the pleased and surprised look on Bill Tilley's face
when they had shaken hands after the match. He shut his
hard brown hand on the money and he looked out the train
window. After a long time he uncrumpled the bills, smoothed
them out against his thigh and put them back in the money
clip and put the clip in his pocket.

Cutler looked thinner, tireder, older. "I heard about it. I
got three letters about it, from dear friends. Get your stuff
out of the Carranak today."

"But I . . ."

"You threw it away. You were nothing. You wanted to
keep on being nothing. Now I'm going to let you keep on
being nothing. Get out of here."

Cutler, he found out later, tried to fix his wagon with all
tournament committees, but because Cutler had as many
enemies as he had friends, it didn't work. Bunny found
sponsorship. He did better in the next few tournaments.
Never top man, but a creditable showing. By the time he was
twenty-one he was a tournament veteran. He knew several
specifics for hangovers. His game was more clever, though
not as powerful. Due to the peculiar customs of amateur
tennis, he lived very well indeed. He had long since given up
U.C.L.A. When not on the tournament circuit, he was a
popular and engaging house guest. And he had learned to
identify the Regina Lorrings of the tennis world at fifty paces,
and to respond to them. From them he acquired his own car,
matched luggage, a Rollex watch in a solid gold case, a Zeiss
camera, cashmere jackets, cruise tickets and, whenever possible, cash.

When he was drafted he sold most of his possessions and
put the money away in a Building and Loan Society. He
went through basic, was given a commission in Special Serv-
ices and assigned to a large camp in the southwest where he
gave regular tennis instruction to field grade officers and
played exhibition games with other tennis stars who passed
through the camp. It was a pleasant life and, but for a
certain unfortunate episode with the wife of a full colonel, he
could have stayed there for the duration. He found himself
assigned to Korea and, as the word had gone ahead of him
through the West Point Protective Association, assigned to
a test area in Japan. He began to work out seriously and

regularly at the Officers' Club near Tokyo. He got permission to enter the All Pacific Tournament and made such a splendid showing he was sent on tour to Australia and New Zealand playing exhibitions.

At the time of his discharge he almost had his big game back again. But he was twenty-five, and he had lost a lot of time. He did get on the Davis Cup squad as an alternate. After that, during the next two years both his energies and his charm seemed to wear a little thin. It is one thing to be called a tennis bum. It is something else again to be called a tennis bum and be knocked down simultaneously.

The week after that happened he turned pro. That change warranted no press coverage. He went on two tours, one slightly profitable, and one not profitable at all. Through good luck, after several jobs that did not work out, he at last landed the job of tennis pro at the Oswando Club in Westchester. There were six splendid indoor courts, and so it was a year-round job. He had found that he liked working with kids. He was thirty-three that first year at Oswando. All he knew was tennis. All he would ever know was tennis. And the future had begun to look very black.

Betty Oldbern came to him to be "brushed up" on her tennis. She was nineteen. She was not attractive. She was too heavy. She was very shy of him. She knew how to play tennis because she had been given lessons ever since she was a small child. Lessons in tennis, swimming, golf, riding, dancing, fencing, conversational French, painting, sculpting, creative writing. She was the product of private schools in Switzerland, France and Philadelphia. And of innumerable tutors. She did many things competently, and none of them with grace or style. She had few friends, and quite a few relatives, all elderly.

And the name was Oldbern as in Oldbern Shipping Lines and Oldbern Chemicals.

She was nineteen and living on a generous allowance and in two more years she would be twenty-one and on that birthday she would receive something like three million. She had had the most sophisticated education in the world, yet she was almost entirely naïve. She still wore her baby fat. She could blush like a sunset. Within a month she was deeply, hopelessly in love with him. It had not been hard to manage. The hard thing was to get her to keep her mouth shut and wait. He explained that she had to be of age first, or all the relatives would cause trouble. He kept his hands off her. That was not a great chore.

Four days after her twenty-first birthday, Bunny made an appointment with Harrison Oldbern, Betty's father. He did not state his business. Harrison Oldbern was on the Board of Governors of the Oswando Club, a thin alert tanned man, sportsman, deep-water sailor, shrewd businessman.

"Sit down, Bunny. First time you've seen the office, isn't it?"

"Yes sir. Pretty impressive."

"Drink? I'm afraid I'm only going to be able to give you about ten minutes."

"I'd like a Scotch and water, thanks."

As Oldbern mixed the drinks he said, "What's on your mind, Bunny? Contract for next year? I think I can personally assure you that the membership wants you to stay. You're doing a marvelous job with the kids. In fact we're going to raise the ante a little. We don't want to lose you."

He brought the drinks over and handed Bunny his. Bunny looked up at him and said, "It isn't anything like that, Mr. Oldbern. Betty and I want to get married."

Oldbern's face stiffened. He stared at Bunny. "Betty? She's just a kid."

"She's over twenty-one, sir."

"How old are you, Hollis?"

"Thirty-five, sir."

Oldbern went behind his desk and sat down slowly. "What kind of nonsense are you trying to pull? What the hell is going on?"

"The usual thing, I guess. Love."

"How long has this been going on?"

"Nearly two years. But we thought it would be best to wait until we were both sure."

"You mean wait until she reached twenty-one."

"It happened to come out that way."

"Yes, it happened that way. Hollis, you're a dirty conniving back-stabbing son of a bitch."

Bunny looked down at his drink. "I'm sorry to hear you talk that way, sir. Betty and I have been hoping there wouldn't be too much friction."

"I'll never permit it."

"Betty says we're going to get married no matter what anybody says. Being twenty-one, I guess she's her own boss on

22

that. I'm not married and I never have been. She's certainly in her right mind. I just don't understand how anybody would go about stopping it."

Oldbern waited long moments. He leaned back in his chair. "Betty is not a pretty girl, Hollis. She is not even close to being pretty. She happens to have three million dollars."

"She knows I wouldn't marry her for her money. She knows me better than that. We've gotten well acquainted over the past two years. She knows I have ideals, Mr. Oldbern."

"You haven't any more ideals than a mink."

"I just hoped it could be handled without friction."

"I'll put a firm of investigators on you. I'll have a report on your past that'll make Betty's eyes stand out on stalks."

"You know, Mr. Oldbern, I haven't looked at another woman for two years. That's the honest truth. I've felt pretty bad about some of the things I've done. That's why I told Betty a pretty complete history. I don't think you could surprise her. She knows I've changed and she knows why. She's watched me work with the kids there at the club. Love can change a man, Mr. Oldbern."

"You thought of everything, didn't you? You've had two years to work on it."

"I'd hoped we could get along."

"Do you have a price, Hollis?"

"What do you mean?"

"I can write a fairly large check."

"I'm not thinking about money, Mr. Oldbern. I'm in love with your daughter. And she's in love with me. We want to be married. That seems pretty straightforward, doesn't it?"

"My God, I wish I knew this had been going on. Have you two been..."

"No sir. I swear that all I've ever done is kiss Betty. I guess I've done that pretty often. And I talked her out of running away to be married last year. She wanted to do that."

"But you knew it might mean a cash loss."

"I don't want to tell you what to do, but I think you ought to face this, Mr. Oldbern. It's going to happen."

The man looked older. "Sit down, Hollis. Let me think."

Bunny sat down. The man sat with his hand cupped over his eyes. He sighed heavily a few times. When he took his hand away, he looked intently at Hollis. "I understand you,

you know. I know what you're doing. She's so damn vulnerable. Are you going to try to make her happy? Are you going to even try?"

"Of course I'm going to try."

"Are you going to ask me to give you some kind of a job with a title? You certainly can't stay on at the club."

"Her income figures out to about a hundred and sixty thousand a year before taxes. Taxes will take a lot, but we can live comfortably on the balance. We're thinking about trying some place along the Mediterranean coast. After the honeymoon, that is. I'm paying for the honeymoon with the money I've saved up."

"White of you, Bunny."

"I think she'll feel better about the honeymoon if she isn't paying for it."

"There isn't anything I or anyone else can do, is there?"

Bunny permitted himself his usual likeable grin. "If there is, I wasn't able to think of it."

"I certainly hoped she'd do better when she married."

Bunny still grinned. "Like you said, she isn't what you'd call a pretty girl. Maybe she's doing about as well as she can do, Mr. Oldbern. Maybe she's doing better than she would have. We think we'd like a small quiet wedding. Just the family."

"When do you want it?"

"A month from tomorrow."

The capitulation was far easier than Bunny had expected. He wondered if Oldbern would have made a more valiant effort to defend his chick had the chick been more decorative, more personable.

Bunny stuck his hand across the desk. Oldbern looked at him, started to take his hand and then changed his mind. "You did this damn neatly, Hollis. But I don't have to shake your hand. I don't have to do that."

"Suit yourself, Mr. Oldbern."

He remembered how jubilant he was as he went down in the elevator. He wished Cutler hadn't died. It would be nice for Cutler to read all about it. The sullen skinny kid from the public courts.

Three zero zero zero zero zero zero.

The wedding had been quiet. The tabloids were noisy. None of the news accounts bothered him. One columnist got a half millimeter under his hide:

"Bunny Hollis, ex-almost tennis great, and bronzed glamor boy emeritus, proved yesterday to fellow refugees from sports headlines that with patience, a file of scrap books and the ability to balance a tea cup, a spotted past can be parlayed into a glowing future. Our Bunny bided his time at the swank Oswando Club where, for the past few years he has been teaching the game he once played well to the children and the wives of the almost rich, the middle rich and the big rich. And yesterday, just a little over a month after a coarse wad of cash was handed over to twenty-one-year-old Elizabeth Oldbern, Bunny cut his notch in that bankroll in a double ring ceremony attended only by the family and exceptionally close friends. The groom, a well-preserved thirty-five, wore a dark suit and a satisfied smile. Though the former Miss Oldbern does not come up to the standards of pulchritude this correspondent has noted among Bunny's previous playmates, we believe that Bunny has at last firmly established the standard of living which for so many years he has tried to become accustomed to. No prior marriages blot our Bunny's escutcheon. And that, fellows, is what we mean by patience. He began giving Miss Oldbern tennis lessons two years ago. They left cozily in a Mercedes-Benz, a wedding present from the bride's aunt, Janice Stawson Fielding Chancellor—who is soon, it is rumored, to become the Baroness Von Reicker."

Bunny remembered the column again and glowered at his own image in the motel mirror. He went back into the bedroom. Betty still slept, in the same position as before. He looked at her fondly and thought, *Good kid*. They had driven down to Miami, with stops at Nags Head and Myrtle Beach. They had taken a boat to Curacao, had flown to Nassau, and flown back to Miami for the car.

He had expected to be bored by the honeymoon, bored by the aura of adoration, but to his surprise he had had fun. It had at first shocked and alarmed him and then pleased him to find that he had married a virgin bride. He was quite aware that the incidence of twenty-one-year-old virgins in her particular social and financial strata was very very small. It had given him a very strange feeling to be able to lead her with gentleness through the fears and pain of the first nights, then through the passive acceptance of nights that followed and then at last into more than acceptance—into a gratifyingly lusty participation. It gave him a strange feeling of

25

responsibility to be the only man she had ever known. And he felt a certain amount of pride in realizing that through gentleness and understanding he had been able to arouse her completely. He knew how easily it could have gone the other way—how through brutality she could have been made frigid for life.

Knowing her for two years, knowing her shyness, her physical awkwardness, he had expected her to be a woman of meager desires. He thought her flames would be turned low and would flicker. But she soon became a woman of considerable ardor, sensitive, imaginative, demanding in her lovemaking. He knew she was not pretty. Her figure was fair, at best. Yet during the last week at odd moments he would happen to notice her with half his mind when she moved, when she turned away from him, when she walked toward him, when she pulled herself onto a swimming float or dived into a breaking wave—and at those moments he would feel a quick surprising surge of desire for her. Her skin was marvelously clear and unblemished. She was tidy as a cat and her body was fragrant. In a dark room her brown hair would crackle and there would be faint sparks when he ran his fingers quickly through it.

He knew he did not love her. But he was fond of her. She had her own quiet sense of fun. And secure in her own conviction that she was loved, she had begun to blossom for him.

He sat on the edge of her bed and put his hand on her waist, shook her gently. "Come on, fat lamb."

She spoke clearly, and without opening her eyes. "Not so daggone fat. I'm being deprived of my starches."

"How long have you been awake, you sneak?"

"Maybe five minutes." She opened her eyes. They were pale gray eyes. He had talked her into using dark pencil on her pale brows, into touching up her eyelashes that were like fine gold wire. It gave her eyes more expression and he realized that while he had been in the bathroom she had gotten up and fixed her eyes, run a brush through her hair, used a breath of perfume.

"And this week," she said, "I shall lose another two pounds. In a few months I will weigh one hundred and fifteen. And then I shall wonder why I wasted all this unearthly beauty on a tired old man."

"Mmmmhmmm," he said. "Tired." He grinned and caressed her.

"Are you being bawdy, Mr. Hollis?" she asked primly.

"A touch. Just a wee bit."

"That's what I hoped," she whispered, smiling, reaching her arms out toward him.

The hard rain came down. The room was gray with the light of the dull morning. Somehow it became a very special time for them. They had a cigarette and then, after showers, got dressed and packed quickly and got in the car and headed north in the dusky gloom of the constant rain.

The sports car was built like a low fleet expensive boat. It squatted low on the road, thrillingly responsive. The wind out of the west did not make it sway. But Bunny saw the hard sway of the palms and the pines and he wondered about the hurricane. They had thought it was going to catch them in Miami and they had talked about it and been excited by the idea and been disappointed when the storm had veered to the west below Cuba.

When they stopped in a roadside restaurant for a late breakfast, the few customers were all talking about the storm. An old man with the long sallow knotted face and pale narrow deep-set eyes of the cracker said, "They *say* they know where it is. I ain't fixin' to listen too hard to 'em, with their planes and charts and all. You get this here rain and then it comes right at you like you had the bar'l of a gun aimed right down your gullet. Nobody knows where it is. Where the hell you think all the birds went? Me, I say it's fixin' to roar right down on us. I got me all boarded up and ready, by God. Try to breathe this here air. There ain't enough goodness in it. You got to keep a-fillin' your chest. That's one *sure sign*."

When they were back in the car Betty said, "He sounded awfully certain, that old man in there."

"So we'll add a few knots and get out of here. It would have been fun in Miami, but I wouldn't want to have to sit it out in a car."

The gray car, gray as the rain, sped through the moist heavy air. It threw up a great spume of spray behind it. When the winds became strong enough to make the car swerve, he had to slow down.

[*Slow down. And in that time of slowing a big dark blue*

Cadillac swings out and passes the Mercedes, and he gets half a glance at the two men in the Cadillac, at the Florida plate.

The driver of the Cadillac gets a certain savage satisfaction out of passing the sleek foreign car. The Cadillac trembles on a long curve and he knows that he is holding it on the edge of control. The smaller man beside him seems about to speak, to complain about the speed, but he does not.

Ten minutes later the Cadillac passes the station wagon which had passed the Mercedes when it was stopped at the restaurant.

Traffic is thinning out. The rain and wind have become too heavy, too frightening.

The cars head north, up Route 19.

There is an impersonality about train and bus and plane. You buy the ticket and you are, for a time, with strangers. You are linked only by common destination, by the need to be at another place at another time. Yet you look at the other, at the cool inward faces, the man with the briefcase, the lame girl with the silly hat, the sticky-faced child, and you wonder about them—casually, with no special interest.

The highway is the coldest of all. You are alone and all other vehicles are mindless, untenanted.

Yet when there is a common destination, unplanned and violent as that destination may be, and when the vehicle engines are stilled, you are with strangers who mean even less than the accidental companions of train, bus and aircraft.]

28

4

Johnny Flagan stood shaving in the light of cold fluorescence in his bathroom. The motor in the shaver made a high whining hum which sagged in pitch when the head bit into the crust of hard sandy whiskers along his jaw. He was a suety man in his fifties, with gingery gray hair surrounding a bald spot the size of a coaster. He stood spread-legged, slabs of fat moving on his sloped shoulders as he steered the razor. He had once been a strong man. But the years had run through the puffy body, the years of the cigars and the bourbon and the hotel room women. Years of the quick meeting and the dickering and the club cars. There were brown blemishes on his lard white shoulders and back, a matronly cast to his hips. But all the drive was still there, the hint of harshness.

He was an amiable looking man. Sun and whisky kept his soft face red. He smiled easily and had the knack of kidding people. He wore round glasses with steel rims and the glasses were always slipping a little way down his blunt nose and Johnny Flagan would look over his glasses at you and grin wryly about his morning hangover and you would never notice that the grin did nothing to change the eyes. The eyes were small and brown and watchful and they could have been the noses of two bullets dimly seen in the cylinder when you look toward the muzzle of a gun.

If you walked down the street with him you would soon come to believe that he knew more than half the people in Sarasota.

But what does he do?

—You mean Johnny Flagan? What does he do? Well, he's got a lot of interests you might say. He was in on some pretty good land development stuff on the keys. He's got a fellow runs a ranch for him down near Venice. Santa Gertrudis stock, it is. He's got a piece of a juice plant over near Winter Haven. Then he's director on this and that. And he's

29

got some kind of interest in savings and loan stuff. Hell, Old Johnny keeps humping.

—He seems like a nice guy.

—Sure. He's a nice fella. Got a raft of friends. You get him going sometime telling stories. He's really something.

—Successful and honest, I suppose.

—Successful, sure. You understand I'm not a fellow to talk about anybody. Gossip. That kind of thing. But you go throwing around that word honest, and there's a lot of people got different ideas of what it means. Johnny's a sharp one. I don't think he ever in his whole life done anything he could get hisself jailed for, but you get on the other end of a deal from him, and you got to play it close. Like that time, hell it was seven eight years ago, there was this old fellow down Nokomis way didn't want to let loose of some land Johnny wanted to pick up. Both Johnny and the old man were pretty damn sure the State Road Department was going to put the new road right through his land. Well sir, one day these young fellows come to the old man's house and they're hot and they want a drink of water. They got transits and so on, all that surveying stuff, and the old man gives them the water and they get to talking and it turns out they're surveying for the road and it just doesn't come nowheres near the old man's land. Very next day the old man unloads his land on Johnny, trying to keep a straight face. Inside fourteen months the new road cuts right across the land and Johnny has himself a bunch of prime commercial lots. That old man just about drove them nuts up there in Tallahassee, but he never could find out just who those surveyors were or where they come from. Sure, Johnny's honest, but he's damn sharp.

—He lives right here, does he?

—Near all his life. Married one of the Leafer girls. Never has had any kids. But they seem to get along good, that is except for the times she's found out about Johnny getting out of line on one of his trips. He travels around a lot. Used to live right off Orange, but some time back he built himself a hell of a nice house out there on St. Armands Key. You ever get an invitation to a party out there, you go. He really lays it on. Bartenders and everything. But nobody holds it against him he's made out so good. He doesn't ever try to hide it from you he's one of old Stitch Flagan's ragged-ass kids. That's Stitch that come down here from Georgia forty years ago and went broke in celery and finally ended up as a com-

30

mercial fisherman and went night netting in the Gulf after mackerel thirty years back and drownded out there, him and two of his boys, Johnny's brothers they were. Johnny would have been along and drownded too, except he was hot after some gal down in Osprey and run out and his old man couldn't find him and took off without him. Johnny must have been twenty-two or so about that time. Husky kid and real woman crazy. Funny thing, it was after Stitch and the two boys drownded that Johnny began to take sort of an interest in money. He begun to go after it the way he'd been going after every piece of pussy from Arcadia to Punta Gorda.

Johnny Flagan blew the sandy stubble out of the razor, coiled the cord, put razor and cord in the plastic box and put the box in the toilet article case he used on trips. He checked the case to see that everything he needed was there, and carried the case into the bedroom and put it beside his suitcase. The air conditioner made a dissonant buzzing sound. Babe slept heavily under a single blanket. Johnny dressed quietly and quickly in a nylon shirt, figured red bow tie, cotton cord suit. When the suitcase was snapped shut he went over and sat on Babe's bed, put his hand on the big warm mound of the blanketed hip and shook her gently.

"Hey, honey!" he said softly. "Hey!"

Babe came walrusing up out of sleep, circling her eyes around and then focusing them on him, frowning and saying, "Wass?"

"No flights today. I'm starting earlier and taking the Cad."

"Huh? You be careful. Don't you drive when you're drinking."

"I'll be careful. I'll phone you when I know when I can get free. Okay?"

"Be careful."

He kissed her and carried his suitcase to the bedroom door.

"Johnny?"

"Yes, honey."

"You going to give that Charlie a bad time?"

"He's got a bad time coming to him."

"You going to fire him?"

"I don't know yet."

"If you could just scare hell out of him it would be easier on me, knowing her and all."

31

"I'll see," he said. He shut the bedroom door behind him. The rest of the house was warmer—muggy and gray and cheerless. It was a big house with long stretches of terrazzo, glass jalousies, graceless furniture. Though they had lived in it several years, it had a flavor of transiency, an uncaring coldness.

Ruth had cleared the newspapers off the dining room table, but she had known enough not to touch the business papers he had laid out and worked on the night before. His orange juice, in a tall glass, seemed the only bright spot of color in the long dim room. The morning paper lay beside his place. It was damp from the rain. He sat down and unfolded the paper and called out, "Ruth!"

She pushed the swinging door open and came out of the kitchen immediately, carrying his plate in one hand, coffee pot in the other, as though she had been waiting there just beyond the door for his call. She was a slim woman, quite tall. She was in her late twenties and she was just a shade or two darker than some of Babe's more heavily tanned friends. There was a look of austerity in her face, the sharp nose and thin lips not at all Negroid. In all the years she had worked for them, she had never looked directly at him. She walked with the contradiction of her nature clearly expressed—there for all to see. Cold face and rigid bearing, no sway or dip to her shoulders. Yet whenever she turned to walk away he would look automatically at the back of her, at the sway back and the strong outthrust hips and the swinging suggestive cadence.

There had always been tension between them. Tension and a certain wary understanding.

"Good morning," she said, her voice crisp and cool.

" 'Moanin', Ruthie," he said, reacting to her perfect diction by becoming so mush-mouthed as to be almost incomprehensible. He knew that it annoyed her, and he knew that she would not show it. He knew that the brain behind that cool thin face was of excellent quality. She expressed resentment through efficiency. The more she despised the two of them the harder she labored to make the house run smoothly, make the food perfection. It was a form of defiance, and she knew that they used and appreciated the products of her defiance. She was well-paid, well-treated, but he knew she felt trapped.

She put the plate in front of him. Three eggs fried, turned

over lightly, thick strips of country bacon, grits with butter and pepper. She stood beside him and filled the coffee cup.

"Coming down hard rain, Ruthie."

"Yes, sir. It really is."

"Got them plenty of leaky roofs down there in Newtown." She had backed away with the coffee pot. "A lot of them leak."

He grinned at her but could not find or meet her eyes. "Ought to tear down half them shacks down there."

"Yes sir," she said and moved quickly to the kitchen, and the door swung shut behind her. It was a petty victory, too easily won this time. As he opened the paper he held in his mind the after image of her hips as she went through the door.

He sensed that part of the tension between them was due to the knowledge that she attracted him physically. Not because she was pretty. The most she could be called was handsome. It was the contradiction which intrigued him, the hint of fire under ice. He had idly daydreamed about her many times while going to sleep—thought of the brown still cold face unmoving on a white pillow, the eyes veiled and unknowable, while, like a separate organism, her hips led their own quick, hard, rhythmic, lubricious life. It could be thought about, but never, never, never could there be the slightest move or gesture which could be interpreted by her as the first step in a campaign to achieve that startling goal. Because that would give her the ultimate unforgettable victory—would give her a stature that could never be weakened.

Just two years ago, if Babe had not been so pleased and delighted with Ruth, Johnny would have fired her. Now he thought that even should Babe become discontented with Ruth, he would manage to keep the woman around. The game had become too interesting. They had both become too adept in their ways of muted conflict. It was like having a pet around that you couldn't quite trust.

Johnny Flagan scanned the headlines and turned to the real estate transfers. He saw that Ross Wedge had unloaded three lots in the Lagoon Park development for eighteen thousand. He knew that Ross had picked up six lots at just about the same time he had picked up ten. They'd both had to pay about two thousand apiece for them, and that was dirt cheap on account of Barkmann had needed the cash money to develop the rest of the area. He wondered why Ross Wedge had unloaded half his holding right now. Better off to wait a while. Lagoon Park was coming along fine. But then Ross was in with Whitey building those new stores on the boulevard and maybe he needed a little cash money. Better keep it in mind though, and see if Ross got rid of the other three soon. If he did so, it would be worth nosing around and finding out if anything was coming up that might hurt Lagoon Park and make this a good time to get out.

Ruth came out of the kitchen and filled his coffee cup.

"Thanks," he said. "You take good care of Miz Babe now, Ruthie. I'll be gone for a couple days. Up in Georgia. Say, I couldn't find my Orlon suit. That light gray one."

"It ought to be back today, Mist' Flagan."

He detected the faint slur in her speech, the slur that was the tip-off to a feeling of guilt. When Ruth forgot something, or did something wrong, the slur became evident. He knew that if he did a little digging he could find out that the suit hadn't gone out when it should have. But it did not seem worth the effort.

After he finished his coffee, he picked up the suitcase and went out through the kitchen to the garage. Babe would have the red Hillman to get around in. She despised driving it, but she certainly couldn't expect him to drive up to Georgia in it. He put his suitcase in the Cad, then paused, turned and went back into the house and phoned Charlie Himbermark again and told Charlie he was just leaving and to be ready.

He drove off St. Armands Key, over the Ringling Bridges to the mainland. The gas tank was nearly full. The big dark blue Cadillac was running smoothly. The rain was a damn nuisance, but he decided he ought to be able to make pretty good time in spite of it. Run right up to Waycross and then it was only another thirty miles to the small Georgia city where Himbermark had come so close to fouling up the entire operation.

He turned south on Orange and, a few minutes later, he pulled up in front of the small frame house on one of the back streets beyond the postoffice where Charlie Himbermark lived. He blew the horn. Charlie came out onto the porch and turned to say good-by to Agnes. Agnes waved at the car and Johnny waved back. Charlie wore a transparent raincoat. He kissed Agnes and came hurrying down the walk through the rain and got in beside Johnny.

"Hell of a morning," Charlie said cheerfully. He struggled awkwardly and got himself out of the raincoat and tossed it into the back seat, then lifted his suitcase over and put it on the floor in back. He plumped himself down and wiggled around and adjusted himself and gave a small sigh of relaxation—all of which irritated Johnny Flagan.

Johnny wished he'd never seen or heard of Charlie Himbermark, never seen his pale sixty-year-old face, heard his high nervous voice. Charlie was a man always anxious to please everybody. When he stood talking to anyone, his whole attitude was that of intense eagerness to be found pleasing. He would lean forward, his eyes eager, his mouth working as you talked. He would laugh before you came to the point of the joke. He would pat you quickly and lightly on the shoulder whenever he could, his wide blue eyes watering.

Charlie Himbermark had come down to Sarasota about eight years ago. His wife had died in the north and he'd had some sort of breakdown. He came down with a small pension and a desire to find something to do. He had been in a big bank in the north, some sort of job in the trust department. After a year or so of looking, Charlie found a job in one of the brokerage offices in town. Two years later he married Agnes Steppey, one of Babe's oldest friends. Agnes had been widowed for over a year, and they met when Agnes went into the brokerage office to ask about some stock her husband had left her.

A year ago Charlie had lost his job. It hadn't been his fault, exactly. The firm had decided to consolidate the Sarasota staff with the St. Petersburg office, and Agnes hadn't felt that she could leave the city where she had been born and grown up, had married, been widowed and married again. So Charlie refused the transfer. There was enough for the two of them to get along in meager comfort, but, as Agnes told Babe, Charlie was restless and depressed because he couldn't find anything to do—anything that suited him. Babe kept mentioning it to Johnny until at last he thought over his current enterprises and picked out something he thought Charlie could do. It was just a temporary job and it was up in Georgia, but Johnny figured he could pay a hundred a week and expenses, and Charlie was very pleased about it. Pleased and eager to please and like a damn kid about it.

So Johnny had sent him up to Georgia, and it hadn't been a particularly delicate situation up there—just a situation where it was wise to have a man on the spot, a man he could trust to do some listening and some soothing and report back frequently until the deal went through, but Charlie had managed to foul it up. Now maybe the whole thing would fall through. Johnny didn't know if he could save it or not. If he couldn't save it, his charitable gesture was going to cost him a substantial piece of money—and the distressing thing was that a man would really have to scramble around to foul up a deal as well set as that one had been. It would be in better shape if there had been no one at all up there.

They turned north on 301 toward Bradenton. Johnny had his parking lights on and he was driving fast. He tried not to listen as Charlie, in his light eager voice, told some interminable and pointless story about how the yard man who came once a week cut down something Agnes hadn't wanted cut down—what Agnes had said and what he had said and what the yard man had said.

"For Christ' sake, Charlie!" he said explosively.

"What's the matter? What's the matter, Johnny?"

"I got another call from Ricardo last night, after I talked to you. Stevenson had gotten hold of Ricardo and told him that you told Stevenson that you didn't think there had to be any organizational meeting before approval of the charter."

"Well, it would be just a formality, wouldn't it? I mean we know who the officers are going to be and all."

Johnny gave him a quick glance. "Charlie, what is it that makes you so God damn dumb?"

Charlie tried to smile. His mouth was trembling. "I ... I guess I just work at it."

"I guess you God damn well do. What right did you have to even talk to Stevenson? I told you to stay away from him. He thinks control should be up there. He thinks that Christy and me are a couple of Florida slickers trying to move in on them. Then you go yap yap yap about no organizational meeting. Christ, I don't care what he thinks after the charter goes through, but now you've made him nervous enough so he's starting to try to bitch it up. And now Ricardo is getting nervous. Whichever way Ricardo jumps, the others will jump. Where the hell did you talk to Stevenson?"

"Well, he came into the office, Johnny. You know. Just passing the time of day. We got to talking."

"Stevenson isn't the kind of guy who goes around passing the time of day. He came in to pump you."

36

"I didn't think so, Johnny."

"Face it. You just didn't think. And I can tell you just what the hell you did and why."

"What do you mean?"

Johnny heard the anxiety in the thin voice and he felt the anger swelling thick inside of him, clotting him, thickening his chest. Gene had told him to try to keep from getting angry.

"I'll tell you what you are, Charlie. You're a damn clerk. You never were anything else but a clerk in your life. You had to have somebody standing right over you telling you just exactly what the hell to do. I should have seen that before I sent you up there alone. You get an office of your own you think you're some kind of a big shot. You weren't a big shot and you aren't a big shot, Charlie. I sent you up there to keep in touch and let me know developments. But you have to prove you can sit at a desk. So you open your mouth and start talking policy. You don't know anything about policy. But you have to hear the sickening sound of your own voice. You have to tell those people up there how important you are. You led Ricardo to believe you'd be in on the operation after we get the charter. I wouldn't keep you up there after the charter comes through if all you had to do was sweep the floor. I gave you this job because Agnes kept after Babe about it, and I didn't feel sure about you and I should have had more sense. Jesus Christ! You up there acting like a big expert, and all the time you were as far out of your league as ... Hell, you were a kitten up there, and those are big hungry dogs. You aren't worth a poop, Charlie. Not one little poop in a whirlwind. And when you aren't paddling around gumming things up, you're a God damn bore."

He felt the anger begin to fade. The hard peak of anger crumbled and fell slowly and softly away. Charlie Himbermark sat small in the seat beside him. He looked bludgeoned and shrunken. Johnny was half amused at his own anger, and he felt a small twinge of compassion for the poor old fool.

"Aren't ... aren't you driving pretty fast, Johnny?"

"Shut up!" There was that much anger left.

The miles ran fleetly under the fast wet wheels of the car. They went through Bradenton, and turned toward the Sunshine Skyway and Route 19. Tampa Bay was obscured by rain. Johnny could not see the bridge far ahead. One incredibly steadfast fisherman stood on one of the smaller causeway bridges, huddled against the rail, back to the gusty wind, line stretching down to the gunmetal water, frothed with white.

"You just didn't handle it so well, Charlie," Johnny said at last, his voice soft.

Charlie responded immediately to the hint of forgiveness, and he sat erect and turned toward Johnny. "I guess I just wasn't too clear about what you wanted me to do up there, Johnny. Gosh, I understand it now. I never would have talked like that if I'd understood all the ins and outs. Now that I've got it all clear in my mind, I can handle it all right for you. You can leave me up there when you head back and you won't have to have a worry in the world. That's it, Johnny. Not a worry in the world. I was talking to Will Wilson last night—he's my neighbor—and I was telling him . . ." The voice faltered and stopped.

"Go on, Charlie. What were you telling him?"

"That it . . . was an interesting job."

"And dropping a lot of little hints about it."

"He wouldn't tell a soul, Johnny. Will knows how to keep his mouth shut."

"If that's true, I should have hired him instead of you. Jesus, Charlie, let's not talk about it. We won't talk about it again until we get up there. I wish to God we could have flown up there."

The big car sped on. St. Petersburg was lost and gray under the thick fat rain. Johnny Flagan sat low in the seat, hands holding the wheel lightly. His mind was not on the road or the weather, or even the problems ahead. He was playing a mental game that was old with him, a game that had begun years ago and had become more satisfying to play each year.

He divided his mind into two parts, like a big white balance sheet with a sharp dividing line down the middle. On one side he slowly listed what he owned. Land, securities, cash, buildings, options. He thought of each item carefully, lovingly, remembering to a penny the cost of acquisition, assigning a conservative current valuation to each one. When he was through, when he could think of no other item, he drew a line and added the figures. Next he listed his obligations, finding the exact total. He did it all slowly, so that the game would last longer. He subtracted one from the other.

Johnny Flagan, at this moment, at this instant of time, you are worth almost five hundred and ten thousand dollars. And, except for Bruce Lovingwell—one of the smartest tax attorneys in the business—there is no one else in the wide world who even suspects that it's that much. Half of a million, Johnny. Now let's get on with the game. A dollar bill isn't quite six inches long, but we'll call it six inches and cut the total down to an even half million. Let's see. That's two hundred and fifty thousand feet. About forty-seven miles. Four point seven miles if it was ten-dollar bills. Or damn near a half mile of hundred-dollars bills. Five hundred thousand-dollar bills. Three thousand inches. Two hundred and fifty feet.

He could picture the money spread flat and even along the highway and it gave him a sensual almost voluptuous pleasure to think about it.

The more there was of it, the easier it was to get hold of more.

The old man thought you worked for it. He thought if you broke your back out there in the celery, you'd make money. Or if you hauled on the nets until your hands bled, you'd make out. And the old man had died because he couldn't afford to take the boat out of the water long enough to fix up the rotted leaky bottom. So he drowned out there in the Gulf, him and Buck and Howie, going down in the black night water, choking in the salt water, flapping and choking and yelling and no one to hear them. If the old man had been fifty bucks ahead, he could have taken the boat out and fixed it.

[*The big blue Cadillac moves fast. He keeps it at ninety as much as he can. His is the type of mind that can remember details that seem unimportant at the time. Some part of him is forever observing, recording, filing. And that knack has made him money.*

Suppose a question were asked: What were the last five cars you've passed, Flagan?

"Counting the ones pulled over on the shoulder?"

Just the moving ones.

"That's easier. Let me see. Five. I'll even tell you in the order I passed 'em. A blue and white convertible. Dodge or

39

DéSoto. Woman driver. Then a beat-up old panel delivery. Then—let me see—didn't get much impression from the next one. Dark. Small car. Dark green I think. Then a foreign job. Fancy. I don't know what the hell it was. Followed him for a time and finally made it when he slowed down some. Some people don't like anybody on their tail. When they try it on me, I walk away from them. Then the last one was that station wagon, loaded pretty heavy. Local plates. Clearwater or St. Pete. How'm I doin'?"

Doing fine in your big car, Johnny.

And he senses trouble ahead. He leans forward. He uses the brakes gingerly and the big car skids, straightens, skids, straightens, slows and stops and he lets his breath out and hopes that the station wagon is going to be alert and not pile into him, or get shoved into him by that foreign job.]

5

About eleven miles north of the town of Crystal River on Route 19, on Florida's West Coast, State Route 40 crosses 19 at a village called Inglis. Forty doesn't go far west after it crosses. Just three miles to a place called Yankeetown on Withlacoochee Bay. The Gulf is that close to Route 19 at that point.

Follow Route 19 further north and it swings inland a bit, through Lebanon and Lebanon Station, then Gulf Hammock. By the time it gets up to Otter Creek, six miles north of Gulf Hammock, it is twenty-two miles from the Gulf. Cedar Key is out that way, twenty-two miles along Route 24.

In that straight six miles of Route 19 between Gulf Hammock and Otter Creek, Route 19 crosses the Waccasassa River. Not much of a river. Not much of a bridge where it goes under the road.

The Waccasassa River empties—ten miles from the highway—into, almost inevitably, Waccasassa Bay. The bay makes an almost triangular indentation into the coast of Florida, just about half way between Yankeetown and Cedar Key. The shores of the bay are dreary, uninhabited. Thick mangrove grows down to the salt flats. Behind the mangrove the land is sodden, marshy. In the Gulf Hammock area, Route 19 cannot be more than six feet above the high tide mark in the Gulf ten miles away.

The bridge over the Waccasassa is a relatively modern concrete highway bridge, two lanes wide. Some years ago it was built to replace a rickety wooden lane and a half structure with timbers that flapped and rumbled under the wheels of the vehicles. At the time the bridge was being replaced, through traffic had to take a detour. Not a long detour, about four miles in all. If you were headed north you had to turn west off Route 19 about a mile before you came to the bridge. It was a narrow sand road, and it angled sharply away from Route 19 for over a mile. It turned north then and crossed a narrow wooden bridge over a vagrant loop of the sleepy Waccasassa, and about three hundred yards farther crossed a second bridge over the main river. Two and a half miles farther on, after bearing almost imperceptibly east, the sand road rejoined Route 19.

When the new bridge was built, construction lasted well into the tourist season, despite State Road Department assurances that it would be done by Christmas. As a consequence, many southbound tourists went over the detour down the narrow sand road that wound through sparse stands of pine and then cut through the heavy brush near the river. Many of the tourists had cameras and a few of them, more aware of pictorial values than most, stopped on the stretch between the two wooden bridges to take a picture of a strange old deserted house quite near the sand road. It was a ponderous and ugly old house built of cypress, decorated with the crudest of scroll saw work. It was weathered to a pale silvery gray. The shuttered windows were like blinded eyes. The house sat solidly there and you thought that once upon a time someone had taken pride in it and had ornamented it with the scroll work. It was like a heavy gray old woman wearing crude and barbaric jewelry.

Then the bridge was opened and there was no one to take pictures of the house. No one to see it except for the infrequent local fishermen who knew the times when snook came up the Waccasassa from the Gulf and could be caught from the larger of the two wooden bridges.

It was almost noon on Wednesday, the seventh of October, that the concrete highway bridge became blocked.

Dix Marshall had picked up the load in New Orleans and it was consigned to Tampa. He knew from the way the rig handled that they had loaded it as close to the limit as they dared. The inside rubber on the two rear duals was bald and it felt to him as though the whole frame of the trailer was a little sprung. It had an uneasy sideways motion on long curves to the left. But the diesel tractor was a good one. New and with a rough sound, but with a lot of heart to it. That was a break. Usually the company kept the best tractors off the flat runs, saved them for the mountain routes. Once he'd made this same run with a job you'd have to shift down three times on a four per cent grade. It was six hundred and sixty-five miles from New Orleans to Tampa, and he hadn't gotten a very good start out of New Orleans on Tuesday. He'd felt so woozy after the fight with Gloria that he'd almost asked the dispatcher if he could have a helper on the run. There was the usual bunk behind the cab seat. But the company didn't believe in double wages for a run this short.

Along about midnight he'd gotten so groggy he'd pulled off somewhere near Pensacola and climbed back in the bunk on the sour blankets and corked off. When he woke up it was still dark and he felt a little better, but he felt he'd slept too long.

He wanted this one to be over in a hurry. There would be a load to take on in Tampa consigned to Atlanta, and a load in Atlanta for Biloxi and maybe a short haul load from Biloxi back into New Orleans—he wouldn't know until he got there. He wanted it to be a short trip because he wanted to get back because every time he thought of what Gloria might be doing, he felt sick enough to gag.

Dix Marshall was a small man in his early thirties with thick shoulders and husky tattooed arms. He had thick brown hair which he wore combed straight back, large rather expressive brown eyes, a long upper lip and very bad teeth. He had been driving a truck since fifty-one when he got out of the army and he had been married to Gloria for the last seven years. They had lived in a trailer until the second kid came and then they had moved to a small rented house on the northeast edge of New Orleans.

He had awakened in the truck and he drove toward the dawn thinking about Gloria and feeling sick about the whole mess and wondering just what the hell you did. Did you kill them? What did you do? He knew that all he wanted to do was get back as soon as he could and talk to her some more and maybe they could figure out how it would be for both of them in the future.

She was still a dish. Not so much of a dish as before, but still a dish. Between the two kids she had been fat but after the second one she'd worked on those diets and gotten down pretty well. Not all the way down to the hundred and fifteen like when they were married, but down to a hundred and thirty about.

She'd been so damn cute. That black hair and those dark blue eyes and that cute build. Just about danced his feet right off him. Couldn't think of anything but dancing. On her feet

43

all day long in that store on Canal Street, and then want to dance all night long. Good dancer, too. Lot of rhythm. She'd had a steady boyfriend when he met her. What was that joker's name? Carl something. *Big* bastard. It all happened like he imagined it happened with just about everybody. You think it's for kicks and then it turns out to be something you want permanent. And that old crap about not chasing a streetcar after you caught it was just that. Crap. God knows how many times it was in the back seat of that old Chev of his, and sometimes in motels and once that time in her own room in her own house when her folks had gone over to Lake Charles that time her married sister was sick. It had made him feel strange to be there in her room with the school pictures on the walls and those stuffed dolls and things.

He wished she hadn't let him. He wished she hadn't let him until they were married and then he wouldn't be thinking what he was thinking now. She probably let Carl too, even though she claimed she didn't.

He wanted it to be permanent. She met his folks and he met hers and pretty soon the wedding was all planned and pretty soon the wedding was over and he was married to Gloria. They could have moved in with either set of folks but they didn't want to, and he put the down payment on the used trailer and they had moved in. My God, that had been one hot son of a bitch in the summertime. Lay there in the narrow bed with sweat pouring right off them, but it was the first summer and they did more joking about it than complaining.

She wasn't real bright. Tell her something and she couldn't remember it worth a damn. Couldn't cook much either, but she got better at that. Not bright but always laughing, making jokes, jumping around. Did all her thinking with her body. Talk a blue streak and not say a damn thing. Always wanting to go to the movies—just like now she can't hardly tear herself loose from that television. Not bright, but good. He thought she was good. And it was good to be married. It made you feel settled. You had kids and it made you think you were doing something, building something. And you settled into the job better and you got more dependable and so you got the better hauls and a better rating.

The house wasn't much, but they'd fixed it up pretty good. They did a lot of inside painting they couldn't get the landlord to do. The kids getting old enough to be sort of fun. Hated like hell to be away from them so much, but the money was good, and they were putting some aside, and it all looked fine. Until Sunday night.

He knew he could live to be a million and never forget a second of it, how it was, how things looked—so clear—like it had been engraved somewhere in his mind like a bunch of pictures in an album.

It was the thing that happened to other guys. And it was an old joke, too. A corny old joke. The guys down at the shop would ride each other. "Who's taking care of that while you're away, Dix?"

"I just fix it before I go so it don't need anything in between."

"Nuts. I bet you got yourself one of them there what they call it chastity belts. Let me see the key, Dix."

"Not you, you bastard. You'll get a copy made and you just aren't man enough to handle it."

You made jokes about it. Sometimes the jokes got a little raw on account of Gloria is really a dish, but you didn't let them see you were getting sore. If they knew they could make you sore they'd never let up on you one minute.

He'd taken one of the usual runs to Denver, the Friday to Monday run, but he got up there, just making it, with the transmission sounding like somebody shaking glass in a basket, and there wasn't a spare for the return haul. He'd phoned in and they told him to take an air coach back and so he got in at dusk on Sunday instead of midnight Monday like he always did. He took a bus on out and walked three blocks to the house. The house was dark and he could see there was just one light on, the kitchen light, and he figured she was out there maybe eating by herself after stashing the kids in bed, and it was probably right in between two of her favorite television shows. He thought he would come up behind her sitting there at the kitchen table and put his hands over her eyes, maybe, and say "Guess who?" So he walked quietly onto the porch and opened the screen door and shut it quietly and just started to head across the living room when there was all of a sudden a grunting and rustling from the couch and the bastard from the gas station down at the corner came running at him and got by him and the screen door banged and he heard his steps on the walk, half running. He didn't know who it was in the dark. He hadn't seen him. But he'd pounded the name out of her later.

He turned on the light and she was there on the couch, her black hair all messed up, her face like chalk, her lips without any blood in them, her hands shaking as she tried to hook herself up.

Who's taking care of that while you're away, Dix?

Fellow named Sparkman that works at the Esso Station. Bob Sparkman. Big blond-headed fellow.

He saw her there and he knew he would never forget how she looked, and he just stood there and pointed his finger up in the air and said, "With the kids asleep right over your head."

He was one yard from her, his fists shut tight, when she found her voice and began pleading, explaining, telling him to wait. He gave her a chance to talk. She said nothing had happened, that it was the first time they'd ever been together, that she'd offered him a beer because it was a hot night and he'd turned into a wise guy and turned off the light and she was trying to get the light back on when he walked in. See, there was the beer can.

He kept after her then. He went after her and he kept after her. He hurt her with his hands and he hurt her with his words and he didn't have all of it until two in the morning. Then they were in the kitchen and she sat with her cheek against the cold porcelain top of the table and she was crying silently, hopelessly, and her face was puffed and discolored where he had struck her, but he had the whole truth, he was sure.

It had been going on for six months. Before that there hadn't been anyone for over a year, but there had been another one and his name had been Schneider and that affair had lasted almost a year. Then the record was clean all the way back to the first year after their marriage when there had been one named Cooper and that had only lasted two weeks and they had only been together three times. She didn't know why she did it. She didn't know how it happened to her. She wanted to be good, she said, but these things happened to her. She couldn't help it. They just seemed to happen. And he was away so much.

She lifted her head from the table and looked at him with tired dazed blue eyes and said, "Dix, honey, I'm so ashamed. I'm so terrible ashamed."

There wasn't any other hurt like that. It was like a rusty knife in your gut that kept twisting slowly. He lay beside her while she was in deep exhausted sleep and he tried to think it out logically. But what did you do? Did you kill them? What did you do about it?

And yet in some funny way the most tragic thing seemed to be the tiny nick on his middle knuckle where she had tried to cry out as he struck her, not hard, and her tooth had cut his knuckle. So how could you hurt her bad? How could you kill her? She hadn't ever been very bright. Just sort of fun. And cute. And real good with the kids. Always full of all that sloppy emotion that came over the television. Dirty little affairs and yet she was probably all the time calling them romance. Like a kid playing games, not understanding just how serious it was. She even kept her dolls until she was married. And now, caught and exposed, she still acted more like a naughty child than a grown woman, a mother.

What did you do?

He wanted the trip over. He wanted to go back and talk to her some more. He could give up the whole thing and leave her. But what would happen to her? He knew he could get custody of the kids. But what would happen to Gloria?

If he was going to stay with her, he was going to have to get off the road. Dear God, Sparkman could be back there with her. Get off the road somehow and stay off it. But he knew he wasn't fitted for anything much other than wheeling a big rig. He just knew he had to talk to her. They had to figure this out together. He wondered if he would ever feel like touching her again.

He ran into the rain south of Tallahassee. It was a hard rain. He started the wipers, turned on his running lights and cursed the rain. It would slow him down. But not as much as it would slow down a less experienced driver. He pushed the big rig along, pushed it as fast as he dared. He barreled through the little towns. Capps, Lamont, Eridu, Iddo, Secotan, Perry, Pineland, Athena, Salen, Clara, Shamrock, Eugene, Old Town, Hardee Town, Otter Creek—thundering south through the rain, throwing up spume from the big duals, sitting high with his hands clever on the wheel, eyes trying to penetrate the murkiness ahead.

The thing that caused it was the color of the car. It was a car as gray as the rain, and the tail lights were not on. The car blended, merged with the rain and the road so that Dix Marshall did not see it soon enough. The car was going at a

47

speed of twenty miles an hour through the heavy rain. It had Indiana plates. It was driven by a retired doctor with a mild heart condition.

The big blue and yellow rig was traveling at fifty-five miles an hour when Dix Marshall saw the faint bulk of the slow-moving gray sedan. Within a fractional part of a second he had known that he could not hope to slow down in time. He had a choice to make almost instantly—to cut to the right and take his chances on the sloppy shoulder—to cut around the sedan to the left and risk a head-on with something coming the other way—to brake as hard as he could and hit the sedan and hope to hit it without enough force to kill.

Marshall was an expert. His reflexes were good—his experience was wide. His emotions, not his lack of skill, had trapped him into this situation. He had been in other tight places and he had survived. During the three-quarters of a second it took him to make his decision, the big rig traveled nearly sixty feet. He decided to take the chance of a head-on with something that might be coming through the gray opacity of the rain. It was a calculated risk. With the difference in the relative speeds of the two vehicles, he would not be in the left lane for more than two long seconds. The rain would slow down oncoming vehicles.

He did not hit the brakes. He hit the gas pedal to cut down the duration of the moments of danger. He swung out and he leaned forward further and stared ahead, looking for the twin glow of oncoming dimmers. He passed the gray sedan. He saw something ahead of him, and he snapped the big rig back into the right lane. He snapped it hard and as he did so he saw that the object was the thick concrete railing of the bridge. It was the bridge over the Waccasassa, but he did not know that. He felt the skid of the two sets of duals on the rear of the trailer. He saw the thick rain-wet railing on the right side, saw the rain bouncing from it, haloing it. The trailer kept skidding and he felt it slam against the concrete. It did not seem to be a hard impact. But in the next moment the cab was angled toward the concrete on the left side. He tried to turn away from it and felt the dizzy sense of the cab tipping, the whole rig tipping. As it went over he knew all at once how he would handle that talk with Gloria, how he could make it come out all right for both of them. There wasn't time to put it into the words of the mind, but he knew how it could be.

The heavy cab smashed into the thick railing, burst through it, and pieces of concrete as big as bushel baskets fell into the river. By then the cab and trailer lay on the right side, sliding with a raw noise of ripping metal, sliding, wedging the big trailer from side to side, across the bridge, while the cab, having punched its hole, was nipped off by the continuing motion of the trailer and fell into the shallow river, making one further quarter turn as it fell, landing with the four heavy wheels in the air, then settling, sighing, suckling against the mud of the bottom, air bubbles bursting against the rain pocked surface. Only the front right tire was completely under water. The two rear tires were locked. The front left tire spun for a very short time, braked by the water that came to the hub cap.

Dr. Dudley Stamm had never driven through such a heavy rain. He kept wondering if it would be wiser to pull over to the side of the road and wait it out. He would have done that had it been a thunder shower. But this rain seemed constant, interminable. He did not wish to spend untold hours along the side of the road, with the possibility of the soaked engine not starting again when the rain let up.

"Ever see a rain like this, Myra?"

"Never in my life, Dud. Never. Do you feel all right, dear?"

"I feel fine. But if we can find anything along here, we better hole up."

"But how about the Sheridans?"

"We can phone them. They'll understand. If it's raining as hard in St. Pete as it is here, they'll damn well understand. Good Lord, it looks like the end of the world."

She studied the map. "There should be nice courts down by Crystal River and Homosassa Springs."

"How far?"

"About thirty miles from here."

"An hour and a half at this rate."

"Are you getting too tired, dear?"

"No. You keep asking me that and I keep telling you. If I get tired, I'll let you know."

"You never do."

He did not know where the truck came from. He did not know it had been behind him. He saw a faint oncoming glint of lights in his rear view mirror and then it was upon him, roaring and steaming by, hurling solid water against his windshield. Dr. Stamm instinctively tromped on his brakes. He heard Myra give a little cry of alarm.

"Maniac!" Dr. Stamm said fiercely.

The wiper cleared the water and he saw it all, not clearly because it was obscured by the rain, a rain that would have made it difficult to see across the street clearly. The truck swung in. The trailer swung and slammed the bridge abutment on the right with a noise muted by the rain roar. The truck swerved and the cab burst through the bridge rail on the left side as the whole thing was tipping over. The cab fell from view and the trailer slid on, slid on its side, wheels toward them and came to a jarring stop as it wedged itself across the road from concrete rail to concrete rail, an immense obstacle. The top wheels, and there seemed to be many of them, kept spinning, hurling the rain from them, encircled by spray.

Dr. Stamm came to a stop just short of the bridge. He opened the door and hurried across the road, hearing but paying no attention to Myra's despairing cry behind him. He slithered down the muddy grassy bank and moved cautiously into the river. The water came up to his knees and then to mid-thigh. He paused and moved his wallet to his breast pocket. The next step brought him up to his waist. He looked at the upside down cab and mentally estimated the height of it and saw that it was in water that would be over his head. He was steeling himself to plunge forward when he felt a familiar constriction in his chest, an odd area of spurious warmth about his heart.

It was the message of the heart that brought him back to reality, to the here and now of a sixty-seven-year-old man who stood drenched in a muddy little river. The accident had made him forget himself entirely. From the moment he left his car until this moment he had been no age. He had been a man who reacted as a man. It had not occurred to him that the body would fail to obey. Now he was himself again, and he felt ridiculous as he stood there. Quixotic and enfeebled old man who had thought the worn body would serve him in the same way it had thirty years ago. He could do nothing for the driver. He realized with a certain grim humor that it would be very awkward to faint at this moment. Myra would have the devil of a time explaining what had happened, both to the police and the Sheridans.

He reached with great care into his pocket, below water

level, and found the little box and took it out. It was dry inside. He opened it and put two of the small white pills on his tongue and swallowed them. He put the box in his breast pocket. He felt the stricture begin to fade, felt the cooling of the deceptive warmth. Only then did he turn slowly and walk back across the muddy bottom to the bank. He heard Myra and he looked up. She stood drenched at the top of the bank, her light flowered dress clinging to her, her gray hair rain-matted against her head, and she was crying, "Come back! Please come back!"

He clambered slowly and with difficulty up the bank. She put her arm around him and they walked back to the car. They got in, wet as they were. He took off his glasses and took a Kleenex from the seat and began to dry them.

Myra was crying and smiling at him. "Oh, Dud! Honestly! Dud, you fool."

"Ancient fool."

"He'd be dead anyway."

Dudley Stamm said slowly, "If not then, he is now."

"He could have killed us too."

He took her hand. His chest felt easier. "But he didn't."

A brown car stopped behind them and a man came up in a green battered raincoat. He knocked on the car window and said, "What's happened?"

Stamm rolled the window down an inch. "Go take a look. It's pretty obvious. The driver is still in the cab."

"How do we get through?"

"I don't imagine we do."

Dan Boltay of the State Highway Patrol was driving north on patrol when he came to the bridge over the Waccasassa. He put on his brakes when he saw the thing across the bridge. He went into a controlled skid and stopped twenty feet from the barrier and stared at it, unable to comprehend what it was for a few moments. It looked as if a metal fence about eight feet high, slightly buckled, had been erected across the bridge. Then he realized what it was.

"Holy jumping Marie," he said softly. He turned on the red revolving dome light to warn oncoming traffic. He started to radio in and then thought he better take a closer look. He got out and put on his black rain cape. He went to either end of the trailer and saw how forcibly it had wedged itself across the bridge. The metal frame members were gouged into the concrete. He climbed up onto the railing and walked around it, leaning his hand against it. He saw the twenty-foot hole in the side rail, and saw the upside down cab down in the water.

Just how the hell, he thought, *did that joker manage to do this?* A fragment of an old joke fled across his mind. Where did he stand when he threw it?

He jumped down to the road on the far side of the trailer. There were three cars piled up. He walked to the first car. Gray Buick. Indiana plates. Old couple inside. Holding hands. Probably scared. Probably saw it.

The old geezer rolled the window part way down.

"Did you see this happen?"

"The driver is still in the cab, officer."

"How long ago did it happen?"

"Ten minutes, maybe a little longer."

"Anybody try to get him out?"

"I tried, but I couldn't get to him. These other two cars arrived about five minutes ago."

Boltay was caught by indecision. Take time to radio in for help. Ten minutes wasn't too long. Sometimes they came out of it. He made up his mind and trotted, cursing, down to the river bank. He stripped down to his shorts, covered his uniform with the black rain cape and went in. He swam to the cab, used the things he could grasp on the cab to pull himself down. The windows were shut. He felt the door handle, turned in the water and braced his feet and, hoping it was not too badly sprung, gave a heave. The door sprang open, the edge of it scraping his shin just below the knee. He went up for a breath, then went down and reached in and felt the man. He got hold of a wrist and the back of the man's neck and pulled him out through the door and came to the surface with him. He pulled the man to shore, hoisted him on his shoulder, carried him up and laid him down on his back. Only then did he see the driver's head. The whole left temple area and the left frontal lobe was crushed inward. Water had washed the blood from it and he could see the white edges of the shattered bone. It was a hole you could have put your fist in. Boltay looked at the driver with both anger and disgust. He was annoyed with the man for being dead.

He looked up and saw five or six people looking down at him, looking at the dead driver with that funny blank expression they always wear when they look at the dead. They look steadily and they lick their lips and they swallow, but they don't stop looking.

Boltay, with a twinge of regret, put his uniform shirt over the man's broken head, dressed in the rest of the uniform and put the rain cape on. He wasn't soaking wet. Just sodden.

He went up and got the story from the old couple.

"How fast would you say he was going?"

"I'd say about sixty, officer. It was very fast for the road conditions."

"How fast were you going?"

"About twenty-five, I think."

"Have your lights on?"

"Lights? Why, no. I don't guess I did. I should have, shouldn't I?"

"Yes, I think you should have."

"My husband is soaked, officer. And he's not well. Can we go now. We'll go back and find a motel."

"Okay. When you get settled phone the State Highway Patrol and tell them where you're located. There may be more questions."

He climbed up and got the name off the side of the trailer and went back to his car. There were six other cars stopped. He made his call. "Boltay in 26. I got a bad one. On the Waccasassa Bridge. Big truck trailer wedged right across it. Cab went into the river through the rail and killed the driver. No other vehicles involved. No wrecker is going to haul it out of the way. We're going to have to use torches to cut it free. It looks like a long job and I'm getting a fast pile-up here. Maybe fifteen cars so far."

He released the button and the metallic voice said, "Is the trailer on its wheels?"

"No sir. On the right side, wheels toward the north. The name on it is Twin X Express, out of New Orleans. I got the driver out of the cab and he's on the north bank, east of the bridge. We'll have to set up traffic control and do some re-routing."

"We'll have to close it at Inglis on the south and Otter Creek on the north. Wait a minute. There's a wooden bridge or something in the area. A detour used quite a few years back. It might still be passable. Hold it while I ask."

Boltay waited. "Here it is. A dirt road that turns off a mile south of you. It turns west. There's two other cars on the way. You check that detour and then call in and let us know if it's passable."

Boltay swung around and ignored the people who shouted questions at him and headed south. He found the turn-off. The road was narrow but the drainage seemed to be pretty good. It was soft, but not too soft. Both wooden bridges were one lane, but they felt solid. Solid enough for passenger cars. He followed the detour until he came out on the highway again.

He called in. "It's passable. Not for trucks, though."

"Okay. We'll set up truck detour signs at Otter Creek and Inglis. You start routing your pile-up over the detour. We'll have signs down to you in another twenty minutes. When Stark gets there, put him on the other end."

Within fifteen minutes the tangle was straightened out. Trucks that had gotten by Inglis and Otter Creek before the signs went up were routed back. The two highway patrol cars, parked crosswise of the road, dome lights flashing, routed passenger traffic over the old detour. An ambulance picked up the body to take it over to Gainesville. The first technicians had arrived. They walked around the trailer and looked at the job and made obscene comments about the job and the rain. They sent for heavier equipment and more torches. They told the highway patrol that if they had the bridge clear by eight o'clock at night, they would be lucky. They planned the job: Cut the ends free. Use two big wreckers to swivel it. Bring in another truck and off-load the cargo. Then, if the wheels were too badly damaged, drag it off the bridge. If not, rig lines and tip it up on its wheels. All this in heavy rain and a wind that was slowly, steadily increasing.

And so passenger traffic rolled cautiously over the old detour, over the two wooden bridges, by the grim old house between them, back out onto the highway. They felt their way through the half world of gray driving rain. They inched across the old timbers of the bridges.

The Stamms found motel accommodations a little north of Chiefland. They had changed to dry clothing, had phoned both the Sheridans and the State Highway Patrol.

Dudley Stamm stood at the window looking out at the rain. Myra sat across the room, talking, talking.

"Honestly, I thought you'd gone clean out of your mind.

54

Dashing out of the car like that when you know you're not supposed to do anything like that. I just didn't know what to think. And then to come after you in all that rain and see you standing down there up to your middle in the water—why it was just about the worst shock I ever had in my life. I don't know what in the world you had in mind. You certainly couldn't do anything for that poor driver. I know it was his fault but I can't help feeling sorry for him. Even though it was terrible at the time. I can't help thinking how *strange* you looked down there, how strange and queer standing there in that river. Do you see what I mean, dear?"

"Yes dear," Dudley Stamm said wearily.

[*By now the great anonymity of the highway has ended in other places. Fallen trees block the road from Shamrock to Horseshoe Point. A clot of cars has gathered and there are frightened conferences, many plans of action.*

Near Lecanto the wind takes control of a car from the unskilled hands of a young girl. She is lucky in that she is not injured. She is less lucky in her rescuers. The car is too deep in the ditch to be hauled out. They take the girl along. They are on their way from Lecanto to Holder, three of them, half drunk, excited by the storm, excited by the clinging wet clothes of the girl. Had the heavy rain not drowned the motor of the truck, she would have come to no harm. But they sat in the rain with her and finished the bottle and opened another one and forced her to drink a great deal of it and later they raped her.

The six vehicles move steadily north, toward inadvertent rendezvous. Cadillac, station wagon, Mercedes, Dodge convertible, Plymouth, panel delivery—toward a road block and wooden bridges and high water and an ancient cypress house.]

6

Billy Torris was awakened by the sound of the rain on the metal roof of the stolen panel delivery truck. While still in half sleep he thought he was home again, sleeping in the room off the kitchen with two of his brothers and Mom was up early and standing at the sink and pumping water into the tin dishpan. But the dishpan didn't get full and the spattery noise didn't change and a few minutes later he woke up and it took him several minutes to figure out where he was. He lay on burlap sacks on the metal bed of the panel delivery and it was really raining. Really coming down.

The rain made him feel safer. There was a gray anonymity in the rain. In the sunshine you felt people were looking at you. They had time to look and you stood out clearly. In the rain they were busy keeping dry and they didn't look at you so directly.

He remembered that Frank had driven all the way through to Tampa. The girl, Hope, had slept here in the back while they were on the road, and he had sat up in the front with Frank. They had stopped about midnight at a crummy looking bunch of cabins near Tampa and now the truck was parked beside one of the cabins, turned around so you couldn't see the plates from the road.

He sat up and felt the stiffness in his muscles. The metal bed had been hard through the burlap. He ran his fingers through his long black hair, combing it back over the temples, fingering the duck tail into shape. You couldn't do it right without a comb. But it didn't make a hell of a lot of difference if it wasn't done right. No matter what you did you couldn't look very sharp in jeans so dirty they felt stiff, and a T-shirt with the rip on the left shoulder.

Frank and Hope were in the cabin. He wondered if they

were getting up. He wondered what time it was. You couldn't tell the time on this kind of a morning. He knelt and tucked his T-shirt into his jeans and climbed cautiously over into the front seat. The place might be surrounded and they might be ready to move in. He could see two other cabins but that was all. He could hear traffic on the highway, but he couldn't see the highway.

He didn't want to go out into the rain. He opened the side door and turned sideways on the seat and relieved himself. He wished Frank and Hope would come out and they'd get going. He didn't feel right about anything when he was alone. But when he was with Frank Stratter everything was okay. You felt better when you were with Frank. You felt like everything would work out the way Frank said it would. But when you were alone you kept thinking it was an awful mess and it was going to get a hell of a lot worse, and never get better.

Billy Torris was eighteen, thin, wiry, with a weak troubled face—the fading honey color that was all that was left of the deep tan he had acquired on the road job, working stripped to the waist under the watchful shotguns of the guards.

He thought about the dishpan sound and wished he was home. But he couldn't go home. He'd be picked up. Even if the old man would let him get near the place, he couldn't go home, back to the farm near Alturas.

The old man couldn't get it through his head that they'd just been horsing around. Just out banging around on a Saturday night in Fowler's old heap. He'd driven the tractor all week long and Saturday night was the time you relaxed. Dukie got hold of two bottles of raw corn and they were drinking that. He and Fowler and Dukie. Then they got tossed out of the dance and they just rode around, like always. Like he told the court, it was Fowler who decided they could have some fun with Marv. Marv had just gotten the job as night man at the gas station. For years they'd always kicked around with Marv, he was so sort of dumb and serious. They didn't have a buck between them, but Fowler pulled right up to the pump and told Marv to fill it up. Marv wanted to see the money but Fowler pretended to get sore and he started yelling and pretty soon Marv filled it up. It was funny thinking of how Marv was going to have to explain where the gas went. Then Marv checked the oil and then he asked for the money and Fowler made a real comedy about going through all his pockets and then telling Marv that by God somebody must have stolen his money. They all started laughing at the expression on Marv's face, and then Fowler tried to start it up but it wouldn't start.

Marv sort of backed toward the station with a hand behind him and he said, "You got to give me the money or I'll call the cops."

Fowler jumped out and looked under the hood and turned to him and Dukie and said, "The son of a bitch took the distributor cap."

They all got out then and started walking toward Marv and Marv kept backing toward the station. Marv should have known enough to give up that distributor cap. He should have known enough not to get funny with Fowler. Billy remembered how indignant he had felt. It was just a joke and now Marv was trying to make trouble.

They backed Marv right into the station and he wouldn't give it up. Then Marv jumped toward the wall phone. Fowler grabbed him and they started wrestling around and that was when they broke the glass case. Fowler got the distributor cap away from him and Marv grabbed a socket wrench and came at Fowler, half crying the way he always did when he was sore. He hit Fowler on the arm and then it was Dukie that swung right from the floor and busted one of the bones in his hand when he hit Marv right flush on the button. Marv went down and slapped his head on the concrete floor and that was when he got the concussion. It scared Billy and Dukie looked scared too, but Fowler started picking up the cigarettes that had fallen out of the broken case and he said, "Let's get out of here."

They all put packs of cigarettes in their pockets and it was Fowler, looking kind of funny and wild, who went over and pushed the no sale button on the cash register. The bell rang and the drawer slid open and Dukie said, "Don't touch the money."

But Fowler grabbed all the bills. They were heading for the car, running, when the county cops pulled into the station. Two of them in the county car. There wasn't time to put the distributor cap in, and they started running down the highway and the county car came after them. They took off across the fields and Billy ran as hard as he could. They started shooting and he tripped and fell and he was too scared to get up. He heard them coming and he didn't dare look back. He tried to crawl and then the steps were close and somebody hit him on the head.

Later, after he came to when they were driving him and Fowler in, he found out that they had shot Dukie right through the head. It made a big stink because Dukie's people owned a lot of land in the county, but it was too late then, and it made it necessary to convict the two that were left so that shooting Dukie wouldn't look like such a bad mistake.

He was two days past eighteen when it happened and he got three years and Fowler got five. The old man wouldn't come and see him and he wouldn't give out any money to any lawyer. He'd never gotten along very good with the old man, and this was the end of it as far as the old man was concerned. Mom came to see him and did a lot of crying and told him how the old man was acting.

He tried to explain how they were just horsing around, how they hadn't meant anything and about the corn they'd been drinking. But there were hard facts. Hard, like stones. Facts like Marv being unconscious for thirty-six hours. And the money in Fowler's pockets. And the cigarettes the cops took off him and Fowler, and out of Dukie's pockets.

After the trial they shipped him and Fowler from the county jail to Raiford Prison, and then from Raiford they were sent with some others down to a road camp near Conway. Fowler seemed to go kind of crazy in the road camp, getting locked in those sleeping trucks every night and they finally couldn't handle him and sent him back to Raiford.

It had been damn lonesome after they sent Fowler back. He was scared by the way some of the men acted. The work wasn't too hard. You had to keep going, but you could take it a little slow, slower than when you were working for the old man.

It was on the road camp that he got friendly with Frank Stratter. It made him feel good to be Frank's friend, because Frank wasn't the kind to be friendly with just anybody. Frank was about twenty-three. He was tall and blond and had one of those builds like a cowboy—big wide shoulders and real little hips. He was in for car theft and Frank told him in confidence that the reason he was in for car theft was because they couldn't make the other stuff stick. He had pale eyebrows and pale lashes and the eyebrows were white against the deep road-camp tan. It gave his face a sort of funny

59

naked look. He never changed expression much. He moved easy and lightly and he always somehow looked cleaner and neater than the others, even after one of the real stinking hot days.

Nobody pushed Frank Stratter around, not even Big Satch, the guard that was nine tenths belly. Billy heard that before he'd arrived Big Satch had beat up on Frank, trying to get him to hit back. But Frank wouldn't hit back and he wouldn't yell and he wouldn't beg. The other guards didn't like it, but they were as scared of Big Satch as the prisoners were. He busted Frank up three times and couldn't get a rise out of him. After that he left Frank alone and went back to concentrating on the Negroes.

Billy remembered how it was the day they took off. It was right after the Fourth of July. They were cutting brush along the sides of State Route 15, keeping a lookout for snakes. For this job there were eighteen in the group and three guards—Big Satch, one they called Stud and a new one. Along about eleven in the morning the new guard all of a sudden fell flat on his face in the road, fell right on his gun. Big Satch cut the work and herded them all into a group and kept his eyes on them while Stud took a look at the guard who'd passed out.

"The heat got him, I think," Stud said. "We better take him in."

"Put him in the truck and take him on in and come on back."

"Maybe we should ought to all go in."

"The hell with that. I can handle this bunch. You take him on in and come back."

It was funny how things changed as soon as the big truck had gone. Big Satch had them back working again, but it was different. All the men were watching Big Satch out of the corners of their eyes. You could see it getting to him. He began to get a little jumpy, looking around too fast when he heard a noise or thought he heard a noise. Little by little it began to get out of control, and you could feel it getting out of control. It made you sort of excited. It was like the noise kids make when they imitate a bomb. A little thin whistle between your teeth, starting low and going higher and louder and louder and then boom at the end.

The boom came when a man named Buck something spun quick and threw the brush hook at Big Satch as hard as he could. Big Satch sidestepped it easily and blew the belly out of Buck with the shotgun. It seemed to happen in a half a second. Then three brush hooks all came flying at once and one missed, one hit blade first and sliced his shoulder open, and one hit his head handle first and knocked him down. A friend of Buck's came rushing in as Big Satch was trying to get up and he took a swing like you swing a scythe. It hit the throat as clean as could be and went on through so easy the man who swung it spun half around looking shocked and surprised. Big Satch's hat had come off when he fell. Now his head came off as easily as the hat. A great black gout of blood came out of his thick neck and he settled down into the road, and the head rolled over slowly twice, so you could see the face each time, and then rolled down into the ditch and ended up face down in the few inches of drainage water in the bottom.

A car came along then, an out-of-state car, and it wasn't going very fast, but it certainly picked up speed and got on out of there. Everybody stood around for a few moments and Billy realized that the object hadn't been to get away. It had been to kill Big Satch and that had been done.

Frank Stratter picked up the bloody shotgun and yelled, "Okay. Let's go. Split up." He came toward Billy and said, "Come on, kid."

Frank said it was wet land east of there, full of lakes and marshes, so they headed south and west, skirted the west bank of East Tohopekaliga Lake and about six in the evening came out on Route 192 near the lake. Frank had kept up a hell of a pace. Billy was exhausted, his mouth like cotton, a great pain blanketing his left side from armpit to belt line. They were brush burned, bitten by a thousand bugs, and muddy to the knees.

"What do we do now, Frankie?" Billy panted.

"Shut up. We got to get a car somehow. And then we got to think about clothes."

The car was almost too damn easy. It was in a narrow lane off the highway. A man and a woman and their little girl were having a sort of picnic. The back of the car was full of luggage. It was just out of sight of traffic on the highway. Frank made the man and the woman and the little girl lie flat on their faces, the little girl between them. The little girl was crying, but there was no one to hear her. They were from South Carolina. The man had thirty-eight dollars, and

61

travelers' checks that Frank didn't touch. The woman had eleven dollars in her purse. Frank guarded them while Billy dug around in the suitcases and found the man's clothing and put on slacks that were long enough but too big around the middle and a sport shirt that wasn't much too big. Then Billy watched them, holding the gun, while Frank changed. The slacks were too short for him and just about right around the waist, but the shirt looked as though it would split if he bunched his shoulders.

Frank told the people to wait right there until dark before going out to the highway. He said they might come back and check. Frank had taken complete charge. They got in the car and they drove to Haines City and then over to Lakeland. It was dark when they got to Lakeland. They abandoned the car there after wiping the wheel and door handles clean. Frank brought along one of the suitcases, with more clothes and toilet articles. They ate in a bean wagon near the bus station after washing up in the men's room in the bus station. They had left the shotgun in the car.

After they ate they took a bus over to Tampa and found a cheap hotel and took a double room. They rented a radio and they sat in the room and, on the eleven o'clock broadcast, they heard the latest news of the escape.

Of the eighteen on the road gang, one was dead, the one Big Satch had shot. Eleven had been recaptured, including the one who had killed the guard. Two of those recaptured had testified against the one who had killed the guard. It was expected that the remaining six would soon be picked up. They were working the swamp lands with dogs. Over a hundred law officers were engaged in the search. Two of the escaped men had stolen a car near East Tohopekaliga Lake. The description of the car was given, and the license number. It had not yet been recovered. The men who had taken the car were believed to be, from their descriptions, Frank Stratter and William Torris. Both men were to be considered dangerous, and Stratter was believed to be armed with the shotgun taken from the dead guard.

The next morning they took a Trailways bus from Tampa to Miami. They found a cheap hotel in Miami.

"Now what?" Billy demanded.

"Let me handle it, kid. We got to have new names and papers to back them up. We got to have a clean car. We can

62

maybe pick up a cheap apartment. For that we got to have some money. So the first thing we do is get some money."

"We stay right here?"

"Why not? You nervous? I know the town. They'll figure we're headed north, out of the state. You got to try to think like they do. We'll do a few operations around here. I'll break you in. One thing, we got to have a cover. We got to have jobs. It doesn't matter what kind. We operate at night. First we got to have papers so the new names will hold up. It isn't hard to get driver's licenses. Those are always good. You got to have a car for that. Tonight we start to operate."

And on that first night in Miami they had operated. Frank took a liquor store. He held a rock the size of a potato in his fist. They went in and he leaned over the counter and frowned at a lower shelf and said, "What's that stuff?"

When the man turned, he hit him solidly with the rock and the man fell behind the counter. Frank got behind the counter and said, "Customer coming. Be looking around."

Billy, his stomach trembling, walked over and stared, without seeing anything, at a wine display.

"I want a fifth of Jim Beam."

"Here you are, sir."

"Where's Joe tonight?"

"He had to go up to Hollywood on business. I'm helping out. Anything else?"

"No. That'll do it."

Billy heard the rustle of the paper bag, heard the door swing shut as the man went out. He turned around and saw Frank empty the cash register, moving with deliberation. He saw Frank open a drawer, take out a heavy revolver, examine it, drop it into a paper bag. He bent over, came up with the unconscious man's wallet, took some bills out of it and dropped it.

"Let's get out of here!" Billy said.

"Relax, kid." They headed for the door. Frank turned out all the lights but one in the back of the store. "He's closed for the night."

"Is he dead?"

"Damn it, what makes you so nervous? No, he isn't dead. Wait a second. Might as well take a couple of bottles along. I got all the prints wiped off. Scotch ought to do."

Frank latched the door behind him, tested the lock, then

wiped the prints off the outside handle. They walked three blocks and took a bus. When they were back in the hotel, they counted the money. Two hundred and twelve.

Two weeks later Billy felt a lot less nervous. His new name was Danny King. He worked in a supermarket, packing orders and carrying them out to cars. Frank Stratter was Bob King, his brother. They lived in a garage apartment, owned clothes that fitted, owned a Buick in good condition, had papers in their pockets to prove their new identity. The road camp seemed a long way off. The head rolling into the ditch was something he had dreamed. Every other escapee had been captured. Frank worked in a big Ford agency, washing cars. Billy wished they could just go on the way they were, and forget the operations. Give them up.

He tried to tell that to Frank, but Frank couldn't understand what he meant. That was the funny thing about Frank. You could get just so friendly with him, but you couldn't go beyond a certain point. There was a wall there.

Frank liked to talk about the operations. "You can't keep pulling the same stuff in the same way. Then they get to know where to look for you. You got to keep loose. But we're messing around with little stuff. When the stake is big enough, we'll try something bigger."

"Like what, Frank?"

"Like maybe a bank. Something where you've got to do a lot of planning, but when you make out, it's worth it."

"I don't want to do anything like that."

"Sure you do. Your nerve is getting better all the time. You're shaping up good. And you handle the car nice. We can't stay on this two bit level forever, kid."

"Let's not rush it."

"No. We won't rush it. I got some things I want to do first. One of them is pick up a friend."

"A friend?"

"From up near Ocala where I come from. You'll like her. She's a good kid."

He had felt all along that Frank was closing him out, keeping him out of the center of things. The girl would be another door closed against him. Frank went after her in late August, taking the car. He was gone three days. It was bad while he was gone. The streets were different. He felt as though people were watching him. He felt as though at any moment somebody would look at him and recognize him and begin to yell. But Frank said people didn't do that sort of thing. Take that man in the grocery store, while Frank had held the gun and he had cleaned out the cash drawer. Frank said if that man saw him on the street he would be a little puzzled. He would think he had seen him before, but he wouldn't remember where or how. Billy hoped Frank was right.

He had been thinking about girls a lot lately. There had only been that one time in the loft of the barn at Fowler's place. He and Fowler and Dukie and that girl Christabelle, the one that wasn't quite right in the head. It hadn't been anything like he had thought it would be, and it had cured him of girls for quite a while, but now he was thinking of them again, and he felt a little unclean the way he was thinking about them. Funny, he thought, how you can be an escaped convict and have been in on fifteen . . . no, sixteen robberies with Frank and still feel guilty about thinking dirty.

While Frank was gone he wondered what the girl would be like. Frank liked things with style. He guessed she would look like something out of the movies, and then the two of them would look down on him, instead of just only Frank. A real smooth dish, with silky legs and one of those wet red mouths and wise eyes. That's what Frank would have. It made him feel small, thinking of how it would be after there were three of them, and he thought he would do an operation while Frank was gone, just to show him he could. He found a place that looked all right and he even went in and bought cigarettes there, but he couldn't get his nerve all the way up to do it and he was afraid the man would see the bulge of the gun in his pants.

So he worked each day and he went to the movies each night Frank was away, and on the fourth day when he got home from the supermarket, the Buick was parked by the garage apartment and he knew Frank was back with the girl.

He went in and Frank introduced them. It shocked Billy when he saw the girl. She was just a plain country girl in a cotton dress and evidently not a damn thing else, standing there barefoot in the apartment, and she didn't look over fifteen or sixteen. She had a kind of wide face and sleepy-looking eyes and she was built a little heavy, but she was really stacked. She pushed out on all parts of that cotton dress. "This is Hope Morrissey," Frank said. "Billy Torris."

"Hi," Billy said.

"Hi, Billy," Hope said.

She had a thin country-sounding voice and she wasn't at all like Billy had thought she would be. It made him look at Frank in a sort of different way, as though maybe Frank wasn't what he had figured he was. Frank didn't think she was too young or dumpy or anything. He seemed glad he'd brought her back, and glad to have her there. They seemed pretty used to each other. She couldn't walk within five feet of Frank without him grabbing her, but she didn't seem to mind or even hardly pay any attention. She'd brush on by like he wasn't there. Anyway it was good to have somebody do the cooking, even if she couldn't cook very good. She wasn't very clean or very good about picking up around the place. Her ankles always looked sort of grubby and she never combed her hair much. Frank got clothes for her, but she liked to pad around in that old cotton dress, barefoot, humming to herself in a funny tuneless way.

She slept in with Frank and just about as soon as they got in the room together, that noise would start and Billy would go on out a lot of the times and walk around until they were pretty certain to be asleep. Frank was at her all the time, it seemed like. Morning and night and then, on weekends, it was just better to be out of there and go to the movies or go over to the Beach. She certainly didn't have anything to say. But after she came Frank would talk a lot more than before.

He did a lot of walking alone in September and having her there made him think a lot more about girls than before. He got so he'd follow them on the street, but nothing ever seemed to come of it. Frank had started his big plans. He wouldn't talk about them. But he spent hours drawing floor plans and going over maps. They did some small operations and one turned out a lot better than they had any right to hope. Over eight hundred, it was.

Then on Monday, the day before yesterday, it all ended in a hurry. It was a hot night. He and Frank had been out looking around and then they went back and got Hope and they left the car right there by the apartment and the three of them walked down about three blocks to a place for some beer. Frank was wearing khakis and a purple sports shirt. Billy had on old jeans and a torn T-shirt. Hope wore one of her baggy cotton dresses and a pair of sandals. The bank roll was behind the loose board in the closet, along with the two revolvers. They had some beer and about midnight they walked back. They were a block from the place when Frank stopped and said, "Trouble!"

Billy looked and saw the prowl car parked out by the curb. They walked slowly across the street. Frank wouldn't let them hurry. They headed on back the way they had come. They went over a block and Frank made them wait while he went back to take a look. Billy was nervous. Hope just stood there waiting, chewing gum, patient as a cow in a field. Frank came back in about ten minutes.

"They're up in the place, looking around. I saw them. We got to get out of here."

"How?" Billy asked.

"We got to get a car and we got to get some clothes. I've got about twenty bucks on me. You got anything?"

"Two dollars."

They took the car out of a used car lot. It was a battered old panel delivery. On the side of it it said *Hollywood Seafood Company*. Frank crossed the wires, and it started all right. Billy got the plate off a pickup parked on a dark street.

Frank said they should leave town. Hope sat warmly, heavily between them. Frank cursed as they drove out of town, through Coral Gables. After an hour or so he seemed to cheer up. He told Billy that they'd had some fun for a while anyway, and it wouldn't be too rough to start over again. But it had to be in a new town. He'd heard New Orleans was a good town. They could operate on the way over, just to get money enough for the trip.

After buying gas and eating, they had just a few dollars left when they got to Bradenton Tuesday night. Frank said he had been thinking about how to pull something quick and simple. He cruised around and they found a bar and he parked a half block away and sent Hope back to the bar. "No bum, you understand," he said. "Somebody that looks like they got a couple of bucks."

"I never did nothing like this."

"You won't have any trouble. It doesn't look like a place they'll throw you out of. Just wiggle it around and let somebody buy you a drink then tell him you know a better place you want to go to. Then walk him up this way and slow down when you get in those shadows there by the edge of that warehouse."

She was gone fifteen minutes. They stood leaning against

67

the warehouse, waiting for her. When she came along with the man, they grabbed him fast. Billy didn't even get a look at him. Hope went and got in the truck while they went over him. He had eleven dollars. Frank was so disgusted with the take that he kicked the man solidly in the head, twice. The next place worked better. The man had nearly forty dollars and he was smaller and easier to handle. Frank said there was no reason why it wouldn't work all the way to New Orleans.

"I don't like doing it," Hope said.

"But you'll do it, won't you? Won't you?"

She gave a little gasp of pain and said, "Sure, Frank. Yes, I'll do it. Gee, you wanta give me a cancer or something?"

She slept in the back on the burlap sacks the rest of the way up to the tourist cabins in Tampa. When they got the cabin, Frank said he should sleep in the truck and Frank and Hope would take the cabin.

Now, in the rainy morning, it seemed like a big mess that would just get worse. It didn't ever seem to occur to Frank that they could get caught. It was as though something was left out of Frank, some degree of fear and judgment that other people had.

Billy wished they'd get up and then they could get out on the road in the rain and start making miles. He wondered how Frank was going to arrange to trade cars. They ought to anyway get some green paint and paint out that seafood sign. He wished Frank hadn't kicked that man so hard. There in the dark shadows by the warehouse it had sounded too hard. Frank had grunted with the effort as he had kicked the man.

It was, he guessed, about an hour since he had awakened. He was wondering if he should go and knock on the door. Then all of a sudden Frank and Hope ran to the truck and they each got in out of the rain, one on each side of him. The girl pressed warm and steamy against him and it made him feel strange.

Frank handed him the keys and said, "You drive. I'm going to get in the back and get some sleep."

"How about breakfast?" Hope asked.

"Save it until lunch, honey." Frank climbed over into the back. "Okay. Let's roll. Stay under the speed limit, Billy. Go up 41 to 98 and cut over 98 to 19."

Frank Stratter lay flat on his back in the panel delivery as it started up. He didn't feel sleepy. He had wanted to think. And he couldn't think and drive at the same time.

Last night he had had bad dreams and he had awakened with a premonition of danger. The last time he had felt the same way he had been picked up a day later and eventually sentenced to five years. It was a very uncomfortable feeling. He knew that soon, very soon, when the very first decent chance came along, he would have to separate himself from these two kids. He did not know how he would do it. It would depend on circumstances. On taking the right step at the right time. It might make sense to double back, maybe head down onto the keys. Let them keep running.

Some day it would be nice to get up near Ocala, just long enough to make a chance to see June Anne. Long enough to hear her yelp at him. That would be very good to hear.

June Anne Morrissey. He'd wasted a lot of time thinking about her while he was swinging that brush hook for the state. And then, like a damn fool, after he'd gotten set up down there in Miami, he had gone up after her, thinking she'd be glad to come along just to be near him. He'd driven up there and he'd had to hide out. Too many people around Ocala knew him. It had been over a day before he had a chance to see June Anne alone. He had to check to make sure she wasn't being watched. Then he had to find a time when her folks weren't there.

She'd met him in the grove out behind the house after the short phone call. Now he knew he was lucky she hadn't arranged for the police to meet him there.

"What do you want?"

"My God, honey, you sound unfriendly."

"What do you need? Clothes? Money? I'll give you what I can and then you get out of here."

"I want you to come along with me. That's what I came up here for. I got a car, clothes, money and an apartment. I think you ought to come along with me."

"I'd as soon go along with a snake."

"What?"

"You heard me, Frank. It's over. It was over a long time ago. You're a known criminal, and you escaped, and a guard was killed. I don't want any part of you. I'm engaged to Sonny Western."

"You'll be marrying a hell of a nice batch of groves."

"That isn't why I'm marrying him."

"You better change your mind and come along. Do some real living, June Anne, like we used to talk about."

"We talked about living well, but not your way, Frank. Not the way you've picked out for yourself. I said it and I meant it. I'd as soon go along with a snake. Now you better get out of here."

She stood tall in the shadowy grove, the house lights below and behind her. He took one step and struck her with his fist and she went down and began to sob. He stood over her, feeling a strange unlikely urge to cry also. Then he stepped around her and went down the shallow hill and past the house and out to the road. He turned down the road to where he had left the car. He heard the running steps behind him. He spun around, fists clenched. He could see by the starlight that it was a girl, not as tall as June Anne.

"Who is it?"

"It's Hope, Frank. I snuck up there and I heard her. I'm glad you hit her."

"She's your own sister."

"Anyhow I'm glad. Frank, I want to come along with you."

He laughed at her. "You're just a kid."

"You haven't seen me in two years. I'm grown up."

"Go on home, Hope."

She moved closer and thrust against him, catching his arm in her hand. "Take me along," she demanded. "They won't ever catch you. Take me along."

He felt the warmth of her. He put his arm around her. She felt like a woman. He looked up toward the dark grove. He thought of June Anne and he smiled. He held Hope a little tighter.

"Want to go get your stuff?"

"I'm afraid she'll catch me."

"Okay. Come along, kid. Come along for the ride."

They rode through the night in the Buick and when he thought of June Anne and her folks he had to laugh to himself. Hope sat very close to him. He did not get a good look at her until he saw her in their motel room in Orlando. The idea seemed to turn sour when he looked at her. She was nowhere near as pretty as June Anne. The heavy glossy brown hair was the same, but that was all. She had a pudding face and rather small eyes. But she was grown up. She had been right about that. She was built low to the ground like her old man. She had big strong hips and big round breasts.

It was strange the way she had acted. The only time there had seemed to be any urgency in her was when she had begged to come along. Once the decision had been made, she settled into a placid acceptance. In the motel there was no girlish shyness about her. Nor any of the devices of modesty. She acted as though this were the thousandth night they had spent together, no more remarkable than any that had gone before. It irritated him that she should take it all so much for granted. He decided then that he would get up first in the morning and drive away and leave her there. It would make the revenge against the Morrissey clan no less sweet.

But he learned that her bovine placidity was due to her almost complete indifference to everything in the world except the immediate gratification of her body. And in that special area of interest she was anything but placid. He knew the next day that he had found a strange one—a highly specialized organism. In her outside interests and accomplishments she was on no more than a third grade level. By morning he had no intention of leaving her behind. He felt obscurely ashamed of himself for taking her along, and he knew he could never introduce her to anyone without feeling apologetic, but he could not part with her.

He could not have parted with her then, but he could now. But only because he sensed danger in staying with the two of them. He would leave her to the kid. He doubted that it would make any special difference to her. She seemed to lack the capacity to feel any special attachment for anyone. She was alone in the world and there was only one other individual in the world. That was Man, and it did not matter what face he wore or what language he spoke. He had to admire her for her single-mindedness, her unthinking drive and purpose. She was remote as a mountain, yet attainable as the next breath. No one would even come to know her— if indeed there was anything to know beyond the physical. So divorced was her preoccupation from normal human emotions that he felt quite certain that had he shared her with the kid from the beginning, it would have made no difference to her at all. It would have been, to her, perhaps a more desirable arrangement. He knew that should he stay with her, he would gradually become more violent with her until, one day, he might kill her. Not out of anger. Just in an attempt to pry up the lid and see if there was anything underneath, or if the box was entirely empty.

He had not yet killed anyone, but he knew that the wanting to do it was buried in him. Buried not as deep as it used to be. Buried not deep at all last night when he had kicked at the head of the stranger on the ground. Seeing the end of Big Satch had clarified the wanting. He wondered why he should wonder about killing someone. It was a stupid thing to do. They hunted you twice as hard. And when they got you, they would kill you in turn.

And, as the truck rolled through the rain, he wondered why he was as he was. A job wouldn't be bad. He'd even enjoyed washing the cars, getting them gleaming clean. And he'd never required much money. He could get along on very little. The fact that it was there made you want to take it. Taking it was a gesture of contempt for all of Them. Taking it was a way of saying something. As taking a life would be a way of saying something. Maybe saying, *Here comes Frank Stratter.*

Sometimes he would have a dream where he heard people in the street going *Ah* and *O.* He would get up and dress and go out to see what the trouble was. They were standing there, all of them, looking up into the night sky and he would look up there too and he would see his name in great letters of steady fire written all the way across heaven. *Frank Stratter.* Then they would begin to recognize him and they would move away from him in fear and go into all their houses and leave him standing there alone looking at his name and how it was written up there, higher than anything in the world.

The small truck droned on. There was a smell of aged fish inside it. The floor was hard under the burlap. He lay half smiling at the roof of the truck and he saw how huge the name was, and how the letters glowed. *Frank Stratter. Frank Stratter.*

[*The boy drives the stolen truck. He is conscious of the placid willing dampness of the girl beside him, and also conscious of the ominous clatter of the worn engine every time he gets the speedometer above forty. He knows motors and it sounds to him as though the main bearings are nearly*

72

gone. Too much push and it will give out entirely. The truck is a junker.

He wishes they had another car. He would feel safer in another car. Something like that big Cad that went by, or even the Mercedes, if that wasn't too rich a dream to dream. But he knows he would settle for the slightly aged station wagon, or the green Plymouth. And certainly for the blue and white convertible that passed him cautiously a few minutes ago, with a woman driving.

The girl yawns and picks at her teeth with a thumbnail. When he glances down and to the side he can see a few inches of the inside of her right thigh. He listens to the clatter of the motor and eases the speed off to thirty-five.]

73

7

Virginia Sherrel drove north through the Wednesday rain in the blue and white Dodge convertible that she and her husband, David, had picked out together for the vacation they were to take—the vacation that David had finally taken alone. She drove north alone as David had driven south.

She had not liked the idea of an urn. The very word had the sound of a funeral bell. Bell? Fragment of an old pun. The New Hampshire farmhouse, on honeymoon. And they had walked too far and it had begun to rain and they had run back. And David had knelt and taken the hem of her tweed skirt and twisted the water out of it and, smiling up at her, said, "Wring out, wild belle." He had made a fire later and they had made love by firelight on an ancient glossy horsehair sofa.

Not the sound of urn. And the urn itself had made a sound when the undertaker, with an almost grotesque callousness, had taken one down from a shelf and opened the screw top with a shrill grating sound and then held it out to her— and she, caught up in the wicked pantomime, had leaned forward a bit and stared inanely down into it and said, "No, I don't think so." Not for David.

So it was a box. A flat bronze box not quite as long or quite as deep as a cigar box. With a discreet border design, a small catch. The undertaker had snapped the catch three times.

It was in the trunk compartment of the car, and she knew how it was wrapped. Back in the hotel in Sarasota she had closed the room door behind her and she had made certain it was locked, and she had untied the cord, unwrapped the brown paper, lifted the lid of the cardboard box.

Inside the cardboard box the bronze box lay wrapped in tissue, resting on a nest of tissue. As she unwrapped it she thought of the presents they had given each other. He had

74

said once, "I think best I like to see you unwrap presents. Such a posture of greed. Such intense absorption. And all the sensuous little delays, such as untying knots instead of cutting them."

All the presents and this, then, is your final present, David.

She lifted the bronze lid and looked wonderingly at the fine grayish ash. She touched it lightly with her finger. It was soft and a few flakes adhered to the moisture of her finger tip and she brushed them off. Here is the receding hair and the troubled gray eyes, lips and long bones, fingers and phallus, blood and pores and the crisp curled body hair. *Here is all of you, my lover.* She closed the lid and it snapped as it had in the undertaker's show room. She wrapped it in the tissue, and closed the cardboard box and refolded the brown paper and tied the cord. Then she went over and stretched out on the bed. Gift from David. Gift of himself. And riding now, tucked away in the luggage compartment, riding through the gray rain, riding north.

Yet it could not be comprehended. It could never be understood in its entirety. This was a grief unspeakable. It was a soiled grief, a shameful agony.

September fourteenth. Ten in the morning in New York. Ten in the morning in Florida. Ten o'clock in the small apartment on the East Side. She went down after her breakfast and got the mail. No letter from David. She went back up to the apartment and poured her second cup of coffee. The sun came in. The apartment was in a building only a little over a year old. The apartment was as they said, a machine for living. Full of an incredible cleverness. You see, this fits here, and then that slides back out of the way. All you have to do is turn this, and adjust that. Special plastics and special metals and lighting that was as carefully conceived as any stage setting, so dramatic that the apartment in daylight never quite lived up to its evening promise. Thus it was a place for people who lived most at night.

She sat and looked at the bills and the circulars and read one letter from an old and dear friend who now lived in Burlington and who wrote, "I suppose it is a sort of modern wisdom to take a vacation from each other, but damn if I like the sound or taste of it. To have you and David indulge in such a thing is to me like the teeter and fall of great idols. Forgive me if I am too blunt, Ginny, but I can't help thinking David needs, more than anything else, a sound spanking."

She was annoyed as she read the letter. In her attempt to be light when writing Helen she had given Helen a distorted picture. It was not a marital vacation. It was a sudden queerness in David, a hint of breakdown.

It was then that the phone rang.

"Mrs. David Sherrel, please."

"This is she."

"I have a long distance call for you from Sarasota, Florida. Go ahead, please."

Dim male voice blurred by miles, distorted by a jangling hum. "David?" she said eagerly. "David, is that you?" And as she asked she could remember the last few lines of the letter she had written him. Lines she had worked over very carefully. "Please know that I try to understand to the extent that it is within my capacity to understand. I know that you feel this is important to you. If it is important to you it is also important to me, darling. But please write to me. I think I deserve that much. I think you owe me that much, David. You have always had imagination. Think of what it would be like to be me, and to be here, and not know."

"David!" she cried to the blurred phone. "I cannot hear you."

"Please hang up," the operator said, "and I will try to get a better connection."

She hung up and sat by the phone and waited. She wanted to hear him say he was coming home, that this frightening thing that had separated them was over.

When it rang again she snatched it quickly. "David?"

"No ma'am. My name is . . . Police Department . . . phone number in his wallet."

"Police? What's wrong? Is my husband in trouble?"

"Sorry to have to be the one to tell you this, Miz Sherrel, but your husband is dead. We got to get a legal identification on him, and I guess you ought to come on down here. Hello. Hello? Miz Sherrel? Operator! Operator! We've been cut . . ."

"I'm still here," Virginia said in a voice that sounded not at all like her own. It sounded cool and formal and controlled. "I'll fly down. I'll be there as soon as I can." The man started to say something but she heard only the first few words before she hung up.

In the first few moments there was the shock, and then there was the sense of inevitability, so strong and sure that she wondered that she had not known at once when the phone had rung—she wondered that she had been so naive as to expect to hear David's voice.

She phoned the airlines and made a reservation on a flight leaving at five minutes of two. She rinsed the breakfast things, packed, closed the apartment, cashed a check, picked up her ticket and, after a short wait at Tampa International, she was in Sarasota a little after eight in the evening. It was a still night, very hot. People walked slowly in the heat.

The man she talked to was large, soft-voiced, gentle. He had her sit down and he told her what had happened. "He'd been staying at a place called the Taine Motor Lodge out on the North Trail. He hadn't been making any trouble or anything, but he was acting kind of peculiar and Mrs. Strickie, she's the manager out there, she was sort of keeping an eye on him. She's got efficiencies out there. She noticed his car was in front of his place yesterday and he didn't go out in the evening and this morning she got to thinking about it and knocked on his door about eight and when she didn't get any answer she used her key and went in and backed right out again the gas was so thick, and called us right away. We got it aired out and he was on the kitchen floor, and this note here was on the table."

She took the note and read it. *"Ginny—It just wasn't any use. It just didn't do any good. I'm sorry."* It wasn't signed.

"Is that his handwriting?" The questioning voice came from far away, echoing through a long metal pipe. She swayed on the chair, didn't answer. The man went away and came back with a paper cup. She took it, lifted it, smelled the raw whisky, drank it down.

She gave the cup back to him. "That's his writing."

"It checks out that he did it about midnight. Was his health bad?"

"No. He was in good health."

"Money trouble?"

"No. He had a good job. He was on a leave of absence."

"What kind of work did he do?"

"He was in the radio and television department of a large advertising agency."

"Any children?"

"No. No children."

77

"You know any reason why he did it, Miz Sherrel?"

"Not . . . exactly. I think it was some kind of a breakdown. His work was very demanding. He felt he had to get away for a little while. He thought that would help."

"If you feel up to it, we can go over and take a look at him now and get that part over with. If you don't feel like it, it can wait until morning."

"I'm all right. We can do it now."

And so it was done. David was gone. The body seemed to be the body of a stranger. It was familiar to her in contour, in the shape of each feature, but no longer known to her. They went back and the man gave her the keys to the car. David's things were packed in the car. She found a place to stay. The next morning she made the arrangements about cremation. Then she placed a call to Jim Dillon in New York, their lawyer, a classmate of David.

"Jim? This is Ginny. I'm calling from Sarasota."

"That's what the operator said. What are you doing down there, girl? How's Dave?"

"David killed himself, Jim. They found the body yesterday morning. I flew down."

"He what! Oh Jesus, Ginny! My God, why? Why did he do that?"

"I don't think we'll ever know. Jim, I need your help."

"Anything, Ginny. You know that. I think I could even come down there if . . ."

"No. No, thanks, Jim. I just don't feel like coming right back and facing . . . everything. I suppose there are legal things that have to be taken care of. There's the deposit box and things like that. There's a will in it."

"How big will the estate be?"

"Maybe thirty thousand. Somewhere around there. Then there's the insurance. The policies are in the box."

"Have you got money now? If you had a joint checking account you won't be able to write checks against it."

"I have my own checking account. There's enough in it for now, Jim. I just want to stay down here for a while. I don't know how long."

"How about the funeral?"

"I . . . I don't think there'll be any. He wanted to be cremated. I'm having that done. I'm going to phone his sister in Seattle and phone my parents. Maybe when I come back I can arrange some sort of memorial service, but I don't know about that yet. Can you do everything that has to be done?"

"Of course. Give me your address there. I'll send stuff for your signature."

She told him where she was staying. He told her how shocked and sorry he was, questioned her as to whether it was wise for her to be alone just at this time. He said he would inform the agency, and let their friends know. She said she would write a note to some of the people. After they finished talking, she made the other two phone calls. They were both bad calls to make. When she talked to her parents she was barely able to dissuade her mother from coming down.

"But what are you going to *do*, Virginia? Why are you staying there?"

"I have some thinking to do, Mother."

"You can think *anywhere*. You can come here and stay with us and think here. This seems so *insane*."

But in the end she won out, won reluctant acceptance. She drove around the city and decided she would rather live at the beach. She found a tiny apartment in a blue and white motel on Siesta Key. Her door opened onto the beach. It was September and it was hot and there were few tourists. In the mornings she would see the high white cloud banks against the blue sky and on many days the hard rain would come down in the afternoon, dimpling and washing the sand and ending with the same abruptness that it had come.

She had wired Jim Dillon her new address. Legal papers came and she signed them and sent them back. Sympathy notes arrived. The most careful and intricate one came from the advertising firm.

She spent her days in a quiet pattern. In the early morning she walked on the beach. Later she lay under the weight of the sun, walking gingerly down to swim in the warm water when the heat became too great. The sun blunted her energies, softening the edges of her grief. She was a tall woman with a strong, well-made, youthful body, with black crisp hair, unplucked black brows, eyes of a clear light blue. The sun tanned her deeply and the continual swimming tightened the tissues of her body. She would come in from the dazzle of the beach and take off her suit in the relative gloom of the small apartment and, catching a glimpse of herself in a mirror, be startled by the vivid contrast of deep tan and the

JOHN D. MACDONALD

white protected bands of flesh. The bronze box was in the back of her closet.

It was a time to think. And to wonder how she had failed. And to wonder what would become of her.

The marriage had lasted seven years. They had met in New York. She was from upstate New York, from Rochester. She was working in the fiction department of a fashion magazine when she met him. David had done two short pieces for them. Virginia had read them and thought them quite strange, but she had liked them. A third piece, according to the judgment of the fiction editor, needed reworking. The fiction editor had made a luncheon date with David Sherrel and had been unable to keep it. Virginia was sent along to the midtown restaurant to meet him, armed with the manuscript, the fiction editor's notes, and some money from the petty cash fund.

They had been awkward and earnest with each other during lunch. David turned out to be tall, slim, blond and—in spite of Madison Avenue manners and clothing—rather shy. He was apologetic about working for an advertising agency. He had curious moments of intensity, after which he would slip behind his façade.

She had been dating several men, but after lunch with David they all seemed very predictable and tasteless. The second time she saw him he was very drunk. The third time she saw him it became evident to both of them that they would be married.

It had seemed to be a good marriage. She felt needed and wanted. She learned to accept his moods of black hopeless depression, accepting them as the evil to be balanced against a gift of gaiety, of high wild fun, of laughter that pinched your side and brought you to helplessness. It was their dream that one day his novel would make them independent of the agency. Often she felt strong enough for the two of them. There was the deep stripe of the erratic in him. He seemed to be always on the verge of losing his job, only to regain favor by some exercise of imagination that not only re-established him as a valuable man, but usually brought a pay raise. Though he sneered at his job and his work and could talk at length about the artificial wonderland of the advertising agencies, when he was in ill repute, he could not keep food on his stomach, nor could he sleep without sedatives.

He had a gift for the savage phrase. He could use words that hurt her. But out of her strength and her understanding

80

she forgave him. His apologies were abject. Their lovemaking was as cyclical as his moods. There would be weeks when it would seem that he could not have enough of her. Then would come the coolness and he would withdraw physically to the point where, should she touch him inadvertently, she could feel the contraction of his muscles. And that hurt as badly as did the words.

David always had very good friends, very dear and close friends who would adore him for two months or three before, out of some compulsion, he would drive them off. No friend remained loyal very long.

In spite of their private difficulties, they maintained a united front. He never spoke harshly to her when there was anyone around to hear him. She was grateful for that, as she knew her pride was very strong. She loved him with all her heart. She wanted his life to be wonderful. She did everything she could to make him happy.

It all began to go wrong right after the first of the year. He slipped, day by day, further into a mood of depression. Yet this depression was not like the others. The others had been like the black clouds of brief violent storms. This was like a series of endless gray days, unmarked by any threat of violence. It seemed to her to be more apathy than depression. He went through his days like an automatic device devised to simulate a man. There seemed to be no restlessness in him—just a dulled acceptance. Though he had always been very fastidious, he began to shave and dress carelessly, and keep himself not quite clean. She tried in all the ways she could think of to stir him out of it. She changed scenes, set stages, planned little plots, but none of them worked. When, in unguarded moments, she would wonder if he was getting tired of her, fright would pinch her heart.

One day, out of desperation, she set a scene so crude that in prior years it would have been unthinkable. While he was at the agency she went into the small study where he had used to work during the evening. She found and laid out the incomplete manuscript of the book. She laid out fresh paper and carbon and second sheets in the way he had liked to have them before he had given up work on the book.

That evening she had taken his wrist and smiled at him and tugged and said, "Come on."

He came along without protest. She turned on the desk

81

lamp and showed him what she had done. He stood and looked at the desk and then he turned and looked at her with an absolute emptiness in his eyes. An emptiness that shocked her. "God, Ginny!" he said tonelessly. "Good God, what are you trying to do to me?"

"I thought that if you . . ."

But he had walked out of the room. He walked out of the apartment. By the time she got her coat on and got down to the street, he was gone. He came back within an hour and he was back down in the grayness of apathy, unreachable, untouchable. She apologized for what she had done. He shrugged and said it didn't matter.

In June there was one day of gaiety. One day when he was like himself. Yet not like himself. There was an ersatz quality to his gaiety, as though it were the result of enormous effort—even as though this were a stranger, a quick study, who tried expertly to become David Sherrel. That was the day they ordered the car and planned a vacation trip. By the time the car was delivered he had no interest in it and she could not get him to talk about the trip again. She felt unused, wasted. The empty days and the empty nights went by and she smothered her resentment and refused to admit to herself that she was thoroughly, miserably bored.

On an evening in late July he was quiet at dinner—it had been months since they had been out together or had anyone in—and finally, as though saving something he had memorized, he said, "I know that I've been a mess lately, Ginny. I don't know exactly what's wrong. I feel as if, somewhere, I've lost all motivation. I want to try to get it back."

"I want to help you."

"I don't want help. I talked to Lusker this morning. They're giving me a six months' leave of absence without pay. Lusker suggested psychiatry. I don't think that's the answer. I want to get away for a while."

"I think it's a wonderful idea, darling. We could go back up to . . ."

"I don't think you understand. I have to get away by myself. I don't know why. But that's what I have to do."

She looked at him and her face felt stiff, tight, as though covered with a fine porcelain glaze. "You have to do that?"

"Yes."

All the angry words were close to the surface. She suppressed them. She stood up slowly and began to clear the table.

"It's all right, then?" he asked.

"It looks as though it will have to be, David."

He left two days later. She packed for him. She kissed him and told him to write. She went down to the car with him. He stood and looked at her and he looked shy and lost and she thought it was like sending a child to camp, or to war. He opened his lips as though to say something, then turned abruptly and got into the car. It was a Sunday morning in Manhattan. The streets were empty. She stood and watched the blue and white car turn the corner. She went back upstairs. She prepared carefully for tears. She put on a robe, stretched out on her bed with a big box of Kleenex at hand. She lay and waited for the tears. They did not come. She thought of the sweet little things and the sad little things, and tried, through pathos, to force tears. But they did not come. She realized she was trying to pump up tears the way some women seek out sad movies. She got up quickly and on that day she gave the apartment the most thorough cleaning it had ever had.

He sent a card from Augusta and one from Jacksonville and a third and final card from Sarasota saying that he would stay there for a time and let her know should he move on. There was an address she could write to. She wrote often, not knowing if he even bothered to read her letters.

Now the marriage was quite over. It had ended.

She lay on the still hot beach, joined plastic cups over her eyes, feeling the sun grind into her body. And she tried to understand.

There were two things that had happened to her, long before David, that seemed to point out the direction of understanding.

One had happened to her in high school, during the first week of a course in Natural History. She could not remember the name of the instructor. He had been a small wide balding man with a sharp penetrating voice and a sarcastic manner. He had a projector and a box of slides. The room was darkened. He put the slides in the projector. They were pictures of prehistoric animals and lizards and birds, cleverly faked.

In essence he said, "These creatures no longer exist. They died out. Their own development brought them to a dead end. They had some fatal flaw which finally made it impossible for them to survive in a changing environment. They could not adapt. It is an oversimplification to call them nature's mistakes. They were just dead ends in nature's endless experimentation."

And so it could be possible to say that David had within himself the flaw which made survival impossible. The flaw did not have to be isolated and described. It could be enough to know that it was there.

The second incident had happened when, in college, she had a date with a young instructor, a man named Val Jerrenson. As he was not supposed to date students, they had to be secretive about it. It had been a warm Saturday in May and they had gone down to an amusement park on the shore. They had been standing talking near a shooting gallery, and Virginia, looking over Val's shoulder, saw the head of Val's department walking toward them, frowning slightly.

Virginia had put her hand out quickly and Val had taken it instinctively. Raising her voice a little she had said, "Well, I have to run along, Mr. Jerrenson. Nice to run into you like this. I'll have to catch up with the other girls." She then looked directly at the head of the department and said, "Oh, hello, Dr. Thall! I didn't know Mr. Jerrenson was with you. I really have to run."

When Val finally came back to the car she was sitting there waiting for him, giggling.

After they had driven far enough to be safe, Val had looked at her with an odd expression, and said, "You know, Virginia, you frighten me a little, you have such a perfect instinct for survival. Such a gift for living. You are an organism designed to function perfectly in its environment. Such strength is a little disturbing."

So add the two together. The flawed organism. And the survival organism. Living together, making a life together. She sensed that the marriage had made her stronger, because it had called on her strength, it had demanded it. Yet she had not wished to be strong. She had wanted a man who could dominate her. In the very beginning she had thought David such a man.

Thus, if it had added to her strength, had it not also added to his weakness? Would not David have been better with a silly girl, a gay careless erratic clinging little thing? Or was the flaw too deep?

There was one thing that she learned during the long days on the beach. She learned that her love was not as great as she had thought it. It made her ashamed to realize that. Yet in all honesty, it was an admission she had to make. And it was the final act which had cut love down to a manageable stature. It had been such a childish and insulting death. It was as though, out of petulance, he had flung something at her, had struck her in the face with sticky unpleasantness. She had cared for herself, keeping herself as handsome as she could, as fresh and alive and sweet-smelling, ready and waiting for his use of her. Through marriage his use of her had been sporadic despite its intensity. His withdrawn periods seemed a denial of her. And now he had consummated the final denial.

She could feel grief, and a sense of loss, and a sense of inadequacy—yet it was not a sharpness that pierced her heart. It was more like thinking of a death that had happened long ago. David had died long ago, and he moved through the eternity of memory, blond, slim, tall, with soft sensitive mouth, dulled eyes, a look of rejection. The ashes were soft and gray in the bronze box. And ashes had no life, no history. They were always old.

She knew at last when it was time to go back. When she awakened on Tuesday morning she knew that she had spent enough time in this place. A healing process had taken place. Wounds were closing. She could go back and face friends, and dispose of his personal possessions and give up the apartment and find something to do.

She looked at herself with utmost clarity and knew that any job she could find would not be enough. She knew that she would look for a man. A strong man. A man with courage and integrity and a sure sense of his own place. She knew that, at thirty, she had never been more attractive. With this man she would find she would be able to breed true. He would not need strength to lean on. He would exude strength and that strength would make her feel like a woman, rather than a mother or a guardian. There would be children, as many as she could have. And it would not be a rebound from David. It would, instead, be an acceptance of the years lost, and a desire to do, with those that were left, what she had been meant to do from the very beginning. And the first step was to find a job which would expose her to the greatest possible number of men who might meet her qualifications.

When she left in the rain on Wednesday morning, she was more than a little amused at her careful planning, at her incredible certainty that the future would be just as she desired it.

[*The woman drives cautiously through the rain that makes drum sounds on the canvas top of the blue and white convertible. When passed by the Cadillac and the Mercedes her mouth tightens a bit with disapproval of people who go too fast in this sort of weather.*

She wonders if this was the same road her dead husband drove on when he came down to Florida. And she wonders how fast he drove and then feels ridiculous for feeling concern about his safety. He is beyond all such fears.

She follows a slow-moving panel delivery truck for several miles and then when for a time visibility is relatively clear ahead she passes the truck.

The cars move toward the bridge, the blocked bridge—the bridge which was actually blocked by the carelessness of a young and foolish wife in New Orleans—a wife who took from her husband a fine clear edge of alertness and coordination—and thus killed him. A wife who now sits weeping again, though she does not yet know the new and greater cause for tears. Soon her phone will ring, because it is always easier to tell them that way than face to face.]

8

Steve Malden picked up a thread in St. Petersburg on Tuesday afternoon. He found the loose end of a thread that had broken in Santa Fe five years ago. Tuesday afternoon at three o'clock he solved a problem that had kept many men busy over a period of years. They had not devoted their entire attentions to it. It was not a major problem. Yet not so minor as to be classified as an annoyance. It had been talked over many times. There was one school of thought which said that after the Santa Fe cell had been broken up, Strellman had left the country. Others believed he had holed up somewhere.

Strellman was not and had never been top drawer. But he was trained and competent and, in the right situation, perfectly capable of making a great deal of trouble.

When the faint Miami lead had come in, there was the question of whether to buck it to the Miami group or whether to handle it on a special basis. Because Steve had worked on the Strellman thing before, he was called off a routine investigation in Rhode Island and he sat in on the conference. As Steve knew no one in the Miami group, it was finally decided that he should go down on his own and see if that faint lead could be worked.

It wasn't like the old days when most of the apparatus had been penetrated, and you could get your check from the inside. Too much of the apparatus had gone underground in the last few years, with new refinements of the cell structure and an absolute minimum of communication. The faint lead had been faint indeed. A conversation overheard in Chicago. About somebody getting off a boat in Miami and being certain they had seen Strellman, older, balder, fatter, walking out of a small hotel called the Joy-a-lee on the crummy end of Miami Beach. Because of the locale it was decided that Steve had best go down as a tourist, so he had driven down in his own car with the Maryland plates, push-

87

ing it a little because the day that Strellman had been seen was already a month, maybe more, in the past.

Steve Malden had checked into a hotel down the block from the Joy-a-lee and he took a few days to make certain that Strellman was not still there. There were four photographs of Strellman in existence, and all four had been taken with a telephoto lens aimed through a hole in the side of a panel delivery truck, but they were reasonably clear. Steve knew he would recognize the man.

As he did not know the hotel setup, or what it could be, he moved in very lightly and indirectly, which was in itself the height of deception for he did not appear to be a man with any talent for lightness or indirection. At a distance he did not look like a big man. At close range he was big with that special quality of hardness that looks invulnerable. Square hard jaw, thick neck, gray-flecked hair cropped close to the round hard skull, beard shadow under the tight skin of the face. His eyes were brown and very deeply set. He smiled readily and often, and the smile seldom reached to the eyes. Through years of deception he had the ability to project himself at any social level—from beer-soaked unemployed truck driver to gentleman sportsman—fitting gestures, habits of speech, bearing, clothing to the impersonation at hand. Sometimes he wondered if, through disuse, the actual person of Steve Malden had ceased to exist.

At the Joy-a-lee he became, as soon as he had made friends with the day clerk, a contractor from Maryland on the trail of a runaway wife. With silent apology to the memory of his wife, he showed the clerk the picture of Dorothy that he had carried ever since her death. The clerk was sympathetic, but the picture meant nothing to her. He explained that he had a pretty good idea of who she had run away with. He said he had sent north for a picture of the guy and it would be coming in any day. A few days later he took her the picture of Strellman and explained that the picture was five years old.

The woman took the picture and turned it toward the light and frowned and said, "You know, I think I've seen this man. I think he's stayed here. I really do."

By then she was a good enough friend to go through the register, card by card. She showed the picture to some of the other employees. It was a maid who remembered it better than the others and came up with what was almost a name. "Purvey or Purvis or Peavy or something like that."

It turned out to be Harry J. Peavis of 1212 Acacia Avenue, St. Petersburg. Steve took a long steady look at the handwriting and saw certain points of similarity with the sample he had studied. He thanked the clerk and she made him promise not to do anything rash. He drove to St. Petersburg, arriving on a Sunday. If Peavis were Strellman, and it seemed reasonable that he was, the contact would have to be made with great care. Strellman was a trained agent, unlikely to be dulled by five years of freedom, and ready to run if alarmed in any way. He would have a new set of identifications ready, and some sort of escape hatch.

At three o'clock on Tuesday afternoon Steve Malden, from a safe vantage point, focused the newly purchased telescope on the small back yard of 1212 Acacia. Harry J. Peavis was tying cord on a tropical plant. He stood up and turned and became Strellman, his face startlingly close. Steve kept watching. He wished there were crosshairs on the object lens and a trigger under his finger. He backed away from the window, collapsed the telescope and put it back in its case. He made his phone call from a downtown hotel lobby. He phoned an unlisted Washington number and when a girl answered he asked for Mac.

"Yes, Steve."

"Jackpot."

"Good! Wonderful! Does he know?"

"I'm no amateur, Mac. I haven't taken the chance of even checking the local background. Harry J. Peavis, 1212 Acacia Avenue. That's all I know. Do you want a pickup?"

"Not until we know what he's doing."

"Want me to stay on him?"

"There's too much chance he might know your face. I know it's a hell of a remote chance, but even that is too much. Put our friends on watch until we can get some boys down there. Make sure they understand and don't detail any clowns to this stakeout."

"Right. And don't send any clowns down, either."

"Insubordination, Steve?"

"Damn close to it. I . . . I have a personal stake in this one."

"And it's the last of the group, isn't it?"

89

"The very last one, Mac."

"You come on back. Take your time. Take a couple of weeks in transit if you feel like it. You've earned it."

After Steve hung up he visited an office building, identified himself, and explained to some sober earnest young men the importance of keeping Peavis under observation. After that was done he was free. He felt the letdown. It had been a long five years. This was the last of the group. No other man in the organization had the same personal stake in it as Malden. His tirelessness in tracking down the others who had slipped away when Strellman did was legendary in his department. It was a special dedication understandable, but still a little frightening.

The reason for the geographical location of the cell in Santa Fe was quite obvious. These members had not been concerned with political philosophies. They were the hard core functionaries, the trained ones. The ruthless ones. They had determined the gullibility of the wife, the silly wife of a young physicist, and learned of the venality of a sergeant technician when another group, equally well trained, moved in on them. Steve Malden had carried more than his share of the load—merely through assignment, not design. And it was his testimony that later dictated the severity of the prison terms. He almost failed to give testimony. He narrowly escaped being unable to give testimony. The package was sent to his home in Maryland. It was addressed to him. It had been mailed from New York. But it arrived a week before his birthday. And Dorothy, who had been doing some mail order shopping, must have thought it was one of the gifts she had ordered for him. So she opened it and died in the fractional part of a second that the explosive, expanding in gaseous violence, took to blow the windows out of the garden apartment.

Not only was the department unable to locate the maker and the sender, but it could never be determined how the traditional anonymity of departmental personnel had been penetrated to the extent that Malden's name and even his address had been made known. Even to his Maryland neighbors he was believed to be a traffic expert working for the Quartermaster General.

But, to the department and to Malden, it was quite obvious that the violent death of Mrs. Stephen Malden was connected with the recent successful defusing of the Santa Fe cell—successful to the extent that four had been picked up immediately, three had fled.

Of the three who fled, only Strellman had been successful. Until now. And now the last dangling thread had been picked up. Malden had seen the face of a fatter balder older man who had carefully tied up some tropical shrubs in the back yard of a house on a quiet street in a quiet city. And that ended it.

It had not been five years of single-minded dedication. There had not been enough to go on. And so many routine tasks had intervened. But the departmental chiefs were aware of Malden's personal stake, and so, during the five years, whenever it was possible to detail him to any aspect of the Santa Fe cleanup they had done so.

It was professional against professional. It was a pure form of counter-intelligence. Malden was glad that it had nothing to do with people who claimed the fifth amendment, or who refused to sign oaths, or who had appeared on the wrong letterhead. They were the perennial amateurs, more annoying than dangerous. The professionals would swear their loyalty, lie under oath, would publicly deplore the disloyalty of the amateurs. Just as our own professionals would know better than to become public martyrs to the cause of Democracy in alien lands.

During his two years of marriage and before, Steve Malden had known that his work was tricky, sometimes dangerous, generally monotonous, and highly essential.

He had not known it was heartless.

He realized that his previous attitude had been absurdly idealistic. He had believed certain holds were barred. Then he stood in the reeking mess of the apartment after they had taken her away. Here, in a tiny moment of time, in a partial second of current history, there had been blown to wet bits the satin and perfumed flesh of the long nights, and gone was the way she laughed and moved and shook her head and touched his cheek, and bent quickly to accept the lighter flame.

He seemed the same. The ones who did not know him very well marveled that he seemed so unchanged, that his testimony had been given so soberly, without hysteria, without the flinch of loss. Those who did not know him well decided that Malden lacked imagination, perhaps lacked even the capacity for great anger. But those who knew him well saw the subtle indications of the change. There had been outside interests. Now there were none. There was laughter at the proper places, but too often it was more an imitation of a man laughing.

Then there was the Seattle incident. Only a very few knew about that. It nearly lost Malden his position. It was a single departure from legality, and no man should ever be made to talk the way that man was made to talk by Malden. But the information gained was valid, and the man's subsequent mental breakdown was not permanent, though he became, of course, useless to his superiors. When a man that tough has been broken, he breaks more easily the next time. Malden got off with a reprimand. Neither the incident nor the reprimand seemed to worry him, to touch him.

Sometimes when he thought about it, Malden would try to put her death in historical perspective. World history was the history of conflict between governments. Conflict created major and minor episodes of violence. In both categories, the innocent suffered. In the wars between the city states of Italy, poison had often been drunk by the wrong persons. All who had been thrown to the lions were not Christians. Bombs killed infants with miraculous efficiency. And four hundred student doctors died at Hiroshima.

Take her death in its historical context and it still remained meaningless, yet not as meaningless as if she had died because truck brakes had failed.

Yet historical perspective was a chilling and comfortless thing. He knew he had to keep his personal involvement in this particular war well in the background or his efficiency would decrease. He had to move and react with coldness. Only once had the wall broken. And then he had been saved because the man who had talked—who had talked finally with bulge-eyed eagerness, spraying spittle in his intense desire to talk and to please—that man had not quite died. And what he had said was later used to prevent a strategic kidnaping in West Berlin that would have certainly been successful otherwise.

Now he drove north through a rain as heavy as any he had ever seen. He drove the dark green Plymouth sedan north, knowing that he would waste no time in transit, would return and report for assignment. He had been offered time off many times in the last five years and he had never taken it. He knew he would not take it this time, and yet this was the first time he had ever felt remotely tempted.

He guessed that it was the inevitable letdown that came from knowing that the last of the Santa Fe project was over. It put an end to the five years. And there should be some way of telling her that the last one had been picked up. But if you told her that, you would have to tell her that no one had ever learned, or would ever learn, who had sent the package, who had given the orders. So there was failure after all.

She had stopped right there at twenty-four. She had been abruptly halted. And the years went by and she was still twenty-four. Now you were thirty-two instead of twenty-seven, and you would become forty-two and fifty-two, while she stayed back there, frozen in that explosive moment of time, still twenty-four, forever slim and clean-limbed, forever three months pregnant.

"Death was instantaneous."

He had often wondered about those words. How did such a death feel? A great blast of whiteness? A sudden roar of darkness? A feeling of falling?

She put the box on the gate leg table by the living room window. She read a letter from her mother first. Then she went to the bookshelf and opened the wicker basket and took out her sewing scissors and went back to the box and cut the cord. ("The firing device was armed by tension on the wrapping cord. With release of tension the firing pin arm, impelled by a spring, was allowed to drop and strike the primer, thus detonating the main charge.")

It had been a warm bright day. The blanket was still out in the back yard, sun lotion, dark glasses and book beside it.

So he drove north on that Wednesday, eyes on the road, big strong hands on the wheel, while back in the silent corridors of his mind the old compulsive dramas were reenacted, the doll figures moving with the stilted precision of puppets too often used. But this time there was a sourness in the corridors, and a dissonance in the unheard music. He felt as though he were a missile that had been fired at an unseen target five years ago. The trajectory had been low and flat and powerful for a long time. The missile has no cause to think or wonder about destination. It flies true. Now the impetus was fading and the arc of its fall had begun to be perceptible. He did not want this to happen. He did not want to be forced to think—to conjecture about what would happen to him. He wanted the flight to continue. He did not want to feel the stir of life again, of decision. It was enough to be aimed, to perform the function of level flight.

The image of Dorothy was now faded. And he despised himself for being unable to maintain the sharpness and the clarity. The fading was a sign of weakness. The slight urge to take time off was another sign of weakness. And he had lived through his strength, and off his own strength.

[*The big man with the face of silence drives the green sedan through the increasing force of the wind. He drives automatically, his mind on other things.*

And then he sees the red rhythmic flashing ahead and he slows the sedan and pulls over to the right as directed, pulls over and stops behind the slick tail of a low wide foreign car. He remembers that it passed him long minutes ago with a Cadillac following it too closely.

He looks back and sees a blue and white convertible stop behind him. He can see the vague blur of a woman's face through the windshield. He turns back and lights a cigarette and settles himself more comfortably in the seat and begins to wait—with the heavy somber patience learned on a hundred streets in a hundred cars during five thousand hours, watching a door, or a window, or an alley entrance.]

9

Hilda, the eighth hurricane of the season, missed Key West. But tons of rain fell on that peculiarly disappointing city at the terminus of a magic highway.

The highway slants down across the bridges and the causeways and the keys—Largo, Matacumbe, Grassy, Boot, Pigeon, Ramrod, Sugarloaf—a shining engineering project—which should lead only to a city fairer than any yet designed by man. Yet it ends in Key West, a shabby, dirty and uninspired town from which it is very difficult to catch a glimpse of the sea, a town of tough bars and honky-tonks, fairies and whores.

Hilda dropped tons of rain on Big Cypress Swamp. They are logging the cypress out of there. The water level used to be high enough to make logging impractical. But with the draining of vast areas of the Everglades there is a faster runoff and now they can get in and get to the giant cypress in the dying swamps. The cypress is cut up and used in the building of the thousands upon thousands of houses that sit in rows on land where the big bulldozers have ripped out the scrub and the cabbage palm. And they sit on made land all the way up the West Coast, where builders have filled in the blue bays with shell from the bay bottom.

Rain fell heavily on the very very rich and very self-conscious little city of Naples. It fell on the fertilized ranch lands and the water ran off and took with it the fertilizer which, later, in the Gulf, would cause the explosive growth of a micro-organism and again the Red Tide would kill billions of fish, sending them in clotted stinking masses against the shoreline and into the quiet bays.

The rain interrupted the operations of the commercial fishermen around Boca Grande, Placida, Englewood, Punta Gorda, Fort Myers. Many of them suffered a monetary loss through being unable to net snook. The snook, with its narrow head, undershot jaw, striped body and vicious fighting heart, is one of the last great small game fish in the world. Its meat is sweet. It is rapidly disappearing from Florida waters.

So, while Hilda moved up the Gulf; the rain moved up the coast, falling on innumerable motels and motel signs, on the raw bulldozed land where houses would soon be built, on the dredges and the draglines that were filling in the bays; it fell on a million pottery flamingos and uncounted shell ash trays; it pounded gum wrappers, ice-cream spoons, broken coke bottles into the sand of the littered beaches; it thundered on roofs that sheltered the twined bodies of honeymoon and the slack bodies of the dying.

And, up and down the coast, the rain softened the earth around the root structure of the Australian pines. There is a city ordinance in Fort Myers prohibiting the planting of these pines within the city limits. That is because the root structure is wide and shallow. When drenching rains precede winds of hurricane force, the pines topple too readily.

Hurricane Hilda, perverse, unpredictable, slowed and made a gentle curve to the northeast, moving ever closer to the coast. She moved to within fifty miles of the mouth of the Suwannee River and there all motion seemed to cease—all forward motion. She was static in that area, the whirling winds churning the Gulf. She drew her great gray skirts closer around her. She had covered an enormous and violent area. Now, in a time when the force of her should have been dying, she shrank into herself and, gaining force from compactness, her winds whistled with a new fury. Already hard gusts of wind struck the coast. The tide had been rising in the Gulf throughout the morning. High tide along the Cedar Key area was predicted at three o'clock.

It was determined later that it must have been at about one o'clock when the hurricane, smaller and fiercer than at any time before, began to move due east toward the Florida coast, moving at an estimated twenty miles an hour, with the winds nearest the eye reaching a velocity that could not be measured.

Slow traffic bypassed the Waccasassa Bridge where technicians worked to free the jammed truck trailer. The heavy rain and the traffic had made the detour less passable. The state policemen on duty had, by one-thirty, evolved a system that simplified traffic control. Dan Boltay had tied a scrap of cloth to a stick. He would hold up a flock of cars until the cars coming from the other direction came through and the last one gave him the stick. He would then give it to the driver of the last car in his batch. He was able to let cars through at half hour intervals. It made a long exasperating wait in the rain. He had radioed in, suggesting that the detour be closed, but it was desired that it be left open.

It was at one-thirty that Roy Stark, on the south end of the detour, having just sent a batch of cars through, began to accumulate another group. Stark was damp and bored. The rain was letting up. The wind was getting a lot stronger. Sudden gusts would make him lose his balance. The corner of the lapel on the rubber rain cape would snap against his cheek, stinging him. When a sheet of rain did come, it was driven nearly horizontal by the wind.

The first car he stopped was a dark blue Cadillac, a new model. He flagged it down and went over to it. The driver rolled the window down. He was a balding, ginger-haired man with a red-faced look of importance.

"What's the trouble here?" he said over the noise of the wind.

"You have to detour around the bridge. One way traffic. You have to wait for a batch to come through from the other end."

The other man in the car was smaller and older, and he looked nervous. "Is the bridge out?" he asked in a high voice.

"No. There was an accident on it. It's still jammed up."

"Anybody hurt?" the driver asked.

"Truck driver was killed."

"How long do you think we'll have to wait?" the driver asked.

"Not too long," Stark said and moved back to flag the next car into line. The next car was slowing down. With the rain letting up visibility was better, and the flashing dome light on the road patrol car was more effective.

The second car was a heavily loaded station wagon with a youngish couple and a pair of kids. They asked the same questions, the questions Stark was getting weary of answering. He noticed that as he stood next to the car answering their questions, the wind from the west was making the car sway.

There was about five minutes before another car came. The storm was making them hole up. Stark decided that it was a good thing it wasn't a day of heavy traffic, like in the middle of the tourist season. They'd be lined up all the way back to Lebanon Station.

Stark was pleased when the next car came along. It made a break in the monotony. He'd never seen any other car that looked quite so rich and haughty. And the damn thing was really low. He saw the name on it as he walked up to it. Mercedes-Benz. There was a couple in it. A good looking guy and a girl who was not as good looking, but looked like plenty of money.

The way the car door opened was the damnedest thing Stark had ever seen. It swung out and tilted up. It was hinged on the roof and counterbalanced. It left a high sill to step over if you wanted to get in or out.

After the usual questions and answers the man said, "Where's that hurricane?"

"I haven't had any report on it lately. I guess it's out in the Gulf, heading for Texas."

"You sure of that? This wind is getting pretty hairy."

Stark looked at the tree tops. The gusts were beginning to seem solid enough to lean on. And the sky, now that the rain had nearly stopped, was an odd yellowish color. "Doesn't look too good, does it?" he said.

The fourth car was a dark green Plymouth with a husky hard-faced guy driving it. He was alone and he had Maryland plates. He didn't ask as many questions as the others. He didn't seem as impatient about the delay.

The car that pulled up behind the green Plymouth was a Dodge convertible, a blue and white one with one hell of a good looking woman alone in it. He answered her questions. He kept looking toward the detour and soon he saw the first car come laboring up onto the main road, straighten out and pick up speed. There were ten cars, and the last one had the flag—two giggling girls in an MG and the driver handed him the flag and he gave it to the woman in the blue and white convertible and told her to give it to the officer at the far end. Not much business this time. Just five of them. He motioned them on and they turned off onto the narrow dirt road. The big Cad and then the station wagon, then the foreign job, and then the husky guy in the Plymouth, and then the good looking woman. Just as the convertible turned into the road, a beat-up panel delivery came along. Stark hesitated and then waved it on. It turned into the road too fast and the back end swung a little before it leveled out. He caught a glimpse of two kids, a boy and a girl, in the front seat and something about Hollywood fish printed on the side.

As he stood there a truly massive gust of wind came along. It slammed against him and drove him back. He turned and took several running steps before he caught himself. The force of it shocked him. He heard a rending crack, muffled by the wind noise, and a big limb fell onto the road, bounced and slid and was pushed over into the far ditch by the wind.

He leaned into the wind and walked to the car. He was on call. He called in and he heard the strain in the metallic voice at the other end:

"The hurricane has changed direction and it's moving in on us, Stark. It's pushing a high tide ahead of it and raising hell along the coast. No more cars go through that detour. Stay there and turn 'em back the way they came. Tell 'em to find shelter. Tell 'em to get the hell out of this. It looks like a bad one. Cruise south and stop everything coming at you and turn 'em around."

Stark started the motor and swung around and headed slowly south, dome light flashing. The wind swayed the moving sedan. On impulse he pushed the siren and kept it on. The sound seemed buried and lost in the new high wail of the great wind.

The Australian pine was a huge one, very near the end of its life span and beginning to die. It stood on the north bank of the Waccasassa River, thirty feet west of the wooden bridge over the main part of the river.

The same gust that drove Stark across the road struck the old tree. It tilted, leaned. There was a ripping, crackling sound and the flat root structure was pulled slowly up on the west side of the tree. The tree fell slowly at first and then more quickly. It brought up square yards of black soaked soil with it. It fell thickly, heavily, onto the north end of the wooden bridge. The great weight of it in free fall smashed the tough old timbers. The bridge folded and sagged, supported the weight for a few seconds, and then with small harsh noises as spikes were pulled slowly from weathered wood, bridge and tree sank into the swollen Waccasassa.

The caravan of six cars came nosing cautiously down the

JOHN D. MACDONALD

dirt road. It crossed the first bridge, the Cadillac in the lead.
The cars jounced over limbs that had fallen into the road.
The caravan passed the ugly old house. The road turned
slightly. The lead car came to the bridge and it stopped.

"God damn!" said Johnny Flagan in an awed tone.

"That tree fell right across the bridge," Charlie Himbermark said excitedly.

"You can sure figure things out fast, Charlie. Damn if you
can't."

"Don't take it out on me, Johnny."

"We got to get out of here."

Johnny Flagan pushed his door open against the wind and
looked back. The cars had piled up behind him and he
cursed. He had no place to turn around. The ditch was too
deep and soft on either side. Somebody started leaning on
the horn.

"Thanks," Johnny said. "Thanks a lot. That helps out."

He got out of the car and the wind buffeted him, pushed
him against the side of the car. As he passed each car he
yelled, "Bridge is out!" and did not pause to answer questions. The last car in line was an aged panel delivery with a
kid driving, a dumb-looking young girl sitting beside him.

"The bridge is out," he yelled. "We got to all get turned
around. We can all turn around back in the yard of that
house back there. You got to be the first one."

The kid nodded and backed the truck. The kid looked
scared. He backed the truck too fast. Johnny stood, braced
against the wind, and saw the kid waver from side to side on
the greasy road and then slam the truck backward into the
soft ditch, putting it in on enough of an angle to block the
road. Flagan cursed softly. The rain had now stopped completely. The thin young fellow from the station wagon and
the husky guy from the green Plymouth joined him.

"We'll have to horse it out of there," Johnny Flagan said.
The good-looking woman in the convertible had backed,
following the panel truck, and she stopped when she saw the
road was blocked. As the three men approached the truck, a
man climbed from the back of the truck over the seats. The
boy who had been behind the wheel got out and the young
girl got out the other side. She had not been prepared for the
force of the wind. It caught her and sent her stumbling
forward. She tripped and fell and rolled across the road and
came to rest in the opposite ditch, skirt wound high over

100

pasty thighs, face twisted into sudden childish tears of pain and fright.

The man who had climbed over the seats got behind the wheel. The three men and the boy caught hold of the truck. The husky man from the Plymouth got behind it, his back against the truck, legs braced against the ditch. The wheels spun and the truck moved and came out suddenly, braking to a stop before driving into the opposite ditch.

It was then that the second tree came down. Johnny Flagan saw the movement out of the corner of his eye and looked up and yelled and trotted back out of the way. It was another pine, not as large as the one that had fallen on the bridge, but it was tall and a good two feet in diameter. It missed the truck. The trunk thudded against the road. The thin man from the station wagon tried to twist away from it, a heavy limb brushed his shoulder and sent him diving into the rear of the panel truck. He hit his head against the back of the truck, slumped onto the bumper, hung there for a moment, and rolled over onto his back in the road. The husky man hurried over to the crown of the tree and Johnny Flagan realized that the young girl had been there in the ditch. The man clawed down through the branches and as Johnny moved over to help him, the man pulled the girl out. She was still crying and there was a long scratch on her cheek, but she was otherwise unharmed. The man who had hit his head was trying to stand up. Johnny Flagan looked at the size of the tree, at the blocked road. A flying limb banged the side of the panel truck. Johnny ducked and cursed and saw the wind knock Charlie Himbermark sprawling on his back, and he suddenly began to feel the queasiness of alarm. It was a long time since Johnny Flagan had been afraid of anything.

Boltay, at the north end of the detour, had received his orders and was headed north, turning back southbound traffic.

The attempt to clear the main bridge was suspended. The coastal power and phone lines had begun to go. Driven by hurricane winds, the tides began to hammer the beach resorts. There were last minute evacuations of exposed keys. Radio stations switched from public power to their own generators.

The casualties had begun.

A child in Cedar Key monstrously sliced by a whirring

flying piece of aluminum roofing. Two elderly women from
Ohio electrocuted when a power line fell across their sedan.
A fisherman at Horseshoe Point drowned while trying to
adjust the mooring lines on his anchored boat.

And the main force of the hurricane had not yet reached
the coast. The great property damage thus far was water
damage. The huge tides smashed sea walls, sucking filled land
out through the gaps in shattered concrete, collapsing shore
houses. Tidal water came up over beaches, across shore
roads, moving into houses set hundreds of feet back from the
normal high tide mark. Thousands of sand bags were being
filled. People fought and worked to protect their homes.

*Emergency Warning Service. All coastal facilities. 2:12
p.m. It now appears that the eye of the hurricane will
intersect the coast line in the vicinity of Cedar Key and
Waccasassa Bay. Unless there is a change in speed or direction, this intersection should take place at approximately
four-thirty. Evacuation of all exposed properties from Dead
Man's Bay to Tarpon Springs is recommended. Highway 19
is now impassable. Warning—this is a highly concentrated
and violent hurricane.*

10

As the wind had strengthened, Jean Dorn had not let her alarm show in her voice or her manner. The wind made driving more difficult. When she looked at Hal she saw that he was sitting very erect, his thin hands on the wheel at ten o'clock and two o'clock, knuckles white with the strength of his grip.

At least there was not as much rain. The sky was more pale than before, a luminous gray in which there seemed to be a tinge of yellow. The look of the sky made her sense how small they were and how very vulnerable. Small car speeding north under the vast yellowish bowl of the sky. Looking down from the sky it would be a little box shape moving along a gray ribbon.

She felt a tremor of completely irrational fear, and for a moment believed so strongly that they were moving swiftly toward some unimaginable catastrophe that she wanted to cry out to Hal to stop the car. She forced herself to relax. All her life she had been vulnerable to the moods of the weather. A bright warm day gave her a holiday mood. Heavy winter snows had made her feel hushed, secretive, tip-toe. On days of rain she had always wanted to weep.

She remembered reading that when the barometer was low it induced an atavistic nervousness and tension in people. It was a primitive warning, and the animals responded to it also. With a hurricane in the area the barometer would be low, and it was not strange that she should feel alarm with no real basis for it. There was another factor, too. During the early months of pregnancy with both Stevie and Jan she had been moody, vulnerable. Only in the later months did she get that warm deep sense of waiting and growing and flourishing.

Yet the sense of alarm had been very strong. Almost strong enough to . . .

She looked again at Hal's hands as the car swayed so

violently that he had to slow down. His lips were thin and tight.

"Maybe we ought to try the radio again," she suggested. He nodded and she turned it on, waited for it to warm up. It buzzed but no station came on. She turned the needle across the dial and she could find no station, no sound except the constant buzz.

"I guess ... it's broken."

"Oh, lovely!" he said. "All we need."

"Hal, darling, don't ... "

"Shut up!"

She turned her head sharply and stared at him, then turned and looked out the window, feeling the warm sting of tears in her eyes. She rode that way for perhaps five minutes.

"I'm sorry," he said abruptly.

"It's all right."

"Of course it's all right. The magic forgiveness. Like turning on a tap. No, I don't mean that either. Don't pay any attention to me, Jeanie. I'm just in a vile mood. And now, for God's sake, don't say 'That's all right' again."

She decided it would be better to say nothing. He was too full of his own defeat. Perhaps too too full. Too close to the edge of self pity. She wondered how and why he had lost his resilience, the core of his courage. Or was he without it in the beginning—and she had not known that because this was the first time it had been tested.

She felt shocked and ashamed of her own disloyalty. Hal had certainly not given up readily. He had maintained his spirits for a long time. She remembered how, during the first two weeks at the warehouse, she would massage his sore aching back muscles each night and how they would joke about it. His hands had become toughened. They had a new harsh feel against her flesh, a hardness and masculinity that was not entirely displeasing.

He had not given up for a long time. The trouble was that when he finally had given up, when he had wept, he had given up all the way, unlocking all the gates and surrendering all the turrets. Jean suspected that it had something to do with his family, with his father. Defeat, to Hal, was the unthinkable thing. The thing that could not happen.

She wondered how it would be for him if he were alone, if he did not have this pressing burden of wife, two children, and new child to come. Already it seemed that she could sense his resentment.

"Accident, I think," Hal said. She looked ahead and saw the red flashing light.

The policeman had them stop behind a blue Cadillac and he told them about the blocked bridge and the detour. Stevie and Jan had begun to get a whining note in their voices and Jean knew they were getting hungry. She opened the glove compartment, took out the box of fig newtons and handed it back to them, with severe injunction to share.

It seemed a very long time before they were permitted to go ahead, along with the several cars that had stopped behind them, all of them following the blue Cadillac. It certainly wasn't much of a road. It moved in aimless gentle curves across scrub flats and then dipped toward heavier trees, crossed a precarious wooden bridge, passed a house set in a grove of big trees, a house that looked gloomy and brooding in the strange light. Hal stopped when the Cadillac stopped, and Jean, looking ahead, saw the big tree down and the ruin of the second bridge. The other cars had stopped behind them. "We can't get through," Jean said.

"Look!" Stevie yelled, leaning over the seat so that his head was between theirs. "Look at the bridge! Wow!"

"Sit back there where you belong," Hal ordered.

The driver of the Cadillac got out of his car and looked back at the row of cars and then walked back by their car. He was a heavy soft-looking man in a cord suit, with a red face and a balding head. The wind made him walk as though he were drunk.

Hal opened the wagon door and got out. "Where are you going?" Jean asked.

He held the door open. The solid wind came into the car and it made her feel breathless. ". . . if I can help . . ." she heard him say. The door slammed hard and he was gone. She tried to look back. She could not see out the rear window because the station wagon was so loaded. She slid over behind the wheel and she could see them in the rear vision mirror fastened forward of the door—see Hal and two other men struggling against the wind as they walked to the rear of the line.

"Where did he go?" Stevie demanded. "I want to go too."

"You stay right where you are. He'll be back in a minute."

"But what is he *doing?*"

"Hush, Stevie. Please. And give Jan another fig newton."

She saw the truck back wildly into the ditch and saw the men walk down to it, tiny figures in the round reflecting mirror. She hoped Hal would be careful. Jan started yelling angrily at Stevie. She turned around and settled the quarrel. When she looked back in the mirror she saw the tree falling. It was impossible drama in the small mirror, a scene from a gray movie, a thing that could not be happening. Hal was partly obscured by the truck. She saw him try to run as the tree came down, saw him come clear of the tree and dive headlong into the rear of the truck, and fall.

She forced the door open against the wind, held it open with her body as she turned and shouted to the children, "Stay right here. Don't try to get out."

Then she was running back toward Hal, feeling the wind buffeting her. It swerved her against a green Plymouth with no one in it, hurting her wrist when she braced herself. Hal was trying to get up. She ran to him. His face was strange and blank, showing neither pain nor surprise, but rather a dulled determination.

She caught his arm and helped him and he got to his feet and staggered back and sat on the rear bumper of the truck. When she tried to talk the wind forced her lips apart, inflated her cheek, blurred her words.

"Are you all right?"

"I'm all right." She could barely hear his words. He looked at her, and seemed to look through her, and there was a puzzled look deep in his eyes. She knew he was not all right. She looked around despairingly. The others seemed busy with their own self-assigned problems. Two of the men had climbed over the tree trunk and were walking toward the other bridge. No one seemed to know or care that Hal was hurt.

A sharp painful memory of childhood came into her mind. Her parents had forbidden any attempt to swim out to the float. But the other kids were out there and she decided she could swim out. She had chugged along, pleased with herself, until she was about twenty feet from the float. And then things had gone wrong. No matter how hard she kicked, her legs had sunk so that she was upright in the water. She had kept paddling frantically, but the paddling merely served to keep her precariously afloat. She could move no closer to the float. She could see them there, brown in the sun, outlined against the blue sky, and they were not looking at her. She tried to call out to them, but her mouth and nose kept going under. She could even hear them laughing, and she saw Judy being tickled by the Gillton boy, but no one would look down at the desperate struggle happening so close to them.

Then the world got all strange and soft and dreamy, and with arms that were loose as feathers, she was trying to climb a green ladder made of soft rounds of silk. Everything was faraway and unimportant, and then she felt sulky annoyance when something grabbed her roughly. Without transition she was then on the float in the bright angry sunshine, gasping and choking and coughing. Water ran out of her nose and mouth and then she was sick. They brought a boat out and took her ashore. Her parents had heard about it and were down on the beach waiting for the boat. She felt lonely and heroic. Her mother had hugged her and cried over her. Her father wore a face like thunder.

Now she stood by her husband, her hand on his shoulder. She looked down at the swelling on the crown of his head, at the blood matting the dark hair. No one seemed to know or care that he was hurt.

He said something and she leaned closer to him. "What, dear?"

"Dizzy," he said, frowning.

"Can you get back to the car?"

He looked up at her. "Where is it?"

"Up there."

People had gotten out of the other cars. They came down to stare at the tree. They had to shout at each other to be heard. The wind suddenly became as strong as an arm pushing her back. It pushed her against the rear of the truck. A palm frond came whirring and rattling through the air and bounced on the road and skipped and cracked her shin painfully. She kicked it away and the wind slid it under the truck.

The men came back and one man came over to her. He was about Hal's age or a little younger. As he walked he braced himself strongly against the wind, planting his feet with care. He wore a bright blue and green sports shirt and gray slacks. His hair was cropped short and he was a powerful looking man.

He came close to her and looked down at Hal and said, "Need help?"

"He hit his head."

"I saw it. He hit pretty hard."

"He acts dazed. He didn't know where the car is."

The man seemed to study her for a moment. He leaned closer to her, his mouth close enough to her ear so he could talk in almost a normal tone. "We looked at the other bridge. Even if we had anything to get this tree out of the way, I wouldn't want to try it. The water is coming up fast. It's over the bridge boards. Stuff is coming up the river and bumping into the bridge. The wind is pushing the Gulf toward us. If it keeps up this road is going to be under water. Do you understand?"

She nodded quickly.

"That house back there is on the highest ground. I think we all ought to try to wait it out there. That man over there thinks we ought to try to walk out."

"We can't do that!" she said. "We've got two small children."

"Are they alone in the car?"

"Yes. I had to leave them when I saw . . ."

"Get back to them. I'll get your husband into that house and then come after you and the kids."

She obeyed without question. When she was half way to the station wagon she looked back and saw the man helping Hal over the trunk of the fallen tree. The others stood in a small group and she saw them dodge violently when a palm frond was whirled over their heads.

When she got to the car both Stevie and Jan were crying. Stevie stopped quickly when he saw her. She tried to pull the door open and could not. She went around and got in the other side of the car. Jan still wept. "Where's Daddy?" Stevie demanded.

"This is a bad storm and we can't drive away in the car, darling, because the trees have fallen down. We're going to wait in an empty house. A nice man is helping your daddy get to the house and then he's coming to get us."

"Why does he have to help him?"

"Daddy fell down and he hurt his head. Now don't start crying again, Stevie. Please. Be a big brave boy."

Stevie gulped the tears back and turned on Jan and said, fiercely, "Stop being a baby!"

Trees to the west of the car swayed dangerously. She looked ahead at the bridge and saw the water was much higher than before. It had spread out on the far bank covering where the road had been. The wind whipped the shallow water, pushing it eastward.

The big man came and forced the door open and got in. He was breathing hard. He nodded at Jean and turned around and grinned at the kids. "Hi," he said. "We've got to do some camping out. My name is Steve. Steve Malden."

Stevie's eyes went wide. "I'm Steve too!"

"And that's Jan," Jean said. "I'm Jean Dorn and my husband's name is Hal. How is he?"

"He's in the house waiting for you. We may be there some time and it may get cold. You better bring some warm stuff if you can manage it."

Jean crawled back over the seat and pried a suitcase loose and got out sweaters and one of Hal's jackets. She put the sweaters on the children, put her own on.

"All set?" Malden said. "We better go out your side. You take the boy and I'll carry Jan. Come on, honey. Climb over here."

"Stay on this side of the cars," Malden said to her as she opened the door.

She went ahead holding Stevie by the wrist. Just as they got into the open beyond the rear of their car, a gust hit them and slammed Stevie against her ankles, knocking her down. She kept hold of his wrist and got to her feet and pulled him up. His eyes were wide with shock and fear and surprise. He said something but she could not hear him. He did better from then on. They passed all the cars and climbed over the tree trunk and soon they were in front of the house. The house cut the hard thrust of the wind. Malden moved ahead of her, climbed the three shallow steps and pulled the door open. She followed him in and Malden closed the door. The relative silence was abrupt. The house was shuttered and it was so dark inside that for a few moments she could see nothing. She tried to release Stevie but he clung to her hand.

There were several people talking at once. Their voices were thin with excitement, edged by fear. She began to make them out, and then she saw Hal over in a corner, sitting on the floor. Malden took them over to Hal. He set Jan down.

Jean turned and said, "Thank you so much for . . ."

109

"I better go get in on this policy meeting, Mrs. Dorn. Holler if you need me for anything."

Jan and Stevie had moved close to Hal. Jean sat on her heels and took Hal's hand. "How do you feel, darling?"

"I'm fine," he said in a remote voice. "Just fine."

"Did you hurt your head, Daddy?" Stevie asked.

In the gloom she saw Hal turn and look at Stevie, look at him in a puzzled way. When she realized what that look meant, fear closed tightly on her heart. Hal was looking at the child without the slightest tinge of recognition. She saw him look in the same way at Jan, and then turn and look at her. His lips opened as though he were about to say something, but his eyes clouded again and he looked down at the floor. Jean folded her coat and put it on the floor beside him. She eased herself down onto the coat, her back against the wall. She took Jan in her arms. She looked at the room.

It was a room with a low ceiling, a long room on the northeast corner of the house. It was paneled in a dark rough wood. The room was completely bare and there was a smell of wet rot. The wooden floor was heaved and buckled, and, near one wall, there were holes where the floor boards had rotted away. There was a small brick fireplace set into the south wall and, to the right of the fireplace, a staircase that went up. The walls of the staircase had been plastered, and the plaster had fallen away from the laths and lay like dirty snow on the stairs. There was a door to the left of the fireplace that led to another room, and another doorway in the west wall that led to what had apparently been the kitchen. She could see the edge of an iron sink, and a row of empty shelves, crudely made.

The others were arguing. Over and under the tones of their voices she could hear the voice of the wind. The wind pressed against the house. It found small cracks where it could enter. It entered and stirred the ancient dust. As it came in the small cracks, and as it twisted around the cornices, it made small wild sounds, full of a supersonic shrillness. The shrill sounds ebbed and pulsed with the changes of the wind. She thought that if she had to listen to that long, she would begin to howl like a dog. She thought she could feel a stirring of the hair on the nape of her neck.

There were cracks in the old shutters. Thin gray bands of light shafted into the house, diffused by dust. She felt the stir of the bones of the old house when the wind swerved and smote it strongly. Over the wind sound there were other sounds from the outside world. Remote and inexplicable thuddings, rattlings, crashings. Something cracked sharply against the back of the house, silencing for a moment the voices of argument. And then they began again.

She moved closer to Hal and took his hand. He did not look at her. His thin brown hand lay slack in hers. She sensed the imminent fulfillment of her premonitions. At some other time perhaps a thing like this could have been a game, something to remember and talk about and laugh about. But not now. Not in a world newly soured by defeat. This was the end of something. An end far more specific and final than their decision to leave Florida.

She sat beside her husband and thought of marriage. You did not think of the big things, the epochal, the stirring. You thought instead of the trivia of marriage. The ludicrous. The absurd. Your mind was cluttered with little things. Like the time that Hal, that afternoon in Central Park, for no reason other than high spirits, had sprung up from the path and grasped a low limb and hung there, grinning down at her, then cautiously hung from one hand, made a face and scratched his ribs with the other hand, then dropped lightly beside her and kissed her in full view of the weary bench-sitters, not one of whom even smiled, but sat there looking at them with what Hal always called "the subway glaze."

The little tragic things too. Turning off the Merritt Parkway in that first new car they had ever owned, and hitting the small brown dog. They had run back and the dog had dragged himself off onto the shoulder. Whining, the dog had bitten his own flank with great ferocity and, quite soon, had died. They had asked at a dozen houses and then given up trying to find who owned it. There was no tag, no collar. She remembered how quickly the flies had gathered. Hal had dug a hole with the tire iron and they had buried the small brown dog. It had saddened the day and the weekend for them.

And the time Stevie, sitting on the kitchen floor, had stared up at them, eyes bulging, face slowly turning blue. She had held him by the heels and Hal had thumped his back and then finally dug into his throat with his finger and loosened the small wooden wheel Stevie had swallowed. She remembered how weak they had both been after it was over.

And the morning when Hal had started out the front door

111

and neither of them had known that the rain at dawn had frozen into an utterly transparent film over the walk. She remembered the way he had gone down, a wild flailing like a comedy sequence, and then the sickening crash onto hip and elbow, how he had looked back at her, face distorted with pain, then the humor fighting with the pain, overcoming it, until they both laughed like fools. But it had been a month before his arm was right again.

Trivia of marriage. Like the lurid pajamas he had bought himself for the first night of their marriage. And the wound he had inflicted on her. He swore that he had taken eleven pins out of the new pajamas, but he had missed the twelfth, the crucial one. The shocking stab of the pin had made her leap and yelp, and in that moment of confusion he had thought her an exceedingly apprehensive bride, rather than someone cruelly and ludicrously stabbed. She blamed his sense of decorum that had made him start with pajamas. And he had said that all he had expected was ten minutes of use out of them anyway, and he asked if there had been any pins in the gossamer nightgown of hers, and who was she to lecture about decorum after whooping and plunging like a singed heifer. She said that she would be grateful for a more kindly simile, so he changed it to spooked mare, but by that time they were beyond the point where the conversation could be continued with any coherence.

You remember little things most of all. She sat and listened to the eldritch whimper of the wind, and the tears ran down her cheeks, heavily, slowly, and she kept her head turned so that the children would not see that she was crying.

11

Bunny Hollis had driven the Mercedes-Benz with the casual co-ordinated grace with which he performed all physical movement. She sat in the seat beside his, and she would look at his hands resting lightly on the wheel and she would say, over and over to herself—Betty Hollis Betty Hollis BettyHollisBettyHollis.

Not Betty Oldbern any longer. Never Betty Oldbern again.

His hands were square and brown with pronounced cords on the backs of them, with long fingers splayed at the tips, with heavy ridged nails that he kept closely clipped. On his left hand was the gold ring, heavily ribbed, a masculine variation of the daintier band on her finger.

Just the way he would open a door, climb stairs, reach to pick up something. It was controlled grace, taut and completely masculine. Finely and perfectly balanced. Not like that one who had been Stella's friend. That ballet one. His grace had been muscular, but of a different breed. There had been a simper in it.

All the days of her childhood and her young girlhood seemed to be compressed into one unending scene—where she walked alone down a street while all the others watched from steps and porches. She walked in painful consciousness of too soft hips, her knees brushing awkwardly together, her head too heavy for her throat, her arms refusing to swing in any rhythm to her walk. There goes that Oldbern girl.

Almost from the very beginning she had known that she was not what Daddy had wanted. Not at all the sort of girl he had hoped for. He had wanted a brown sunny laughing girl. A girl like Stella or Janie or Sue or Cindy. A girl who could *do* things, and talk to anybody in that bright pert way that she had never been able to manage. When she had tried to talk that way people had looked at her in an odd way.

That was why Daddy had sent her away, of course. To all those schools so far away. It was something you had to

113

accept. You weren't what was wanted, what had been expected, and so you had to go away. And she had sent back the very best marks she could get. And the medals given for those marks. It was a small gift, but the only one she had to give.

Eating so much was part of it too. But she had never clearly understood how that was so much a part of it until lately. Eating had been just about the only fun. And in a sense it had been scary fun. Gobbling all those heavy pastries and thinking that each new pound put you a little bit further from any possibility of being ever wanted by any man. And that was a relief, because it was a problem you'd never have to face if you were too fat. And she had really been terribly fat that day she had first seen Bunny Hollis. About a hundred and sixty-five. And for a small-boned girl only five foot four, that was really gross. Mirrors had always been the enemy, and being that heavy had been sort of a way of getting back at the mirrors.

She knew she would never forget that day. She had been bored and restless and she had driven over to Oswando Club, a place she usually avoided. She had sat alone at a table under an umbrella and ordered a sundae and ate it there and wondered about ordering another and watched the man who was teaching tennis to two brown towheaded boys of about thirteen. The day was still and hot and she could hear his instructions clearly. "Billy, the reason he keeps passing you is because you wait to see where your ball is going. As soon as the ball leaves the racket, you should be on your way back to position. And you're trying too hard to hit 'em where he ain't. Just concentrate on getting it back smoothly and moving back to center court. Let's try again."

She decided he was quite a nice man. He seemed so patient and so anxious to have the kids do well. He stood by the net post and watched the kids. She was aware of him, but not specifically aware. Then, as she watched casually, he put both the boys in one court and he took the other side of the net and began to volley with them. She watched him. She saw the shape of his shoulders, the long straight line of his back, the way he moved with style and precision, the way his head was set on the round strong column of the neck.

She watched him and she felt a rising of warmth within her, a slow stirring that brought a hot flush to her cheeks. For the first time in her life she felt strong, specific, physical desire—desire that had an immediate target. She had had crushes, but they were not like this. It was as though for the first time her femininity had a focus and a purpose. She had thought of men and of physical love and wondered often how it would be. Her anatomical knowledge was sound and specific. But her wonderings had always made her feel faintly queasy. The actual act seemed to be so ludicrous, so animal, so intimately degrading. And suddenly she had seen a perfect stranger and the act, which had been so appalling, seemed all at once to be logical and necessary. Yet even as she drew mental pictures that shamed her, she realized the absurdity of her position. Fat girl in the umbrella shade going all sticky over the tennis instructor at the club. He was so old. He must be nearly thirty.

She could not get him out of her mind. She learned that he was Bunny Hollis and he was well liked at the club. The next week she made an appointment with him and showed up with tennis equipment to take lessons. It was by far the bravest and boldest thing she had ever done. He had been polite and distant. They had played a few games so that he could find out how well she played. Then he had called her up to the net and she had come up close to him, ashamed of the way she was panting and sweating and trembling from the unaccustomed exertion.

"How old are you, Miss Oldbern?"

"Nineteen."

"I think I can help your game, but you have to co-operate. I'll be frank with you. If it offends you, I'm sorry. You're much too heavy. The first exercise you better practice is pushing yourself away from the table." He grinned to take the sting out of the words.

A week later when she fainted during a lesson it was because she was weakened by hunger. She came out of it after he had carried her into the shade. She opened her eyes. He was rubbing her wrist and looking down at her with a strange intentness.

"How much have you been eating, Betty?"

"Practically . . . nothing."

"Do you want that badly to be good at tennis?"

"No . . . I mean I guess I do."

After that she sensed the change in his attitude. He seemed thoughtful, and quite aware of her. Lots of times they would talk instead of practice. She told him about the schools,

115

about how she had lived for nineteen years. And he told her how he had lived for thirty-three years. Fourteen years' difference in age didn't seem so much if you said it quickly. And when she was fifty, he'd only be sixty-four.

When it turned cold they moved the lessons to the indoor courts. That was all there was in her days. The lessons. There was nothing else worth thinking about. There was a lesson on a gray day in November. When it was done he turned out the court lights. Gray light came down through high windows. They walked toward the doorway. She clumsily dropped her racket and it clattered on the floor. They both bent to pick it up. They straightened up, close together. She had the racket. He looked at her and put his hands gently on her shoulders and pulled her closer to him and then put his mouth on hers and kissed her hard. She had been kissed before. But it had never done anything like this to her. From far away she heard the racket fall again. He kissed her twice and then held her close. She was down to a hundred and forty-four by then.

He released her and turned away and said, "I didn't mean to do that, Betty."

"I love you," she said. It was the only thing she could think of to say—the only thing that was indisputable and explanatory.

"You don't mean that. I shouldn't have kissed you."

"You can do anything you want to me, Bunny."

But he wouldn't take her on that basis. Within the next month they began to talk cautiously of marriage. She was not a fool. She was accustomed to rejection. She was quite aware that the world was full of men who would be delighted to pretend love in order to marry all that money. And she sensed that Bunny was one of those. She was certain that Bunny was one of those. By then she had learned enough about him so that she could not blame him too much for being one of those. He had never had money. She tested him by pleading with him to run away with her when she was twenty. It alarmed him. She could see that. He didn't want the applecart upset. Nor would he make love to her. She took that as a tribute to her unattractiveness, and as a sample of his caution. She knew what a fool she was making of herself, and yet she decided to go ahead with it, to wait and to marry him, knowing that she was merely buying something important to her, and could never buy the truly precious thing, a return of the love she felt for him. For despite her awareness of his greed and his design, she could not help loving him.

And, of course, it was the only way that the money would ever be of any use to her.

The family—her father and all the elderly relatives—raised absolute bloody hell when she made her plans known. But she was twenty-one and there wasn't a single thing they could do about it. There was no way they could turn her against Bunny.

She weighed a hundred and thirty-seven on her wedding day. The flesh was stubborn, clinging. The softness was gone and the remaining excess was firm and too durable.

After the ceremony she began to be afraid. She had had two years in which to anticipate climax. Soon she would be taken by him. It was the penalty he would have to pay for his carefulness and his greed. She hoped he wouldn't be rough. He was so terribly strong. His strength frightened her.

It was absolutely no good. He had been gentle, almost tender, but it was no good. It had been strange and awkward and it had hurt, but not badly, and if this was what the world was all about then a lot of people had been kidding a lot of people in a lot of different ways for thousands of years. It was no good at all. And then it was bearable. It became something you could do without it bothering you too much if you didn't think too much about it. If you made a sort of passive acceptance.

And then, like a light being turned on, like a window being opened, it made sense on that first night in Curacao. It made her feel as though she had been particularly obtuse about getting the point of a very obvious joke. It made her feel stupid that it had taken her so very long to learn what this could be. What had been harsh and alien and alarmingly masculine about him became suddenly dear. It all became simplified, like the logic of the dance. Harshness was meant to be enclosed in softness. Giver and receiver. The very physical configurations of them, the differences between them, became as logical to her as night and day. And in the very midst of this new acceptance, in the sudden certainty that what she was doing was inevitable and good, there came upon her wave upon wave of a pleasure so keen that it was beyond anything she had ever imagined. The pleasure stretched beyond the point where she could bear it without crying out, and just as she did so there was a bursting, a fulfillment, a shuddering torrent that left her feeling boneless, spent, heavy and soft as rich whipped cream.

The next day she went about full of a heavy-lidded wonder, full of a warm sweet stupor. It seemed the most precious and miraculous thing in the world to know that it could happen again and again. She held that knowledge close to her. She could not look at Bunny the same way, ever again. She looked at him with warm, strong, knowing lust, and wanted him when she looked at him.

She tried to tell him all of it, half laughing as she tried to tell him. He laughed too and held her and said, "It appears, Mrs. Hollis, that the honeymoon has begun."

"You have been very patient, Mr. Hollis."

"Patience has been richly rewarded, Mrs. Hollis."

And in the tropic nights, in the lazy mornings, in the afternoons after swimming, she learned that each time could be better than the last. She learned that she was a lusty woman, and, having always been uncertain, shy, rejected, she felt very proud that here was at last an aspect of life which she could seize cleanly, firmly, strongly.

And she also learned that this coming alive had strengthened her desire to look well for him. She knew that the better she looked to him the stronger would be his wanting, and the stronger hers would be. She learned to be constantly aware of him, and to so handle her body that she would look her best. She learned little tricks to entice him, amazed and amused at her own ability to devise such tricks. In her flowering she learned to handle herself more gracefully. There was more confidence in her walk, more fun in her talk.

Little by little, and with the utmost caution, she began to permit herself to believe that she might be loved. She began to believe that if Bunny were acting a part, he was by far the most clever actor in the world. With the new confidence that came from accepting the possibility of being loved, she became Betty Hollis. And the other one, that Betty Oldbern, was long dead, long buried. She could not grieve for Betty Oldbern, not for that fat awkward stupid girl, that wolfer of pastries, that dull talker, that winner of gold medals for excellence in French composition.

"There isn't so much rain now," Bunny said. "But that damn wind is getting a lot stronger."

"I've been thinking about something," she said.

118

He gave her a quick glance and looked back at the road. "Hmmm. Important?"

"I think I'm going to have an operation."

The car swerved and came back into line. "What the hell kind?" His voice sounded angry, and she was pleased because she knew it was concern and not anger.

"There was a girl I was in school with in Philadelphia. She had a real grim set of buck teeth and practically no chin at all. Much worse than I. They used to call her the beaver. She had an operation right after school was out and when she came back in the fall she was really lovely. They did something to her jaw. Some sort of bone graft or something. And they fixed her teeth too. The funny thing about it was that her eyes had always looked sort of close together, like mine do. But that was because of her chin going in. I covered up my mouth with a towel this morning and looked and it really does change my eyes. I'm going to find out what she had done and get it done to me."

"That's a lot of nonsense, Betty. You look fine."

"You're a kind man. But I'm going to have it done."

"Why?"

"Because you deserve the best I can provide, mister."

"Damn it, I don't approve of . . . Hey, what's all this?"

She saw the flashing red light too, saw the two cars waiting. The state policeman waved them to a stop behind a loaded station wagon. They found that the bridge was out and that they would have to take a one way detour. Some other cars came along and stopped. Finally they were permitted to go. Bunny complained aloud about the condition of the road and the low clearance of their car. The detour seemed to be a long one. They crossed a narrow wooden bridge and not very far beyond it the two cars ahead of them stopped.

When Bunny saw the ruined bridge he turned to her and said, "Something tells me, my fat lamb, that we are going to have to sit out a hurricane." His voice was casual, his smile was easy, but she saw a certain tautness in his face, a tinge of apprehension.

"We'll just all have to turn around and go back, darling."

"That might be quite a trick."

The other men went by toward the rear of the line, but Bunny stayed where he was. Betty felt slightly irritated with him. He ought to at least go and try to help the others.

Bunny turned the motor off. The wind made the car tremble.

"I've never liked storms," he said.

"What's holding things up?" she asked.

He got out, swinging the door up, stepping over the high sill. He looked back and then he got in quickly and he looked pale. "Another tree's down!" he said nervously. "We're blocked off here. Damn it, why did they have to send us over this cow path? They should have known it wouldn't be safe."

She turned and saw the others back there. "Well, let's go back and see what everybody's going to do about it."

When the wind caught her, nearly hurling her from her feet, she felt a wild high surprise. It snapped her hair against the side of her cheek, stinging her. It pressed her skirt tightly against her, and the hem fluttered against her legs, making a rippling fluttering sound. Bunny caught her arm and grinned at her and shouted something over the noise of the wind. They went back to where the others were, and she saw a man sitting on the back bumper of a panel truck, a woman standing beside him, her hand on his shoulder, looking tense and worried.

An older man with a red face came up to them and told them angrily that the water was rising fast and the other bridge looked dangerous and maybe they'd all better hole up in that empty house back there and wait it out.

Bunny said, over the wind sound, "These things last a long time. Maybe we ought to walk back to the highway."

"It's better than two miles and there's low places the water will be over. And the wind's getting stronger. There'll be stuff blowing around. Besides we got two little kids in the group, and that fellow there, being helped toward the house, he got hit on the head when the tree came down."

"We're going to walk back to the highway," Bunny said.

"Suit yourself," the man said, and turned away.

"Mind a little hike?" Bunny said to her. His mouth had a pinched look.

"We better lock the car first."

He looked back uneasily. "You wait right here. I'll go lock it."

"Bring my blue jacket, will you, please? It's right behind the seat."

He hurried off, leaning against the wind, half running. He came back with the jacket. They climbed over the trunk of the fallen tree and walked by the house and onto the other bridge. The floor boards of the bridge were completely under water. Some sort of big log was caught against the bridge and the current was coming up from the Gulf, holding the log against the bridge, spilling water over it. The water was a deep green brown and it made dirty foam where it swirled over and around the log.

They both ducked as a palm frond crackled by just over their heads. They saw a big tree fall beyond the bridge. It fell silently, the noise of its falling lost in the roar of wind and water. The water level was rising visibly.

She looked at Bunny and was shocked at the way he stood, shoulders hunched, under lip sagging, fear visible in the way he stood and the expression on his face. She took his hard arm and shook it angrily. "We better go back to the house."

He straightened, looking relieved. "I guess that's best."

"Are you afraid, Bunny?"

"Don't be a damn fool. I'm worried. Anybody would be worried. I'm not afraid."

"That's good. I wouldn't want you to be afraid."

They went back the way they had come. They were the last ones into the old house. The six automobiles were empty. It was a relief to be out of the claw and tug and pull of the wind. When her eyes were accustomed to the light, Betty counted noses. Thirteen of them. Five, counting the little girl, were female. One tall very handsome and poised looking woman—a dark-haired woman who had been alone in the convertible. And the nice looking and perhaps slightly pregnant blond woman, the mother of the two children, wife of the man who had been hit on the head. And a young doughy-looking, ripe-bodied girl with a scratch on her cheek. She seemed to be with the two rough-looking boys. She was crying. And Betty was the fifth.

Eight men. The red-faced one in the cord suit. An old frail looking one who seemed to be with Red-face. The two hard-looking boys. The father who had been hit on the head. And a massive powerful-looking man in a sports shirt. And Bunny. And the little boy.

Not exactly, she thought, *the sort of list I would make up for a party. Would any of them be on such a list? That dark-haired woman. Maybe the big husky man. None of the others, certainly.*

121

They stood by the fireplace and Red-face came over to them. "Decided not to try it, eh?"

"It began to look a little too rugged."

"I've been checking the house. There isn't any big stuff close enough to fall on it. It looks solid enough, even if some of the floors and the sills are rotted out of it. I'm Johnny Flagan by the way. This here is a business associate of mine. Charlie Himbermark."

"Hollis," Bunny said. "Bunny Hollis. And Betty, my wife."

"I guess we might as well make ourselves comfortable, folks. It's going to get a lot worse before it gets any better. I've been through a mess of these things."

"Is this really a hurricane?" Betty asked.

Johnny Flagan laughed. "Lady, this is the front edge of it. It hasn't got warmed up yet. And my car radio said it's coming right smack dab at us. It sure fooled those weather boys. It swang around and it's moving right out of the west. Just like that one a few years back they lost track of in the Gulf and it came right on in and took a sideways smack at Clearwater then moved on up and stomped hell out of Cedar Key. Really mashed that little town up. I'm telling the others and I'm telling you, anything you want to get out of your car, get it now. If you got any food or anything to drink, make sure you get that and bring it in and we'll put it all in the pot and draw for whoever needs it most."

"I guess we haven't got anything," Bunny said.

"But darling," she said. "How about the coffee in the thermos, and the bag of oranges?"

"Better get those while we can," Mr. Flagan said.

Bunny gave her a quick angry look. He went to the door. He hesitated and seemed to brace himself and then went out. Mr. Flagan touched her shoulder lightly. "Don't you fret about it, little lady. It's the low pressure that makes you feel nervous like. We got to all get along here as best we can."

Bunny was back in a very short time, bringing the thermos, the oranges, and a woolly car robe. Flagan took the coffee and oranges into the kitchen. Bunny looked around and then said, "Let's take a look in the other room."

The other downstairs room was as barren as the first one. But it was empty of people. He spread the robe down in a corner and they sat on it, their backs against the wall. He lighted cigarettes for them both. His hand shook as he gave her her cigarette.

122

He looked beyond her and said, "I guess I was scared, Betty. I guess I still am. I'm sorry."

And any last dreg of anger and scorn left her entirely. He had always seemed almost too capable, too ready to meet anything that came up. Now he had showed her weakness, and he had confessed it. It made her feel warm and strong and protective. She wanted to tell him that whatever he was afraid of, she wouldn't let it come and get him. She cupped her hand against his cheek and said, "I'm just too dumb to be scared, I guess."

"Fat lamb," he said softly.

He put his arm around her. He held her waist and then she felt his hand slide up to her breast and cup it, and she felt the almost instantaneous swelling and tautening, the almost laughable readiness of her body.

"Darling, darling," she whispered, her head sagging against his shoulder.

"There ought to be a private room in this hotel," he said. "Shall we ask the desk?"

"Ask Mr. Flagan. He's the manager."

"And Himbermark is the bell captain," he said.

"And that sorry-looking little girl is the dishwasher."

"The Windblown Arms," he said. "With plenty of running water."

They laughed together and she turned and kissed the side of his throat.

12

When the tree came down and nearly smashed that young fellow flat, Charlie Himbermark shocked himself with the intensity of his wish that the tree had managed to fall on Johnny Flagan. That would have made a nice thing to see. A nice direct hit, driving that ginger skull down between those flabby knees, bursting the self-important belly, turning Flagan into a nuisance on the road, like a tromped frog.

The image was so vivid that he looked at Johnny Flagan's neck with a feeling of warm satisfaction. He looked at the back of that thick red neck, at the deep horizontal wrinkles, and he felt warm and glad that the tree had shut Johnny Flagan's mouth forever.

But the tree had missed and the satisfaction ran quickly away.

It certainly was a comedown in life to have to take the punishment that came from Johnny Flagan's mouth. To have to sit meek as a lamb and say yessir and nosir, and never contradict. Flagan with his stinking little deals. Flagan couldn't possibly know what the big time was like. He'd never be able to understand a business that was conducted with dignity and purpose and understanding.

Like handling the Willoughby portfolio for over twelve years. Georgiana had been so proud of him when Charles had been given the Willoughby portfolio. He remembered how, every Tuesday, when he left for the bank she would make certain that he hadn't put on one of those shirts with the frayed cuffs, or a necktie that was the least bit soiled around the knot. Because every Tuesday afternoon at three-thirty he would leave the bank and go out to the Willoughby place and have tea with old Miss Anna Willoughby and Roger, her brother. They would chat and have tea and then they would go over the summary sheet he had brought along. The sheet would show any changes during the week.

Percentage and dollar change in quotations of both the bonds and the stocks. Proxies, stock splits. With old people like that you had to be certain that you were getting the maximum current return from the holdings, rather than playing for a continual increment in the total value. At the time of Anna Willoughby's unfortunate and unexpected passing away, the value of the portfolio was over nine hundred thousand dollars.

Flagan had no feeling for dignity. He had no style. It was laughable to think of Flagan ever trying to hold a job at The Bank. Grossinger would have fired him during the first week. The Bank was no place for loud talk, flamboyant clothing and a whisky breath. There was tradition there. Quiet sound tradition.

Georgiana understood how it was at The Bank, and she was proud of him, proud of the job he was doing. They had both liked the life, liked the pleasant apartment, enjoyed their friends. Georgiana would never never have approved of Johnny Flagan.

He wished there was some way he could tell Georgiana about Johnny Flagan. He could imagine how shocked she would have been had he been able to tell her about the other trip he made to Georgia with Flagan, and about the cheap woman Flagan was friendly with up there. A woman just as obvious as Flagan, just as coarse and cheap.

But Georgiana was dead and now he was, incredibly, married to Agnes, Babe Flagan's friend. Whenever he thought of Georgiana and Agnes at the same time, he felt guilty and ashamed. He knew that Georgiana could never have conceived of his getting remarried. He did not even quite know how it had happened himself. Agnes wasn't as coarse as Babe and Johnny. But she was certainly a more ... a more robust woman than Georgiana had been.

Compared to Agnes, Georgiana seemed rather dim. Of course she had never been a very well woman. Those cruel migraines had come upon her so often, and she would have to spend the whole day in a darkened room, suffering the tortures of the damned. She was so brave about it though. Such a small frail brave woman.

Who could have guessed that she would die when she was only forty-eight? The bitter blow had broken his health. She had been there, and then she had been gone, the apartment empty, the flower smell still lingering, the rooms silent. It was like the days when she had had migraine, and he would tiptoe around to keep from disturbing her.

His health broke and Mr. Grossinger was very decent about it. As he had only put in twenty-six years in The Bank he could not expect the full pension, of course. But Mr. Grossinger had done the best he could with the Board, and they had put him on a forty per cent pension. It was even fortunate in a way that his health had failed. He would have had to leave in any case. It would have been unbearable to stay there where nearly everything in the city reminded him of Georgiana. But if he had just left, there would have been no pension at all.

The job in the brokerage office had been pleasant work. He had enjoyed it. Of course he had still missed Georgiana dreadfully, but it was nowhere near as sharp an anguish as it had been up north.

And then Agnes Steppey had stopped by to ask advice. She was a rather nice looking woman of about fifty-five. She was tanned a deep brown and she wore an orange blouse and what seemed like quite a lot of costume jewelry. She had a rather deep laugh, and sparkling dark eyes. She looked almost, that first day, as if she were some kind of a gypsy.

He studied the list of the stocks her late husband had left her and he saw at once what the trouble was. Carl Steppey had been buying growth stocks, and from the dates of purchase it looked as though he had done quite well indeed. They made a healthy capital gains picture, but they certainly weren't producing income.

He explained very carefully to Mrs. Steppey what ought to be done, how she should unload all but one or two of the items on the list and reinvest the funds in the type of security which would bring her an adequate guaranteed income. She caught on quite readily, and after it had all been juggled around she had lost a certain amount of face value through taxes and brokerage fees, but her income had been jumped from about twenty-one hundred a year to over thirty-eight hundred.

They got on well together. She got into the habit of stopping in when she was downtown, and he would go around the corner with her for coffee. It was inevitable that they should talk about losing a wife and a husband. It surprised him to find she had three grown boys. One was an engineer in an aircraft plant in California. One had gone to

Annapolis and was making a career of the Navy. The youngest was homesteading in Alaska. She showed him pictures of them, of their wives, of her three young grandchildren.

There was one thing about Agnes that had distressed him in the beginning. It still distressed him, but he didn't see quite what he could do about it. She had a certain coarse turn of speech sometimes. She loved indecent stories, and actually told them very very well. But it did not seem to him to be a proper thing for a lady to excel in. They talked about how lonely it was to be single, and without his ever quite knowing how it came about, they were suddenly talking about marriage and a month later they were married.

There certainly was a great difference between the first wife and the second. Georgiana had always been so sensitive and rather shy. She had never talked about the sexual side of marriage. When he had married Agnes he had not thought very much about the sexual aspects of it. He had even hoped that Agnes would agree that they had both outgrown that sort of thing—outlived it, rather. But buxom, earthy Agnes had other plans. At first it made him feel quite ridiculous, but soon he began to take a peculiar pride in being able to respond almost as well as when he had been a very young man. Agnes distressed him with bawdy comments about the food she bought for him, and he had been very reluctant to go to a doctor for those injections. But when you overlooked that side of Agnes, she was really a wonderful person to be with, and he felt lucky to have married her. Except when he thought of Georgiana, and then he felt guilty about marrying again.

The nearest he had come to a quarrel with Agnes was when she had said, "That Georgiana of yours must have been a poor man's version of Alice Blue Gown. An original gutless wonder. Did you ever get up enough nerve to go to bed with her?"

Agnes had apologized later and he had forgiven her. Agnes seemed to think there was nothing strange or unusual about their leading a personal life that would have been normal for a couple in their thirties. Charles liked it, but he could not quite get accustomed to it. You just had to face the fact that Agnes and Georgiana were two different types. Agnes was more like Babe Flagan than she was like Georgiana.

There was another difference too. Georgiana had always

127

treated him and his work with respect. But Agnes was always puncturing his dignity. "Please, I beg of you, don't start telling me again about that mausoleum of a bank you once worked in. Carl used to say all big city bankers are disappointed undertakers. If you *must* keep dithering around looking for a job, let me see what I can do, dear."

And the job working for Johnny Flagan was what she had done. But Johnny had misrepresented the job. That was what had caused all the trouble. Johnny had made it sound as though all he wanted was a sort of spy and errand boy. So Charles had decided to show Johnny that he was capable of accepting responsibility, even if the job was a great deal smaller and less important than the job in The Bank.

But Johnny didn't want anyone to accept responsibility. He wanted to do it all himself. He had to be the king pin. Nobody else could have a chance.

It was too bad that tree had missed Johnny Flagan. Because he was certain that the reason Johnny was taking him back up to Georgia was to humiliate him. Flagan had come from nothing, and he had to prove his worth by stepping on everybody else. Flagan was small town. He'd never be anything but small town. He'd be lost in the city. He was probably shrewd enough for a small town, but that was as far as he'd ever get.

He realized Johnny was saying something to him.

"What's that, Johnny?"

"Go get the bags out of the car and take them to the house, Charlie."

"Sure thing, Johnny." He felt the willing smile on his mouth and turned his back and walked toward the Cadillac. *Now I'm a bell hop. A flunky. Carry my bag, Charlie. Go get this. Go get that.* He was so intent on his hatred for Johnny Flagan that he was almost unconscious of the renewed fury of the wind.

He got the idea just as he reached the car. Stevenson was a nice man. Stevenson was easy to talk to. If Ricardo and the group pulled out, Johnny would be unable to swing the charter. He knew that Johnny had told Stevenson he could handle it all by himself if need be, but Charlie knew that was a lie. Johnny had told him in confidence that if Ricardo pulled out he wouldn't take the chance of taking over all those shares himself. The idea was still a good one. Maybe Stevenson would listen to a proposition. Get Ricardo to pull out. Then Johnny would too, and they'd withdraw the application for a charter. Then Stevenson and Ricardo could form a new group and re-apply for a charter. And, because of the information Charlie had given them, they might in return let him have a few shares and give him a position.

Agnes would be very annoyed. She wouldn't want to leave Sarasota, especially to live in a small town in Georgia. But he thought she would agree. It would be nice to be associated with Stevenson.

And it would be particularly nice to get even with Johnny Flagan for calling him stupid and calling him a clerk and a bore.

Johnny would find out who was a clerk.

He carried the bags back. They were hard to manage in the wind. The wind kept banging them against his thin legs. As he reached the house he saw that the young couple who had decided to walk out had changed their mind and were on the way back. He carried the bags inside and Johnny took his bag without a word of thanks. Charlie Himbermark had been nervous about the hurricane, but he was nervous no longer. He knew that it would be over sometime, and they would get up to Georgia sooner or later, and when they did he would find a chance to have a private chat with Stevenson. A chat between gentlemen. A little dignity and mutual respect.

Whatever happened to Johnny, he had asked for it. He just didn't know how to handle people.

Johnny motioned to him to come out into the kitchen. Charlie went out. Johnny had opened his bag. He took a quart of bourbon out and broke the seal and unscrewed the cap and handed it to Charlie.

"Take a knock, Charlie. Then you'll stop jittering."

"I'm not jittering."

"Then you should be. This is going to be a real ass buster of a hurricane."

"What can happen?"

"The damn thing you better think about is the water coming up high enough to wash this castle away. The second probability is it getting blown down. Take a drink."

Charlie stared at him. Johnny looked serious. And he knew this country and these storms. Charlie took three shallow swallows of the tepid liquor. It scalded his throat and heated his belly and spread warmth through him. Johnny

129

took the bottle, wiped the neck on the palm of his hand, upended it and drank deeply, his throat working. He lowered it, said, "Haw hoo wow!" recapped it and put it back in the bag.

"It would blow this house down?" Charlie asked incredulously.

"Snatch the roof off then blow the walls down, Charlie, my boy. Don't tell that to the others, though. If you do we'll have to waste bourbon on them. Now don't tag along after me. I'm going to go make the acquaintance of that big black-haired dolly with the tan and the nice big boobies."

Charlie watched him swagger out of the barren kitchen. After he had gone the wind seemed louder. It seemed to threaten to move the house. There was a calendar on the wall between the boarded-up windows. Charlie walked over to it and tried not to hear the whine and whistle of the wind as he looked at it. July 1926. The paper was curled and yellowed. The twenty-fourth of July was crudely circled in red. Above the month was a colored picture of a canoe on an indigo lake passing in silhouette in front of an enormous yellow moon, with a girl and boy in the canoe. The advertisement at the top was for a garage in Gainesville. He wondered idly what the date meant, why it was circled. Was that the day they had left the house? Or a date of death?

The wind slammed the house again and started something vibrating, a loose board or lath or piece of roofing. Himbermark rubbed his hands together and discovered they were damp. In between the wind sounds he could hear the others talking.

He thought of the trooper on the road. He would learn that the other cars hadn't gotten through. They would investigate. Help would come. It was inconceivable that they would all be ignored. Yet suppose the main bridge was cleared just after they started through, and the trooper got word over his radio. If there was a trooper at the far end, he might not expect another group of cars through the detour. And the trooper who had let them through would think they had made it all the way.

He moved cautiously to the doorway and looked into the dim room. No one was looking toward him. He ducked back and got the bourbon and this time he took a longer drink. It did not burn his throat as much, nor was the heat of it as evident. He recapped it and hid it away.

130

Stevenson would be easy to talk to. Stevenson wasn't like the other men in The Bank, but he was more of a gentleman than Flagan. And he didn't think that Stevenson thought much of Johnny Flagan. He had seen the pained look on Stevenson's face that time he had met him in Johnny Flagan's suite at that hotel. The three of them had been talking in the parlor of the suite. The door to the bedroom was closed. Right while they were talking the bedroom door had opened and that woman had come out, pouting and sulky, dressed only in one of those skimpy little terrycloth beach robes that came down just below her hips. She had tousled reddish blond hair and a thick sleepy-looking face and she said, "How long's all this quack going on, Johnny? We're outa liquor and now I'm outa cigarettes, damn it."

Johnny had grinned and jumped up and given her a fresh pack of cigarettes, turned her around gently, then hoisted the back of the beach coat and given her a sharp palm crack on the bare whiteness of her. She had made a little shriek and jumped back into the bedroom and slammed the door. Then Charlie could hear her laughing in there. He had been embarrassed and he had looked over at Stevenson and saw that Stevenson had looked pained and disturbed.

"Sarah Jean gets herself all nervous and restless," Johnny said.

"Maybe we ought to finish this up some other time," Stevenson said.

"Hell no, Steve. She'll keep. She's a good kid. She came over with me from Augusta yesterday afternoon."

And in a few moments they were back into the conference again, discussing the new shares that Ricardo had lined up, and talking about the way the charter was going to go through. Charlie found he wasn't following it very closely, that instead he was thinking of the girl in the bedroom, wondering just how Johnny had met her in Augusta and how it happened that she was willing to come along with him. He wondered what sort of person she was, and what kind of boldness it was that Johnny had that enabled him to bring her over here so casually and treat her with such affectionate contempt.

He went down in the creaky elevator with Stevenson afterward and he wondered if he should say anything about the woman. Something casual and sophisticated. Or maybe express distaste for the arrangement.

But he couldn't think how to say it, and Stevenson didn't say anything, so the opportunity passed.

Yet it was undeniable that Stevenson had looked disapproving. He had good reason. It was his home town, the place where he was raising his kids. And he was associated in business with a man who would bring a woman like that to his home town.

Perhaps Stevenson was looking for some chance to get Johnny Flagan out of the picture. Then it could be a new life, a new job, a good start.

The warm tide of pleasure ebbed quickly away. He looked at his thin hands, at swollen arthritic knuckles, grainy skin on the backs. Stevenson wouldn't want him. You couldn't think of a new start at this age. It was funny about age. Funny how easily you could forget that you were old, be trapped into thinking a young man's thoughts. He remembered how it was at forty, when you could think that if you were lucky and healthy, there could be just as much life ahead of you as there was behind you. But when you were over sixty, you knew the biggest part was behind you. And you didn't know if you had one more year or ten. Or even fifteen. Sometimes fifteen seemed like a lot of years. Other times it seemed like a meager unfair amount, like you were being cheated. That was when you looked at the young ones and felt stinging envy and thought how if you had their life, you wouldn't waste a moment of it. Not a single second.

Stevenson wouldn't want him. Johnny was disgusted with him. Johnny had a right to be. He'd known he shouldn't have talked, shouldn't have tried to make a big impression up there. But you had to let people know you were alive. That you meant something.

A small girl came out into the kitchen and looked up at him. She was a plump pretty child. She had been crying recently. She sucked on her fingers and looked up at him.

"Hello, honey. What's your name?"

She took her hand out of her mouth. "Jan. My daddy's sick."

"That's too bad."

"His head is hurt."

A small boy came out into the kitchen and took Jan's hand impatiently. "You come on back. Mother wants you. Come on." He towed her into the other room.

Himbermark heard Johnny Flagan's voice, raised above the wind sound, and he went to the doorway to hear better.

"...all stuck here until this thing blows itself out. It's pushing the Gulf in on us, and we may have to move upstairs before it's over. Now this pile here is the stuff out of the cars. We haven't got much food or much to drink. I'll take charge of it and dole it out to whoever needs it most if nobody's got any objection."

He paused and looked around expectantly. "Okay then. If you got anything in the cars that can be eaten or drunk up, we ought to get it before this thing gets any worse. The water may get kind of deep out there, and maybe we ought to get the luggage and stuff in here and get it all upstairs. I introduced myself to some of you. I'm Johnny Flagan. The Dorns over there, the couple with the kids, had some bad luck. Mr. Dorn got smacked on the head when that tree went down. Most of you can get your own stuff. But somebody should get the Dorns' stuff out of the wagon. And get Mrs. Sherrel's stuff too. I noticed a cistern out in back of here. The pipe running into the kitchen is dry, but it may just be clogged up, and there may be water we can drink in the cistern. I'll go out and check that over. If there is, we'll fill everything we got."

"There's some pots and pans in our station wagon," Mrs. Dorn said.

"Fine. We ought to get those in here. And don't forget flashlights. Bring all the flashlights in. Blankets, car robes. We've got to figure on being here all night the way this thing looks. We got to have some kind of sanitary arrangement too. We aren't going to be able to go out in this mess. There's a little room off the kitchen, a sort of pantry. The floor is rotten and some of it is gone, but the rest of the floor feels solid enough. We'll use that as a kind of a privy. There ought to be water under the house pretty soon anyhow. Now let's get this thing organized. Your name is Malden? Suppose you and Bunny Hollis unload the Dorn car and the Sherrel car when you get your own cars emptied. Mrs. Sherrel, maybe you can get on the door and open it and close it for people as they bring stuff in. Just bring it in and put it in this room. Charlie, suppose you and these two young fellas carry it upstairs as they bring it in. We'll get ourselves all straightened out here, and we'll be cozy as if we were in a hotel."

Charlie could sense the relief the others felt at having somebody take over. And he felt a reluctant admiration for Johnny Flagan. The thirteen people had stopped being enclosed in their own isolated small groups and had become members of the larger group, co-operating for survival.

13

Hope Morrissey had been thinking about her father's grove as the panel truck rattled steadily northward through the rain, Billy Torris driving, and Frank asleep in the back. She thought of how it was when the trees were in blossom. Then you would lie on your bed at night and the sweet heavy smell would come in through the screen and the blossoms made the trees look pale at night.

She liked to think about the grove, but she did not want to go back there. Her father, Sam Morrissey, was a silent man who drove himself every hour of the day. He had set out more trees than one man could handle, yet he made himself finish the work that had to be done, the endless spraying, pruning, fertilizing. He walked with a long, tired, lunging stride, big hands swinging, and when he came into the house he brought with him a smell of sweat so sharp and tangible that you thought it should be visible around him, like a cloud. He seemed but barely aware of his children, and spoke to them only when it was necessary. For all his labor he did not seem to gain ground. He was an unlucky man. The wind would change unexpectedly and drift the protective smudge away from the tender trees in the frosty night. When any piece of equipment broke down it was never an obvious and readily replaceable part that failed. It would be some obscure gear or pinion that was seldom known to fail. The parts would not be in stock. The equipment would sit idle until a new part could be obtained by air express from the factory. And then, more often than not, it would be a part for a different model. He could have made up for his bad luck by the intensity of his labor were it not for the streak of quarrelsomeness in him. He continually felt wrongly used by the pickers, the truckers, the packing plants, the Association. He brooded about the way he was being wronged while he worked. And when he could stand it no longer he would stop work and find the man at fault and tell him off.

Sometimes these discussions erupted into violence. And though Sam Morrissey was a powerful man, he was not difficult to knock down. The excess of anger made him squinch his eyes shut and charge with both big arms swinging wildly. Any man who kept his head could knock him down.

Elena Morrissey, his wife, was a soft, pretty, careless, silly woman. She felt that she had married beneath her station. If so it was a social distinction too narrow to be measured by any outsider. She liked gay colors in the house, but despised housework, and did only the bare minimum necessary for existence. She liked flowery print dresses and large-brimmed hats and tiny pocketbooks. She was a woman with a fabulous memory for dates, names, places, relationships. She spent a great deal of her time calling on friends. When she asked Sam to do something for her, which was often, she used the high clear patronizing voice of the mistress of the manse speaking to a groom.

They named their firstborn Jonathan. June Anne was born two years later, and Hope was born four and a half years after June Anne. Elena had her children with an ease and a quickness that seemed to her shameful and peasant-like. No nausea and very short labor. She had always considered herself delicate. The doctor who attended her when she had Jonathan told her she was as healthy as a horse. She did not become his patient again.

Jonathan died, quite grotesquely, when he was twelve. He was a sturdy boy and he spent every possible moment with his father. Because he imitated his father's walk and his father's silence, he seemed a rather solemn boy. His best friend was Taddy Western, younger brother of Sonny Western. They were almost the same age to the day. On Taddy's twelfth birthday he asked for and received a bow and arrows. The bow was much too big for him. It had a fifty-pound pull. Neither boy could draw the arrows back as far as they should go.

The two boys were together on a bright sunny afternoon after school. Taddy found that he could draw the bow by sitting down, hooking the bow over his toes, and pulling the bow string back with both hands. As Taddy explained it later, they were taking turns rocking back onto their shoulders and shooting the arrows high into the air. Sometimes they could watch the arrow throughout its flight. Other times it would disappear in the high thin air, and then there would be a moment or two of delicious fright while they raced to the shelter of a tree and waited for the arrow to thud down, burying a good half its length in the ground. Jonathan fired the arrow that killed him. They lost it in the air. They ran under the tree. They waited. Taddy heard a flickering sound as the arrow came down through the leaves. Jonathan stood a moment by the tree, with four inches of wood and brightly feathered arrow end protruding from the top of his skull. Then he fell down and bled from the ear, but not very much.

After Jonathan's death Sam Morrissey became more silent and sour than ever before. And he worked harder. He left the house at first light and many nights he worked by the blue glare of a gasoline lantern. Elena felt truly afflicted. Her firstborn, her only son, was dead. Her youngest child, her second daughter, Hope, was feeble-minded. June Anne seemed to be the only one left. Her mother would often look at her and weep. That made June Anne uncomfortable.

At the time of Jonathan's death, Hope was five and a half years old. She could say a few words. She could not dress herself. She could feed herself messily. She was monstrously fat, dull-eyed, drowsy. Her skin was coarse, hard and shiny and there were bare patches on her skull. She slept between sixteen and eighteen hours out of each twenty-four.

By the time she was seven she had not improved. She was a great burden to Elena. Elena decided that Hope would be happier with other handicapped children. Elena took her to Jacksonville. Sam was too busy to go along. The people at the home seemed quite pleasant. Elena felt no sense of loss in parting from the child, though she simulated grief. She was shamed by her own high spirits on the way back. She felt as though the weight of the world had been lifted from her delicate shoulders.

Two months later the home requested that she and her husband visit them. They drove up on a Sunday. The people at the home seemed very proud of themselves. The family doctor had missed what seemed to them to be a rather obvious diagnosis. Hope had been born with an underactive thyroid. Her serious hypothyroid condition had so dulled her mind and body that any layman would have thought her feeble-minded. "In such cases, Mrs. Morrissey, medication seems to work an actual miracle."

A miracle it was. A fat little girl with a clear skin, able

to walk and talk and play and feed herself. She had a limited vocabulary, of course, way behind her age, but her eyes were reasonably alert.

They thanked everyone and took Hope home with them. Even though it had been explained, Elena could not feel toward Hope as she felt toward June Anne. Seven years was too long. In seven years she had become too accustomed to thinking of Hope as an ugly burden. She kept seeing the child in the light of the past years, and she could not feel love. It was an effort to simulate affection. Hope progressed quite rapidly. She was able to enter the first grade when she was eight. In the beginning she seemed both affectionate and eager to learn. But affection was too often repulsed. And all the children in the school knew her history. Many of them had seen her the way she used to be. They told the others, with suitable exaggeration. Hope withdrew quietly, sullenly, into herself, convinced that she was different, ugly, unloved, unwanted. Maybe, without June Anne in the house, it might have been different for her.

June Ann was a girl born to the adjective "most." Basically she was a normal decent girl, adequate mentally but not brilliant. Well co-ordinated, but not exceptionally graceful. Friendly, but not overly charming. But a rare beauty befogged the eyes of the beholder. A rare and unusual perfection of both face and figure guaranteed that she should be considered brilliant, graceful and charming. In due time she believed herself to be as others described her. She accepted the knowledge without humility, yet without arrogance. She was as she was, and pleased by it. For her alone were her father's rare gestures of affection, her mother's constant ones.

Hope was the disinherited. Though she had a dull mind, she was not too impassive to be hurt. Nor to wonder about herself and find a refuge of sorts in the limited play of her imagination. It was an imagination that needed props, and props were there in the timeless legends of "The Ugly Duckling" and "Cinderella." Both those stories made a deep and lasting impression on Hope Morrissey. Through childhood she felt as though she waited for her inheritance. The chrysalis would open and she would step out. The glass slipper would fit to perfection. When she was ten she quite suddenly became thin, nervous, unable to sleep. A series of basal metabolism tests showed that the thyroid had somehow reactivated itself. She ceased taking medication. She regained weight, and placidity. For a time she had thought that the princess was emerging at last, but it had not been true. Not this time.

There was no acceptance for her, not at home, not at school. Perhaps in a larger place than the small town near Ocala she could have found another outcast. But there she was entirely alone, and without resource. A more sensitive child could have been driven into mental illness by the isolation. But Hope was aware only of a restless discontent. A great dull gray weight of discontent.

By the time she was fourteen she was a doughy, ripe-bodied girl, heavy, soft-fleshed, with no-color hair, dull blue eyes, careless of her person, uninterested in clothes. Though her teachers tried to force her assimilation into the group, the other children would have none of her. No boy cared to be seen with a girl he considered spectacularly unattractive.

During her fourteenth year her father broke his right arm in a fall. A man came to work for him. He was a migrant worker who had last worked up around Orange Springs, a lean stringy man in his middle twenties who looked much older. He was not so much evil as primitive. His name was Dinty Seral. He had a hawk's face, pale weak eyes, a manner of servility, self-effacement. He watched the girl carefully and he stalked her with brute purpose. He raped her one rainy afternoon in a tool shed at the far end of the grove, and terrorized her with a knife blade at her throat, explaining precisely what he would do to her if she told. She did not tell. She met him whenever he demanded. Her abject fear of him faded quite quickly. She began to look forward to the quick and merciless interludes. They were, after all, the only change in the flat gray of her days. And it was the only acceptance she had achieved, ever. She took to following Seral about until he savagely ordered her to stop, fearing that her manner would arouse suspicion. She obeyed him.

It was in this way that Hope Morrissey found what was, to her, a satisfactory reason for her existence, a fulfillment, and a constantly growing need. The colors of her world were vivid at the times she was with Seral. At all other times they faded into grayness. Throughout the seven months that Seral worked for Sam Morrissey, her role altered subtly until by the time he was paid off and left, she had become, in her soft demanding way, the aggressor.

After Seral left her life was gray again. She had established her function, dimly classified it as the act for which she had been born and patterned, found that it was the only area of acceptance for her—and was then denied it. Had she more boldness she might have gone about in the community trying to find a substitute for Seral. She could probably have found someone with more need than taste. But she was caught up in the habit of isolation.

She performed the single positive act of her lifetime on the night that Frank Stratter paid his unsuccessful call on June Anne. Hope knew that Frank was wanted by the police for something. That did not matter to her. She asked with unexpected boldness and was accepted. It did not occur to her that his acceptance was a gesture of revenge against June Anne. She was fifteen when Frank took her away to Miami with him. She was not interested in the city. She did not concern herself with what Frank and Billy Torris were doing. She was satisfied to be wanted, to eat and sleep and live, and accept this new life.

It was too bad that they had had to leave the apartment. She had grown to feel quite at home there. And it had frightened her a little—not very much—when Frank had made her bring those men back to the darkness from the bars. She hoped she wouldn't have to do that very often. It didn't seem right.

She rode along in the truck, her hands clasped loosely in her lap, heavy white thighs stretching the cotton dress, wipers flapping at the rain, truck swaying in the wind.

She thought of her father's grove and she wondered vaguely how they were. She had no desire to ever see them again. Particularly June Anne. She realized she was getting very hungry and she wondered if she should turn around and wake Frank up and tell him. But Frank might get angry. When he got angry he would hurt her by pinching or hitting her. She balanced pain against hunger and decided she could wait a while.

She swayed forward when Billy stepped on the brake. She saw the police car ahead, the blinking red light. She saw the man beckon them on. Frank knelt in back, his head between them, voice sharp as he said, "Okay. Keep going. Down that road. That's where he wants us to go."

They caught up with the other slow-moving cars. It was a narrow wet, rutted road. When the cars stopped she got out with the others and the wind caught her and tumbled her into the ditch. The force of the wind shocked her. It was almost the same panicky unbelieving shock as when Seral had first forced her down on the dirt floor of the tool shed. The feeling that this cannot be happening, not really.

Then the great green top of the tree came swinging down at her. She could not get out of the way. It came down with a great wet sighing smashing sound, driving her down into the ditch, hurting her face, thumping hard against her hip. A big man tore the branches apart and got hold of her and pulled her out. She stumbled and he caught her. Her cheek was bleeding and she was crying. He examined the cheek and told her it was just a scratch. Her bruised hip made her limp a little. She could see that the cars couldn't get out. She didn't know what they were going to do. The wind was frightening. They climbed over the tree and went back into an old house. It was boarded up and quite dark in there. All the people came in. She stopped crying and felt quieter inside. Frank had a white strained look. Billy seemed very nervous. She stood between them and the three of them leaned against a wall.

After a while a sort of fat-looking man made the boys work. People brought things in, suitcases and things, and the boys had to help carry them upstairs. She felt tired and hungry. She eased herself down gingerly and sat with her back against the wall and felt as if some time, pretty soon, she would begin crying again. And she kept thinking of the grove. She wished she could stop thinking about the grove.

Frank Stratter meekly obeyed the orders of the big mouth who had taken charge. He carried endless suitcases up the creaky stairs and put them in the narrow hallway. There were four small upstairs bedrooms that opened off the hallway. Upstairs the wind sound seemed louder, and he thought he could feel the house sway.

He met Billy at the head of the stairs and Billy said, wide-eyed, "What are we going to do?"

"Shut up!" The kid was getting too nervous. This would be as good a time as any to take off, to leave the pair of them right here. With a hurricane coming in, the police were going to be too damn busy to bother looking for any fugitive from Miami law. He decided he would find the right chance and take off. He had what was left of the money they had gotten in Bradenton. And the clothes he wore. And a pocket knife with a four-inch blade. Nothing else. And it was pretty obvious that some of these people would be carrying a nice chunk of cash. The couple from the Mercedes for example. Or the big-mouth with the Cadillac. He knew he'd feel better if he could take off with some of that money. And it looked like it would be one hell of a long time before anything he did here could be reported.

The tactical problem was complicated by leaving Billy behind. The kid would talk. And that might cut down the time margin. Also, it would rule out New Orleans. And he wanted badly to go to New Orleans. He wished he had told the two of them they were headed for some other city. He wished he had a gun.

He stopped suddenly, half way down the stairs and wiped the palms of his hands on the thighs of the khaki pants. There was one way that would diminish all complications. When he thought of doing it, the breath was shallow in his throat. Billy stopped behind him and said, "What's the matter?"

Frank turned. "Go on back up. I want to talk to you."

They went into a far corner of one of the small bedrooms. "We can't stay here, kid. When they come in to get all these people out of here, they're going to ask a lot of questions. Who are you? Where did you come from? Like that."

"I guess they will," Billy said.

"So we don't stay."

"It's pretty rough out there."

"And it's rougher on the road gang, kid."

"I guess it is. When ... when do we go?"

"It's going to get darker. I want a good chance to take some money off these folks. Then we light out. We can make it to the highway okay. Then we take our chances from there. Okay?"

"Hope'll be pretty scared to go out in this."

"She'll have to come along. We'll have to make her come along."

Billy looked dubious. "All right, Frank. Anything you say. But how do we get another car?"

"We'll get one. Now go on down and get another load."

Frank watched the kid leave the room. He wiped his hands again. He felt a trembling anticipation within himself. He put his hand in his pocket and clenched it around the closed knife. You wondered about doing it. How it would

142

be. There could never be a safer time or place. Three of them would go into the dark storm wind. Only one would reach the highway. Even if the bodies of the girl and the kid were found soon, the details would be all confused. He wondered if it would be easy to do. Or hard. He imagined it might be pretty easy to do. He thought of the dream sky and the way he saw his name in the giant glowing letters. *Frank Stratter.* He thought of the swing of the brush hook. He felt again the jolt of his foot as he had kicked the man. This might be easy to do. Just once. Just to see how it was. And maybe never do it again. Because it was a damn fool thing to do. If they found out about it, they really came after you. And when they caught you, they killed you.

He stretched his shoulders, arched his chest, sucked his belly in and thumped himself in the pit of the stomach where the trembling feeling was strongest. He went downstairs. On the next trip up he carried a child's crib.

14

Virginia Sherrel had not been particularly aware
of the big man until he came over to her and asked her
if her keys were in the car. She took them out of her purse,
and handed them to him. "This one is for the trunk. Really,
I could get the things myself. Mr. Flagan seems to feel that
women are helpless."

He took the keys. "His conditioning, I guess. Southern
womanhood or something. Anyway, it is rough out there.
And he gave you a job being doorwoman."

She smiled up into his face. He had a look of massiveness,
of implacability. There was the slightest glint of amusement in
deepset eyes, a surprising hint of sensitivity in the set of his
wide firm mouth. "I'll bring everything in."

"Is it necessary?"

"This is flat country, but I think the water is going to
come a lot higher. Don't let me make you nervous."

"I'm not in the least bit nervous."

He stared at her, then smiled again. "You don't look the
type who is too stupid to be scared."

"Well! Thank you."

"I guess you're just a remarkably steady woman. We may
need you around here." He turned and left. She kept smiling
for a few moments after he left, and then the smile faded. It
was rarely that any man gave such an impression of enormous quiet competence. She wondered what he did for a
living. He very obviously did not work behind a desk. There
was no hint of softness.

She opened the door for them as they came in laden with
luggage. It took nearly all her strength to hold the door
against the twisting clutch of the wind. Had the door been
on the windward side of the house, it would have been
unusable. When they came in they looked frayed and breathless.

When the big man called Malden brought her things in, set them down, she saw the box that contained the bronze box of ashes. It shocked her that they should be brought into this house—and it surprised her to think that for a little time she had forgotten them. For a few hurtful seconds she missed David so intensely that she nearly cried out in the suddenness of pain. For this was the sort of thing that David could and would have risen to. His gaiety would have been infectious, his courage unquestioned. Calamity had always sharpened his wit and his perception. It was almost as though the life he led had never demanded enough of him. In spite of his look of blond frailty, he had been planned for a more violent age. Perhaps, during the Korean war, before she had known him, he had lived completely. He had been a naval aviator, a fighter pilot.

Malden stood close to her and said, "Is something the matter?" His perception surprised her.

"No. Nothing's the matter, thank you." She forced a smile. And then began to wish she had told him. But that was absurd. You did not tell a man you had just met that you were disturbed because he had brought your late husband's ashes into a room where you stood.

He studied her for a few moments and then said, "Know anything about hurricanes?"

"Just what everybody knows, I guess."

"It's pretty dramatic out there right now, and not too bad yet. Not as bad as it's going to be. It's worth taking a look at. If you wish, we could go out and take a look at it. When you understand something, it isn't quite as terrifying."

"I don't think I'm terrified, Mr. Malden, but I would like to see it."

"I'll keep you from being blown away, Mrs. Sherrel."

They went out into the full noise of the gale. It caught hard at her as they passed the corner of the house, and his hand was strong on her upper arm. They climbed over the fallen tree and went to the shelter of the blue and white convertible. From there they could look west through a wide gap in the trees. All the sky was a strange dark coppery color. Long cloud banks moved swiftly toward them. Her eyelashes were pushed back against her eyelids, her black hair snapped at the nape of her neck. When she tried to speak the words were blown out of her mouth.

He had to speak loudly, his lips close to her ear, to be heard. "The name comes from *huracan*. That's a Taino word. It means evil spirit. See those higher clouds? Altostratus and alto-cumulus. With clear spaces between. They're moving east. They radiate out from the eye. Now see the low stuff? It's moving northeast. That puts us in the bad quadrant, where you can get the worst violence. This is a small one. The eye won't be more than four or five miles in diameter and it ought to be off in about that direction." He pointed slightly northwest. "And not too far off the coast. Those cloud ridges will go up to seven or eight miles high. Oh-oh, here comes another rain squall." The first wind-driven drops stung her face. Malden opened the car and they got in. She slid over under the wheel. The rain struck so violently it sounded like hail. The car rocked with the push of the wind.

"When is the worst coming?" she asked.

"In an hour. Maybe a little more, a little less, the way it looks."

"How do you know so much about it?"

She saw a faint grimace, like a fleeting expression of distaste. "It used to be sort of a hobby, meteorology. I had the usual gadgets. Wind velocity, rainfall, aneroid barometer. Drew my own weather maps. But ... I gave it up." His expression changed. For a moment he looked almost boyish. "This is the first one of these babies I've ever seen."

The clouds overhead were very black. There was a sudden piercing blue-white flash, a great crack of thunder. She started violently and forced a smile and said, "Is it supposed to do that too?"

"Sure. It does everything. It has everything. Electrical disturbances, tornadoes." The blackness moved swiftly by. Another one was coming. In the interval the rain ceased and the day was temporarily brighter, but it was the brightness of dusk, and was suffused with the odd coppery glow so that the colors of all things looked strange, unreal.

"We better get back," he said, and opened the car door. He started to step out, and then turned and frowned at her and said, "We're going to have to wade back. Look here."

She looked. In that short interval the water had come up a frightening distance. It was nearly to the car hubs. Malden did an astonishing thing. He cupped his hand, scooped some up and tasted it.

146

"What in the world?" she said.

"Salt. We're getting this from the Gulf. They must be catching hell along the coast."

She took her shoes off. He took them from her and put them in the side pockets of the jacket he had put on. He helped her out. Her feet were toughened from walking on the beaches. There was a dip before the house where the water was deeper. She clung to him, holding her skirt above her knees with her other hand. They went into the house, into the relative quiet of the house where the thousand evils of the wind were muffled. She felt warm and glowing and oddly drowsy.

"I guess that was a fiasco," he said. "I'm sorry."

She looked at him in surprise. "But it wasn't! I loved it! I wouldn't have missed it."

"You got the hem of your skirt wet."

"Not very much, really." He gave her back her sandals and she slipped them on her wet feet and smiled up at him.

He looked at the others. The man named Dorn was being helped toward the stairway. Everything had been carried upstairs. He turned back to her and took her over to a corner away from the others. He spoke so only she could hear. "I don't want to alarm you, Mrs. Sherrel."

"Virginia."

"All right. Virginia. I'm Steve. I don't want to alarm you, but this place isn't too sturdy. The sills are rotten. Some of the foundation has crumbled. It may go."

She put her hand to her throat. "What then?"

"I'll stay close to you when the worst comes. I'll try to get us out of here. And maybe the two of us can help with those kids. I don't like the way Dorn acts. It may be a skull fracture. When the house starts to go, if it does, we get out fast. The water will be deep by then. I don't know how deep. Just west of the south bridge, on this side, there's land that's a little bit higher, and some trees that are dense and look easy to climb. Got that direction?"

"Just west of the south bridge. Yes. I've got it."

"Good. I wasn't going to tell you and then I decided you wouldn't panic."

"What made you decide that?"

"I don't know, exactly. I just decided you wouldn't, Virginia."

"And if the house doesn't go?"

147

"I think we're going to be here some time. We better each stake out a soft piece of floor upstairs. I imagine your husband will be worried about you when he doesn't hear."

She looked down at the rings on her left hand, looked up at him. "He died, Steve. The middle of last month."

"I'm sorry."

She felt the tears in her eyes. "I was terribly sorry. But when somebody wants to die, when they take their own life, you can't feel quite as sorry, can you? Angry and hurt and ... lost. But not quite as sorry. Do you have a wife, Steve? I'm sorry. That's a bold question. I guess hurricanes make you ... skip the usual devices."

He answered her expressionlessly, his face like a mask. "No. I have no wife. I'd better see Flagan and find out if there's anything else he wants done."

She watched his broad back disappear as he went up the stairs. She wondered why the mention of a wife was such a taboo. There were odd depths and silences in the man—like areas of old pain. A strong man. Strong all the way through, all the way to the bone. The song of the wind was but a minor distraction to her, a matter of little importance, while she thought about Ma¹den. It was disconcerting to feel such a strong attraction to him. The very strength of the attraction made it suspect, gave it the flavor of rebound, made her wonder if it was but the reflection of her own vulnerability. His hands were good and his eyes were good. She wondered what it would be like to be kissed by that firm mouth, held by those strong arms. She suddenly realized that she was thinking like a schoolgirl dreaming of the new boy in class. It was ridiculous.

A great hand pushed against the house. She felt a subtle shift of the worn flooring under her feet. For a moment her heart closed her throat. Then the floor was steady again. She exhaled a bit tremulously. This was a time to be practical. She remembered the pair of jeans in her luggage. Dress properly for your hurricane. Jeans and a blouse and a cardigan. And a scarf for her hair. At least it would be a temporary project.

Upstairs, in the hallway, rain water pattered with tin sounds into the pots and pans set under the roof leaks. Flagan straightened up from peering into one of the pans and smiled at her and said, "This is one way to get some drinking water. Better get yourself a boudoir staked out, Miz

Sherrel, before all the best suites are gone. Why don't you bunk in with the Dorns? They're in that room there. Maybe you can help a little with those kids."

"I'd be glad to."

"That lady's got her hands full. I'm in this room here with Charlie Himbermark and Steve Malden. The three kids from the truck are in that room, and the newlyweds have got that last room over there. I don't know which is your bags, but you find them and take them in with the Dorns, will you?"

"Yes, Mr. Flagan."

"We got the commissary set up in my room. Cookies and candy and oranges and some coffee. The water'll be in there too. You'll have one of the only two rooms with doors. The newlyweds grabbed onto the other one."

She found her two suitcases and the box in the room where the two boys and the girl from the panel truck were. They were without luggage. The girl lay on the floor, on her back, looking blankly at the ceiling. The younger boy stood at the window, peering through a crack in the blinds. The older one sat crosslegged cleaning his fingernails with a long bladed knife that glittered in the dim light of the room. Virginia Sherrel thought him an odd-looking young man. He had a trim powerful look, but a strange blankness in his face. The features were good, but his eyes were peculiarly expressionless.

"These are my things," she said brightly. "I have to bunk in with the children."

"You wouldn't mean in here, lady," the blond boy said.

She stared at him. "Of course not." The other boy had turned from the window and was staring at her. She was annoyed to find that she was blushing. "In with those Dorn children."

The blond one smiled at her. "Why don't you stay right here with us, lady? We'll tell jokes and sing songs and all that stuff." He managed to give the words a sound of the promise of evil pleasures. His smile was crude and impertinent.

"No thank you."

"Suit yourself, lady."

The girl had turned her head. They all looked at her with much the same expression. A sort of blank obscene amusement. She had planned to make two trips. But she got the box under her right arm and picked up the two heavy suitcases. No one made any offer to help her. She went awkwardly out bearing the heavy load. She was very glad to leave that room.

The door of the Dorns' room was open. The man lay on folded blankets, his eyes shut, his head half turned toward the wall. The woman was shushing the children and struggling with the folding mechanism of the crib. She looked at Virginia Sherrel with an expression of exasperation close to tears. Virginia set her things down and hurried to help the woman. Between them they soon had the crib set up. They introduced themselves in low tones. She was Jean Dorn. She had a pleasant pretty face, drawn with lines of strain.

While Jean put the little girl in the crib, Virginia looked around the room. The room was tiny, no larger than ten by twelve. The Dorns had been carrying a great deal of luggage in the station wagon. The most incongruous item was the set of battered golf clubs in one corner.

"I won't be crowding you too much?" Virginia said.

"No. No, I'm glad you're here. I'm afraid to be alone. You go to sleep, Jan. Please, honey. Stevie, you go back and lie down where I told you."

"How is your husband?"

"He acts so strange. It scares me. He acts as if he hardly knew us. As if he was way way off some place. I can't even tell if he's sleeping or unconscious. When I shake him he mumbles but he doesn't seem to wake all the way up. He ought to be in a hospital." The helpless tears began to run down her face.

Virginia put her arms around her. "Take it easy, Jean. Try to take it easy. We're stuck here but they'll be coming after us as soon as the storm is over. He'll probably be all right."

"He's hurt. He's badly hurt."

Virginia comforted her as best she could. She took her bags into a corner, closed the door, put on jeans, a heavier blouse, a pale blue cardigan. The storm seemed louder, more violent, when the door was shut. She opened the door again. Steve Malden stood in the hallway, talking to Flagan and Himbermark. Steve saw her and motioned her over.

"How is Dorn?" he asked.

"In a sort of stupor. Semi-conscious I guess you'd call it."

"He collapsed when we got him to the head of the stairs," Flagan said. "We had to carry him into the room. Kids okay?"

"She's got them quieted down."

"Now I guess all we have to do is wait it out," Mr. Himbermark said.

Virginia looked at them and knew that Steve hadn't told them his fear that the house would go. She looked quickly at Steve. He said, "That's a better outfit you've got on, Virginia."

She smiled at him. She thought of the house going. She thought of all the worldly goods of the Dorns piled there in the small room. Her smile went away rather quickly and she felt pale.

"Come visit our bachelor quarters a minute, Miz Sherrel," Flagan said. "Got something for you." The three men followed her into the room. Flagan uncapped a thermos and set out the four small plastic cups from inside the cap. He ceremoniously filled each with bourbon. They lifted the plastic cups.

"To a house by the side of the road," Flagan said.

They drank. The bourbon was tepid. It scalded her throat, but spread out within her, bringing its spurious warmth and courage.

"Those three from the truck are strange acting," she said.

"They'll stay right in their room," Steve said.

She stared at him. "Why?"

His smile was odd. "We smell each other," he said.

"What on earth do you mean?"

"As soon as I tried to talk to the older one we smelled each other, Virginia. A scent unmistakable. I smelled a thief and he smelled the law."

She stared at him and felt that it did not fit, that he could not be the law. But as she continued to stare she saw all at once that he was. That he was stamped with it. That it was a part of his strength, and perhaps more. "So that's what you do."

"On a federal level."

"F.B.I.?" Flagan asked.

"No. But I've gone through quite a few of their courses." He didn't offer any further explanation. Virginia lifted the plastic cup to drink the last of the bourbon. At that moment a great fist of wind struck again and the house trembled and seemed to shift. She spilled some of the bourbon and her eyes went wide.

"Jesus!" Flagan said, his head cocked, as though listening for it to happen again.

151

"Johnny!" Himbermark said. "The house is all right, isn't it? Isn't it, Johnny?"

"Shut up, Charlie," Flagan said wearily. He walked over to the window and looked through a fairly wide gap in the boards. It was a gap that kept this room lighter than the others. They saw his heavy back stiffen. He whirled around. "Come take a look at this!" His voice had lost its heavy aplomb. It sounded thinner and younger.

Virginia stood beside Steve when she looked, aware of his comforting bulk beside her. The water had come up. She looked at her car first. It was even with the lower edge of the windows. Scud whipped along the top of the brownish water and small waves slapped at the windows. The fallen tree trunk was covered. She could not see the lead car, the Cadillac, very well. The road was slightly lower there. The water was half way up the windows. The hood was covered. The gleaming roof was above the water, shiny as the wing case of a water beetle.

"Faster than I figured," she heard Steve murmur. He touched her shoulder lightly. "Stick around. I'm going to take a look downstairs."

When Steve reached the foot of the stairs he saw that the water had come into the house. It stood about six inches deep in the room. Wind that came through gaps ruffled the surface of it. When the house shook the tremor of the walls made ripples that met at the middle of the room. In the faint light the water looked black, oily. He decided he would try to estimate the rate of climb. He could see the slight hump on the surface of the water where it was boiling up through the place where the floor boards had rotted away. He looked at his watch, found a mark on the far wall that seemed to be about six inches above the water level. He sat on one of the steps, took out a cigarette and lighted it and began to wait.

As he waited he thought about the Sherrel woman. Damned attractive. All woman. Strong shoulders and good hips and legs. Deep breasts. Handles herself well. Talks well, and has that knack of looking right at you. That could be an artifice. If so, it's a good one, because it gives such a strong flavor of sincerity to her. Dorothy had that same look, the same way of looking right at you, a way that closes out all the rest of the world during the moment that she looked.

Fooled too many times though. It's stupid to try to find a

substitute. They can seem all right at first. But soon you find something wrong. Like Connie. Connie came the closest. Then you found out that was only because she was a born chameleon. She had the knack of sensing what you wanted her to be, and immediately taking on those characteristics. She would take your dream and make herself the fulfillment. After a while you found that there wasn't any real Connie at all. Just a mirror in which you saw what you wanted to see.

He did not think Virginia one of those. But with the suspicion born of loneliness, of too much hurt, he knew that there would be something wrong with this one too— something irremediable. Perhaps she was one of those who has to devour you, to possess every atom of you, to control you utterly. There was that look of strength about her. And her husband had recently killed himself. Maybe after years of her feeding upon him, there was little left to kill. Like the empty husk of the tiny male spider that remains weightless in the web.

Yet he could not talk himself into indifference. She attracted him, both physically and emotionally. He was wary of the standard trap of pure physical attraction. And he sensed that the very oddness of their predicament hastened mutual interest, mutual knowledge. He felt a certain resentment toward her. He felt competent to survive, should the house go. But now, somehow, it had become of great importance to him that she survive also—even if the final end of it was to find that once again he had been mistaken.

Would Dorothy have had her for a friend?

That was one of the easiest tests, the one often used, the test that so quickly eliminated them. This one? Yes. She could have been a friend. He remembered the voice of Dorothy, faint and distant across the years. "One thing I despise is a woman's woman. The bridge club, fund-drive type, completely equipped with claws, talons and meow. They all seem too damned dainty and ominous. I have no point of contact with them. They always make me feel as if I had forgotten my girdle. Give me a man's woman every time, Steve. I can talk to that kind. Because I'm one myself. We're the ones who don't make a kind of warfare out of marriage. We're stupid enough to want to be a wife and a friend both. Oh, not the jolly fishing pal type. But a friend you drink with, horse around with, go to bed in the middle of the afternoon with. We don't think there's something nasty about a roll in the hay. We don't think it's indecent to say exactly what we mean. And—you lucky boy you—we don't have to be constantly petted and fussed over. We work like dogs for you—and like the dogs you are, you don't appreciate us. Until you get married to the other kind."

Virginia Sherrel passed that test quickly and easily. She had the same flavor of frankness and lustiness that Dorothy had had. Yet it could be ersatz.

He did not hear the footsteps on the stairs behind him until they were quite close. The storm sounds had obscured them. He whirled quickly and saw that it was Virginia.

"Hi!" she said. "Jumpy nerves? I was wondering if you'd drowned down here. What are you doing?"

He moved over on the stair to give her room. "Measuring our intake. In another couple of minutes I'll be able to tell you the rate."

She sat beside him and looked at the water. "Good gosh," she said. "Look at it! Wouldn't it be awful if it was your own home, all your things, and you had to watch the water coming up and up?"

"Drowning the television? Sopping into the broadloom?"

"Well, not so much the actual *things* as the feeling of the place. You know. Fireside and everything. And thinking of having to hoe it all out afterward. Gook and slime. Say, it's getting darker, isn't it?"

He looked at his mark. He could barely see it. The water had almost reached it.

"Quite a bit darker."

He listened to the wind sound and heard that it had changed in character. It was less intermittent. It seemed steadier. And the sound had climbed the scale, had moved up another half octave. Within the constant screaming he could hear various soft lost sounds—thumpings and crashings and flappings as though outside there was some great sad imprisoned animal that fought dully for release.

Somewhere upstairs a door banged with a noise like a far-off shot and he thought he heard the tinkling of glass. He felt Virginia shudder and he took her hand, laced his fingers in hers.

She looked down at their hands, barely visible in the gloom. "Silly," she said.

"What is?"

"I'm a big girl now, but it feels awfully damned good to have my hand held."

It was something Dorothy could have said. Would have said under the same circumstances. The mark was touched by the water. He looked at his watch. "It's coming up at the rate of a foot every twenty minutes. But it will slow down."

"How come?"

"For every foot it rises, it has more land to spread over. It takes that much more water."

"Hey, it's getting really dark!"

"I think the bar cloud is coming."

"Bar cloud? What's that?"

"That's the one that means the real business, Virginia." Her face was pale in the darkness of the stairway. She shivered again and her fingers tightened on his.

"Now you're getting me scared again," she said.

On impulse he leaned over awkwardly and kissed her lips. She made no attempt to evade him. He moved slowly so as to give her a chance to turn her head if she so desired. Her lips were warm and soft. She put her arm around his neck and quickly, convulsively, increased the pressure of the kiss and then moved away from him.

"I suppose that's heartening too," she said.

"I guess that's what I meant."

"Once upon a time I was in a hurricane and a man kissed me."

"Virginia, I didn't mean to . . ."

She stood up. "Got to go see how the kids are doing." She went up the stairs. The water had come up to his feet. He had to move up a stair. She had done everything right so far. He felt absurd to be testing her, weighing her. She was Virginia. She should not be measured against preconceived standards. It was an indignity to her to so measure her.

Three strong ones out of the group. Virginia, Flagan and himself. And one old man. And one vulnerable family group. And three mean kids. One very rough looking punk. With all the earmarks. One younger kid, more uncertain, but showing promise of turning out like the older one. And one moronic girl.

It would have to be Virginia and the two small kids. Somehow. Get them together, get them out, stay with them. If the house should go.

Suddenly the quality of the fading daylight changed. It

became much more clear. The room brightened. The wind increased in violence. He was puzzled until he remembered from his reading that visibility becomes crystal clear just before the bar cloud and the worst of the storm arrives.

He decided that he would like to see a bar cloud. It should be visible from the room the newlyweds occupied. He went quickly up the stairs and knocked at their door. The man opened it. The wind sound was now so loud he couldn't hear what the man said. He gestured toward the window. The man nodded. He went to the window and looked west. He saw it approaching, a massive black bar. It looked to be two miles up. It seemed to stretch as far as the eye could reach. It came on inexorably. He sensed the impossible force of the storm, the improbable violence. The look of that bar cloud made you want to grab something solid, close your eyes and hang on. It brought an atavistic fear to him. It made the hair prickle at the nape of his neck.

He turned and looked at the man named Bunny Hollis. The man stood with eyes wide, mouth and throat working, hands washing each other. The young and not very handsome bride went to her man and put her arms around him. He held her and put his head down into the hollow of her shoulder, his eyes shut and his shoulders hunched against an anticipated blow. The girl looked at Steve and there was a mute pleading in her eyes. Perhaps for understanding.

Another strong one, he said to himself, *I miscounted. She has it too, though he hasn't. I hope you make out, he thought. I hope, Mrs. Hollis, that you have strength enough for two. It looks as if you will need it. And soon.*

156

15

"This is Station WAKJ transmitting on standby power. Our power lines went out at a few minutes after five. The time is now six-eighteen. Hurricane Hilda intersected the West Coast of Florida at six o'clock at the mouth of the Suwanee River, moving in an east northeast direction at approximately eight miles per hour.

"Though we have no reports from the area, it is believed that wind damage will be enormous in the area from Adams Beach to Rainbow Point. Lake City and Gainesville can be expected to undergo heavy winds, though not as heavy as at the coast line, since it is predicted that the storm will diminish in fury as it moves inland. It is already estimated that water damage along exposed coastal areas will run into the hundreds of millions. We received one report from Sundown Cove about twenty minutes ago. Because the intersection of the coast line came at a time when the tide would normally be high, water damage is ... well, it's just stupendous. The ham radio report we got said that the municipal pier has been carried away, that all waterfront homes and buildings have been destroyed, that the water has come up so high that huge combers have been breaking in the heart of the town, smashing the shops. The ham radio report said that loss of life has been heavy and that many residents have taken refuge in the bank building and in the Baptist Church.

"Folks, if you are within the range of my voice and you are in the path of this hurricane, take every possible precaution. This is a great calamity. A great tragedy. It will be many days before we know the full extent of the damage. About all we can do is pray for those folks at Stephensville and Steinhatchee, at Horseshoe and Cedar Key and Yankeetown. That's mighty flat land through there. That water is being pushed a long way inland. We've had a report that it's pretty deep across Route 19 in a lot of places.

"Just as soon as the wind makes it possible, planes will be going in there dropping in supplies, and helicopter rescues will be attempted, I'm sure. The Red Cross, of course, will be standing by, ready to go into the area just as soon as they can.

"Here's another report. The eye of Hurricane Hilda has just crossed the town of Wilcox. Wait until I look at my map here. Yes, that would indicate that she has picked up a little forward speed. The report says the winds have diminished a bit. At Wilcox they're down to a little less than a hundred miles an hour. And she seems to have turned a little bit more north, probably enough so that Gainesville will miss the worst of it, although they have winds of gale force there already, with gusts up to seventy miles an hour. As an amateur I'd just be willing to venture a guess that Hilda will keep on turning north and blow herself out somewhere up west of the Okefenokee.

"For those of you who called in before the phone lines went out, I have to tell you that until the emergency period is past we can't use the facilities of this station for messages to loved ones. I'm sorry, but that's the way it is. This is a small violent hurricane and nobody expected her to switch around and come in on us like she did. She really came in. They'll be talking about this one for years. I want to tell you that just about the best thing you can do is stay safe until this goes by, and then get out there and do every doggone thing you can to help those who have really taken it in the neck.

"I'm under orders here to just keep on talking about this thing and give out the reports as they come in. And I can tell that before this night is over I'm going to have to say some things that are going to make me and a lot of people pretty sick at heart. It'll all be built up again. They can't lick us. But they can sure put us back on the ropes for a spell.

"Here's a new one. A navy plane just bucked the heavy winds and followed the coast line all the way up. Visibility is pretty good in the wake of the storm. The pilot reports that the water is so high and came so far inland that he can't pick up the familiar landmarks. The whole coast line looked altered to him. He thinks he located Cedar Key, but he wasn't certain if he had the right place. If he had the right place, it took a whale of a beating. Pretty soon now the tide should drop and we ought to start getting a runoff of all that extra water.

"Right now I'll play a record to sort of cheer you folks up and if anything important comes in, I'll cut the record right off in the middle and let you have it, so keep listening. This is Pete Alderman over at WAKJ operating on standby power broadcasting a running account of Hurricane Hilda as a public service to West Coast Florida."

They own the white houses on the low beaches. Houses with Florida rooms, jalousies, terrazzo floors, cypress paneling. They own the neat yards with protective sea wall, the graceful clump of coconut palm, the silvery punk trees. They claim not to understand the mental processes of Italian peasants who willingly live on the vulnerable slopes of Vesuvius. Yet they have builded their white houses as close as possible to a sleeping giant, to a placid shallow Gulf of Mexico. Gulf front land is the most costly. Their children swim in the safe shallow water, they sieve the small plaid coquina shells from the wet sand, they hunt for the blue-black discarded teeth of sharks—like small arrowheads with serrated edges.

At dusk they sit on their terraces and watch the sun slide down into the slate Gulf, and the glasses are cool in their hands and the west breeze makes a dry rattle in the palm fronds.

Their houses went very quickly.

First came the very slow deep swells that precede the hurricane. Then came the first fitful winds. They were evacuated then, and it seemed like a picnic. Take the jewel box and a few bottles and the portable radio. Board up the picture windows. Move inland to a motel. They had done it before. It was a hurricane party. It was excitement. Come back later and exclaim over the new contours of the beach, the salt-ruined plantings, the forgotten window where the rain had driven in.

This time it was not at all like that.

A house went quickly. The water came up and up until the brute waves could smash directly against the sea wall. The sea wall stood. It stood until the solid water, cresting over it, sucked the fill from behind the wall, sucked it down through small openings in the wall. Soon, without backing, the sea wall twisted and crumpled. When the waves retreated they carried slabs of concrete and left them sprawled on the beach to be picked up by the next wave and hammered against what was left of the wall.

Now the pattern was clear. Each great wave came up, smashed, sucked back what had been torn loose. The fill was pulled from under the terrace. Then it was pulled from under the house. When enough of it was gone, the terrazzo block

159

cracked and sagged under its own weight. The house broke in the middle and sagged into the hole. Furniture slid down toward the place where the spine of the house was broken. Now the waves struck the front of the house itself. They smashed the weakened structure. As each wave pulled back, sucked back out of the shell of the house it brought with it the things from within the house. Bright plastic dishes. An aluminum kitchen chair. Toys. Sodden books. And the next wave would lift, pick up the bright debris and smash against what was left. After the walls went, the roof slid down in one great piece, but was soon lifted, turned, dropped, broken.

Then the way was clear and for a time the waves reached and smashed and wiped the place clean of any sign that a house had been there. But the tide and the wind were increasing and soon the tips of the greatest waves could reach the next line of homes, the homes of the people who either could not afford the Gulf frontage, or had been wary of storms.

In the motels the hurricane parties were gay. Until the portable radios began to bring in the knowledge of the extent of the damage. Then they listened, turning the volume above the wind sound, sitting in the white glare of the gasoline lanterns, laughing no longer.

It struck in greatest violence along the least populated area of the West Coast. It could have as easily struck at the Venice-Sarasota-Bradenton area. Had it done so, damage would have been in the billions. Yet even so the high water caused much damage in that area, and more damage in the St. Petersburg-Clearwater area.

At Sundown Cove the huge combers, slightly flattened by the great winds, swept unimpeded from the Gulf, swept across the area where the municipal auditorium had been, where there had been stores and a supermarket and parking lots—swept across the area they had cleared and smashed against the stone flank of the bank building.

Johnny Flagan drank directly from the bottle and recapped it. He counted the drinks he had had. They seemed to have no effect. He wanted an effect. He wanted a glow of confidence and courage. He wanted to get to the point of where he could stop thinking of water and of swimming. He had never learned how to swim. That was the way the old man had gone. It made him think that after all these years the Gulf was coming in after him, reaching for him.

It wasn't time yet. There was too much to do. Too many things to straighten out. He stood there listening to the fury of the wind and feeling the trembling of the house. He tried to play the game of adding up what he had and what he was worth, but he couldn't keep the figures straight.

"Mister?" The voice was directly behind him. He turned around and saw the blond boy, the good-looking hardfaced kid.

"What's on your mind?"

"Would you come over to our room a minute? My girl friend is acting funny. I think maybe she's sick or something."

Flagan was glad to have something to do. He went down the short hallway and into the room, the young man following him. The girl and the teen-age boy stood by the window, looking at him in a strange way.

Johnny Flagan turned to question the blond one. The door was shut. The blond one stood in front of it. He had a knife in his hand, a knife with a long slim blade. He smiled and waved the blade back and forth.

"What do you think you're doing?" Flagan demanded.

"Take your wallet out and toss it over to the kid."

"Are you out of your head? My God, this isn't the time or the place to be . . ."

"Take it out, dads, or I'll cut you a little. I'll cut you up with this here knife. And move your hand slow when you reach for it."

Johnny studied the boy. The boy didn't look nervous or upset. He seemed to be enjoying himself. There was a certain professional competence about him. Johnny took his wallet out carefully and tossed it behind him.

"Take out the money, Billy. How much?"

After a long silence the younger one said, "Two hundred and twenty."

"That's nice, dads. You carry a nice roll. It goes with that Caddy. Now just move back against the wall over there. That's right. Right there. That's where we want you. Billy, now you go hunt up the old boy that was traveling with dads here and tell him dads wants to see him in here."

The younger boy went out. "What are you planning to do?" Flagan asked.

"Get a little money and get out of here. We're taking off."

"You won't live long out there, kid."

"We'll make out. I've been in blows before."

"Don't take the wallet along. It's got papers in it that are no use to you."

"You telling or asking?"

"I'm asking. As a favor."

"You be nice and I can be nice. Sure. We'll leave it for you. Right out in the front yard."

Flagan cursed him softly. The boy laughed and then gestured with the knife. Flagan closed his mouth. The door opened and Charlie Himbermark came in, wearing his eager please-like-me smile.

"You want to see me about something, Johnny?"

"This kid with the knife wants your money, Charlie."

Himbermark noticed the knife for the first time. He looked at it with severe disapproval. He looked at it the way a school teacher might stare at sloppy homework. "Now see here!" Charlie said with prissy indignation.

"The wallet, Charlie," the boy said. "Just toss it on the floor."

"I most certainly will not," Charlie said firmly.

The boy waved the knife and took a step toward him. "Don't get brave, Charlie. I'll cut you a little."

"You won't cut me at all, young man. And you won't take my money. Who do you think you are, waving a knife around?"

"Watch it, Charlie," Flagan said warningly.

"Are you afraid of this ... this pipsqueak?" Charlie demanded. Flagan looked at Charlie in astonishment. This was an aspect of Charlie Himbermark that he had not anticipated. No situation had arisen that gave any clue to Charlie's physical courage. It bewildered Johnny to find that Charlie had all the defiance and spirit of a scrawny little fighting cock. It was ludicrous, and it was dangerous. Charlie seemed unaware of how dangerous it was.

"Pipsqueak," the blond boy said. He smiled. The knife flickered in the semi-darkness of the room. The boy stepped back. Charlie looked down at the front of his white shirt, at the shallow slice in the fabric and the flesh beneath. Blood began to stain the white shirt.

"Now the wallet, Charlie," the boy said, "before I draw me an X on the front of you."

Charlie stared at the boy. He opened his mouth and made a screeching sound, a thin sound of rage and indignation and sixty-year-old fury. Before Johnny Flagan could say a word,

162

before he had any chance to do anything, Charlie jumped at the boy and grasped the heavy young wrist with his frail fingers, screeching again. The startled boy pulled back, wrenched his arm free, drove the four inch blade into Himbermark's chest, pulled it out, drove it in again and pulled it out and backed away.

It had been many years since Flagan had seen violence. He had never seen violence as quick and brutal. It seemed impossible that it could have happened. And it was so senseless. So meaningless. Such an irritable tawdry way to die. The boy was crouched, the knife ready, the blade no longer gleaming, his face strangely animal in its slackness, blond hair falling across the forehead.

Himbermark stood there, quite dead. He looked down at his shirt and he half lifted his hand as though to brush at the front of himself, the gesture of brushing away lint. He half turned toward Johnny Flagan, the left side of his face illuminated by the pale glow from the shuttered window, the right side in shadow. He looked at Johnny and on his face there was an expression of troubled apology. A self-deprecatory expression. Quite as though he wanted to say, *Look at what I've done now*.

He went down onto his hands and knees and the storm sound concealed the sound of the bony knees striking the board floor. He coughed a small amount of blood onto the floor and then his arms folded slowly so that his face rested in the blood on the floor, his thin backside still canted in the air in the ludicrous position in which infants sometimes sleep. Then he went over onto his side. Flagan went to him, ignoring the knife. He knelt by him and touched his shoulder and wanted to find some words of great apology. He sought one phrase that would make up for everything, make up for a man's whole life. But there were no words.

He turned and looked up at the knife and the eyes behind it. He didn't feel fear. He felt contempt. "You silly young bastard," he said. The knife wavered. It did not strike. They ran for the door, the three of them. Flagan still knelt there. Then with great weariness he got up onto his feet. He tried to listen to them on the stairs. He could not hear them. The wind sound had changed. Underneath the shrillness there was a heavier noise. Like the sound of great freight trains running through resounding caverns. He saw his wallet on the floor and picked it up. The money was gone. On impulse he wedged Charlie's wallet out of his hip pocket and opened it and looked inside. Charlie had nineteen dollars. A ten, a five and four ones.

Steve Malden, looking for Flagan, came out of the room just in time to see the two boys and the girl from the panel truck hurry down the narrow staircase. He hesitated only a moment. He knew with the sure and automatic instinct of the law man that the procedure was to stop them first and find out later why they were running. The water was much further up the staircase. He hesitated for a moment before he waded down into it. They were at the door. They had gotten the front door open. As Malden started toward the front door, the girl, apparently alarmed by the water, tried to pull back. He heard the thin sound of her protest. The younger one pushed her and the blond one pulled her by the wrist and they forced her through the door. The girl looked back toward him, crying out again. Even though she was obviously in terror, her features were too dulled, too indistinct to register fear. She looked like a querulous angry baby.

They went out into the deeper water, and were immediately swept off to the right. Malden reached the doorway. The water inside the house was up to his waist. He held onto the door frame and looked for them. The blond boy was swimming, a long smooth powerful crawl, angling back across the front of the house toward the trees on the far side of the invisible road. The cars were covered by water. Only the radio aerials showed, thin steel wands like some strange water weed.

He saw the other two struggling, their heads close together, arms flailing the water, and he saw that the girl had gotten behind the boy and was clinging to him. Malden took off his jacket and dropped it behind him and dived out through the doorway. He was not a graceful swimmer. He used a short powerful choppy stroke and kept his head high. But it was a stroke he could maintain for a long period of time. The current that swirled around the house was astonishingly strong. It carried him quickly to the two who struggled there. They were both wild-eyed, in panic. The current moved them along rapidly. Malden's knee hit something and he realized that it was the top of one of the cars. He did not know which one.

He pulled the girl free and yelled to the boy to swim back to the house. The girl fought to wrap her arms around him.

Malden levered her back, waited until he had the right opportunity, then hit her sharply with his fist on the point of the chin. She went loose in the water, eyes glazed. He turned her around and got his hand under her chin. The blond boy had reached the trees on the far side. Malden heard his thin hail over the wind roar. He struggled against the current, towing the girl. He fought with all his strength toward one of the radio aerials. He reached it, grasped it, got his knees against the car top and rested there, breathing hard, the girl trailing out in the water in the current behind him.

He looked around. The blond one was holding onto a tree. The younger boy was swimming doggedly toward the other boy, swimming diagonally against the current. His progress was painfully slow. Malden watched him, fascinated. He saw the boy's arms moving more slowly, saw him stay even with the current for a few minutes, and then begin to lose ground. He began to thrash in panic. Had he swum with the current, there were trees he could reach. He was swept away into the gloom. Malden saw one arm upraised and then nothing but the boiling surface, the wind-swept scud. He looked over at the other one. They looked at each other across the dark water. Then the other boy turned and started swimming strongly toward another group of trees further from the house. Within moments he was out of sight.

Malden began swimming again, toward the house. He fought the current. He counted the heavy strokes in his mind, savoring each inch that he gained. He determined not to swim to the limit of his strength, but to save some should he have to turn and find other shelter. The girl was a dragging weight. Yet he gained slowly.

The cramp came suddenly. It jackknifed his right leg. The pain could have been no more sharp if the muscles were being torn from his leg. He released the girl. He took a deep breath and doubled up in the water and kneaded the knotted calf with all the strength of his hands. When his face rolled to the surface he took another breath and began kneading again. He felt the tension slowly relax. Within a minute and a half of the time the cramp had struck he could swim again. He lunged as high out of the water as he could, looking for the girl. He could not see her. He was tempted to swim back and see if he could locate her. But he felt that there was little endurance left. He turned back toward the house again, swimming slowly but cautiously, favoring the leg. Slowly he came closer to the house. The current seemed stronger there. It flowed inland from the Gulf, sweeping around the house.

He watched the corner of the house. He was not gaining an inch. He felt panic. He had used up too much of his strength. There was not enough left to turn back, to try to gain the safety of the trees. He saw her in the doorway, saw Virginia standing in water above her waist, holding onto the door frame, watching him, calling to him. He could not hear her. He called on some deep resource and was able to swim again with all his strength. The corner of the house came closer. He moved slowly toward her. She held onto the door frame and reached out to him. With one last convulsive effort, the last effort of which he was capable, he surged forward the last foot and reached out and caught her slim wrist. She pulled him strongly to the safety of the doorway. He caught the door frame and pulled himself inside. He was able to stand. There did not seem to be enough air in the world to fill his lungs.

She half supported him as they waded across the room, felt for the stairs, found them, climbed above the water level. He sat heavily, panting, head bowed. When he looked at her, trying to smile at her, he saw the tears on her face.

"I . . . I lost her."

"I know. I saw it. I thought you were both . . . gone."

"Cramp. I let her go before I thought. Then she . . . was gone. Saw them running down the stairs. Thought I ought to stop them. Couldn't do it. Why were they running? Why did they go out in that? Two of them drowned."

"They killed the man with Mr. Flagan. The older man named Himbermark. They killed him with a knife."

He stared at her. "Killed him?"

"For his money. He wouldn't give it to them."

He forced himself to his feet. "I better go up and see what I can do."

She stood up beside him. "I'm glad you made it back, Steve. I'm terribly glad. If I saw you couldn't, I was going to come after you."

He looked at her and saw that she meant it, saw how she meant it, and felt very proud and very humble. He felt the sting of tears in his own eyes. He put his arms around her and held her close. They stood on the stairs in their soaked clothes and held each other tightly and it seemed a very good moment to them.

He lifted his head. The wind had become deep-throated, thunderous. The house trembled, shifted, tilted. He stopped breathing. The moment did not continue. It had turned and tilted and wedged itself in a new position. The stairway was slightly canted.

"It's here!" he shouted to her, over the roar. "Here's the worst of it."

They went up the stairs. Just as they reached the top the northwest corner of the roof was wrenched off. The newly-weds came stumbling into the hall. The blare of wind was deafening in the exposed hallway. He looked at the torn edge of roof. He saw another section twist and rip free. He held the woman tightly and braced his back against the hallway wall and waited.

Frank Stratter had clung to the tree and watched Torris drown. Billy went under with the money from Flagan's wallet still in his pocket. That had been a tactical error. But there had been no time to transfer the money.

Stratter had had no idea that the water had gotten so deep, that the currents would be so strong. It was like being caught in an incoming tide. He saw the big man trying to save the girl, trying to tow her back to the house. Stratter felt uneasy. Some of his confidence had gone when the old man had jumped at him, grabbed at him, screeching. The look Flagan had given him, kneeling there in the gloom, had diminished his confidence further. And finally the astonishing strength and depth of the water had shaken him.

He looked back toward the house, the wind like a weight against his face and shoulders. All the world was gray, the roof corners of the house almost indistinguishable against the inky racing clouds. Spume stung his cheeks and the current tugged at his legs. He turned and looked the other way, saw trees fifty yards farther, let go and swam toward them with the current, saving his strength, keeping himself afloat, letting the current carry him on. The wind was so strong that it had an odd effect. Low as he was in the water it seemed to catch at him and thrust him along. He sensed that the wind had grown stronger since he had been in the water. There was a deep note in the heart of it, like the constant bowing of a string on a bass.

He reached the trees and held to them and rested for a few moments and then went on. Soon it would be dark. He wanted to reach the main road before full dark. He suspected that it would be higher, high enough so that he could get out of the water. It should not be over another half mile away. He could barely see another clump of trees ahead. Pines. They were slightly to the side and he swam toward them. When it looked as though he would be carried by them, he swam as strongly as he could and reached them. He held on to a tree on the east side of the cluster, a tree a foot in diameter. He shook the water out of his eyes and looked above him and saw two soaked miserable raccoons on a limb in silhouette against the lesser darkness of the sky.

He began to feel confident again. It was a good possibility that none of those back in the house would survive. Even should the one named Malden rescue the girl and learn his name, he would not live to tell. When the water finally went down they would find the truck, the other bodies, and suppose that he too had drowned. It would come out all right. Everything had always come out all right. You used your head and took the breaks and things always worked out.

He hooked his right leg around the tree and turned and looked east, looking for the next group of trees, the next stopping place. It was getting dark. All this water and the darkness like the end of the world. It had been the end of the world for Billy Torris.

The sudden heavy pressure against his right ankle made him cry out in sudden fright. He grasped the tree with his arms and yanked hard, but he could not free himself. He could not understand what had happened. Then he saw the altered angle of one of the other trees. The rush of water had loosened the soil around the roots. The wind and the current had canted the tree over until it rested at an angle against the tree to which he clung. The two trunks met about four feet below the water level, imprisoning his leg between them, locking it just above the ankle.

He made himself take a series of slow deep breaths. He thought it out and saw a way he might free himself. He locked his arms around the trunk of the tree, raised his left leg and got his left foot planted firmly against the trunk of the tree that had tipped. Slowly he exerted his strength until he was blinded by the effort and he could hear a red roaring in his ears. His shoulders popped and creaked and the cords of his throat stood out. At his maximum effort he felt a tiny diminishing of the pressure on his leg. He tried to rip it free. It moved a few inches and then the larger tree moved and settled more firmly against his. He felt the ankle socket go, a slow inexorable crackling, as of a soft round stone caught in the slow turning of a vise.

He screamed with the pain and screamed again and the world blurred and he sagged into the water. The water revived him and he lifted his head again, coughing the water out of his throat. He made himself be calm again. It took longer. He took a deep breath and went under, twisting himself awkwardly against the current down to where he could feel the leg where it went between the two trunks. It felt sickeningly flat. He tore at the bark with his fingers. He felt how the leg was caught in a sort of inverted V, and had he pulled down instead of wrenched upward when he felt the first pressure, he might well have freed himself.

He thought of what could happen. The tree might shift again, releasing him. He sensed that he was bleeding. He might faint and drown. He tried to think of what he should do. He could take off the purple shirt and use the knife and cut a strip for a tourniquet, and fashion another longer strip into a sort of sling and tie himself to the trunk so that should he faint, his head would stay above water. But suppose his own tree should go while he was tied there? The thing to do was keep the knife handy, ready to cut himself free.

As he started to take off the shirt, he was annoyed by the wind-driven crests breaking into his face. He tried to hitch himself and realized that he could not. He stared at the trunk and up at the limbs and as he realized that the water was getting higher, panic came quickly. He fought hard, exhausting himself quickly, sobbing aloud as he fought. The trees were as unmovable as pillars of concrete. He rested for a time. The water was higher. He had to keep his chin tilted up in order to breathe.

With his head uptilted, he could see the thin shadows of the two raccoons. Animals would sometimes gnaw off a leg to escape a trap. He thought of his knife again. He took it out of his pocket and it slipped out of his trembling fingers and was gone. He looked woodenly upward. He sobbed again and hugged the rough trunk and tried to tear his leg free. The effort did not last long. From then on he struggled to breathe, straining up for each precious quarter inch of height, holding his breath when the chop broke over his face.

JOHN D. MACDONALD

Several times he sucked in water and was able to expel it
and find air. He held the trunk as high as he could reach. He
thought that this could not be happening. It was not a true
thing. Then he could find no more air. He expelled water
and breathed in water and it filled his lungs. His lungs
worked in spasms, sucking in and expelling the alien element,
and he strained upward, and his eyes were wide open under
the water. The lungs quieted and his hands slipped and the
world faded quietly away from him. Caught there, his body
trailed out in the current, three feet below the surface. When
both trees went slowly down together, he was released and
the current moved the body inland. The two raccoons swam
sturdily toward other refuge, eyes alert in the bandit faces.

170

16

When the house shifted and turned and caught again, Flagan lifted his head and waited. He got to his feet. The house was steady again, but it was a precarious steadiness. He got to his feet and walked heavily into the hallway. It was tilted enough so that it was difficult to walk there. His right shoulder kept thudding against the wall. It was not that the slant was steep. He remembered a house at an amusement park long ago, and how Babe had giggled as she tried to go up the stairs. When a house was just a little off line, it affected your balance.

He had felt a curious lethargy since the death of Charlie Himbermark. It had made his own focus, his special interests, less intense. It had made him feel ridiculous and unimportant. It had made him feel as if it were important for him to explain something about himself to a disinterested bystander. Perhaps to Ruth. Explain himself carefully to that dark still face. It was incongruous to think of her. And he did not know what it was that he would tell her. Perhaps just say, *I am me. I am Johnny Flagan and I am older than I had thought.* Charlie's death had seemed to uncover an area of gray weariness, the way a bandage might be taken from a wound that could not be healed. He wondered if he would walk on the streets again, waving, smiling, talking to friends. If so, it would not be quite the same. *Why should the death of Charlie have such an effect,* he wondered. *Charlie was a nothing. An incompetent, irritating old man. Or am I just more aware of my own death? Aware of its inevitability even should I survive this monstrous roaring thing. Aware of this sagging much-used flesh, of broken blood vessels, of matronly belly and breasts. I who was so strong. Work the nets all day and tom-cat all night and be out there again in the pale morning, watching for the leap and flash of the mullet.*

He heard the scream then. The long unforgettable scream of anguish and loss. It came from the room where the Dorns were. As he went in he felt the wrench and roar as part of the roof was torn away, felt the thrust of the unimpeded wind on his back that pushed him into the room.

Both children were crying, their voices inaudible in the storm. The Dorn woman lay half across her husband. Flagan went over to her and looked at the man's still face, at the trickle of blood which had run from his left ear, and understood. He felt an overwhelming tenderness for this woman he did not know. He gently pulled her away from her husband. He had to reach around the back of the man's neck to pry her right hand loose. When he did so he inadvertently touched the top of the man's head and felt the queasy shift of the loose bone at the crown of his head. He thought, wonderingly, *We're not lasting well. Not well at all. We're going one at a time here.* The woman strained back toward the body on the floor, then turned into Flagan's arms, trembling violently. He held her and wondered that he now held a woman he did not know, yet held her without lust, without need. Held her because she was afraid. Because they were both afraid.

There was another screeching, ripping sound, a faint thumping overhead. With his mouth close to the woman's ear he said, almost shouting, "The kids! You got to look after the kids!" He repeated it and for a long time he thought he hadn't reached her. Then she pulled away, not looking at him, and went to her children. The house shifted a little, less than before. He went over and pulled one of the blankets from underneath the man and spread it over him. The wind flapped it and tried to pull it away, but Flagan knelt heavily and tucked the edges under the body, wondering as he did so what sort of man this had been, this lean dark man with the tired face. It made him feel like a man of God to be performing this small service. He wished he knew words he could say.

As he straightened up he became aware of a new sound, a repeated thudding that shook the house, a thud that seemed to come at three- or four-second intervals. With each thud the house trembled. He looked at the woman and saw that she had heard it too. She knelt there, an arm around each child, looking at him, her head cocked to one side.

Flagan left the room hurriedly.

Betty Hollis watched her husband for a few moments, then

stepped forward and slapped him as hard as she could, as hard as she could swing her arm. It hurt her hand. The blindness did not go away. She swung again and again. She stopped and looked at him. He came out of it like a person coming out of sleep. He looked at her and the madness of panic was gone from his eyes. His mouth worked. He looked ashamed. Her fingers had left white stripes on his cheek, stripes that were quickly changing to dark red.

She looked at him and she wanted to cry. She knew that if they lived, they would stay together. But the best part of it was over. They would stay together because he would not give up the money, and she would not give him up. But the good part was gone. She remembered a kind of candy she had always liked. It was from France. It came in a metal box and each piece was individually wrapped. You could tell what each piece was by the shape of it inside the tin foil wrappings. Her favorite had been the coffin-shaped pieces usually wrapped in green foil. They had bitter-sweet chocolate on the outside, and the inside was of chopped cherries in a sweet heavy liqueur. Once she had purchased three boxes out of her allowance. They were expensive. A school friend had gone up to her room while she was out, had opened every box and eaten every one of the special pieces. Every one.

She remembered that she had eaten all the rest of the candy in the boxes, but she had eaten it with sadness and regret and muted anger.

Now, in this marriage, the very best part was gone. They would both know that. It would color all the rest of it. He would forever be aware of her knowledge that he was something less than a man. It would change him like slow poison, and it would change their lovemaking. She knew she could never forget this scene, this horrid, babbling, jittering breakdown, this hulk of tan muscle with the wild scared eyes of a child. The hint of timidity, so long as he had kept his pride, had been endurable, even rather sweet. But breakdown was something far different. It was strange that it could not be excused, forgiven, forgotten. From now on it would be less a marriage of woman and man, more a marriage of woman and child. He had lost the right to demand possession. He could only beg for it, with humbleness.

But, diminished as he was, she still wanted all that was left of him. She saw the shame in him. She let him move close and put his arms around her. "Betty ... "

She let him talk into her ear. She listened to the explanation. She did not give it her full attention. She was thinking of what they could do to assure safety. And she listened to the odd thudding sound that was making the whole house tremble, an evisceral trembling, as of a home built near the tracks of a railroad where a train went endlessly by.

Steve Malden stood in the half shelter of the west wall of the bedroom and looked through the window hole where shutters and glass and frame had been. The room was open to the sky. The house was tilted to the east at about a six degree angle, he estimated. The water was perhaps a foot below the second floor level. It did not seem possible that it could come higher.

He saw movement and a flash of light behind him. Flagan came in with a flashlight. He turned it off as he neared the window. The sky was lighter in the west. A thrust of wind caught Flagan and he moved aside, away from the window, stood close to Malden. Together they looked out at the water. The water had come high enough, and enough trees had gone down so that the water was getting an almost unimpeded path. With such an open sweep the wind had picked up the water into waves now big enough to crest had not the wind kept the crests flattened. The waves thudded against the west wall of the house with stubborn regularity.

Flagan put his mouth close to Malden's ear and yelled, "Last much longer?"

"Not with that going on."

"Dorn is dead."

Malden looked at Flagan, saw the unexpected look of grief in the man's eyes. Flagan no longer looked like the man who had taken charge. He looked incapable of the exercise of authority. Not so much disheartened as uninterested. Malden wondered if the change in attitude had been due to the death of Himbermark. The two men had not given the impression of being very close.

"Let's get everybody together," Malden yelled into his ear. "Get some kind of a tool to get the doors off. Tear boards loose and find something to tie them together with. Neckties. Anything."

The house shuddered again. The two men staggered and looked at each other and waited a moment, then headed for the door, each of them walking with odd caution, as though too heavy a footfall might be the last impetus needed to send the house sprawling and rolling into the current.

The only room still completely roofed was the one assigned to the Hollises. The eight of them gathered there. Malden closed the door. Though he still had to speak very loudly, it was relatively quiet. He turned the flashlight on the faces of the adults in turn.

"The house is going to go. I don't know how soon. We've got to get hold of anything that will float. Bring it in here. Kick the shutters off that side window and be all ready for it. Mrs. Dorn will stay right here with the kids. The rest of us work. We have no tools. Do what you can."

He looked at them again, at the frightened eyes. The Dorn woman looked dulled, apathetic. The Hollis man looked dazed. The smash of the water against the side of the house seemed stronger. But he could almost believe that the wind violence was less. If not less, at least it maintained the same steady raw-voiced note. He did not believe that it could have blown any harder than it was blowing ten minutes ago.

"Virginia, you and Mrs. Hollis gather up anything we can use as rope. Go through luggage. Anybody's. The men gather boards and doors. Okay. Let's move fast."

He saw at once that Hollis was not going to be of much help. He seemed afraid to go into the exposed hall. Flagan went to work at once. Steve went to the room the Dorns had been in. He closed the door and then hurled himself at it until he had broken the hinges free of the old wood. He took the door back to the Hollis room. The wind, swirling down into the open hallway, made it difficult to handle. He found Flagan in the room with Himbermark's body. Flagan was straining to rip up floor boards. Steve helped him, trying to keep the long boards from breaking as they pulled them up. It was too dark below to see where the water was, as it had covered the lower windows. Steve directed the flashlight beam down and saw the black surface of the water about eighteen inches below them. A palm tree rat swam there, eyes red in the beam.

He and Flagan carried the load of boards back. There were four flashlights. One of them was the type with a standard. It rested on the floor, the beam illuminating a corner. The three women knelt there with the two children, tying makeshift life belts to them. They were using belts and neckties from the luggage, and as floats they were using what watertight containers they had found among Jean Dorn's

175

household goods—a pressure cooker, cannisters, jars with screw tops.

Steve looked at them. It was a tableau demonstrating the eternal resiliency of women. He could hear their voices faintly above the wind, the thin nervous gay cajoling tone with which they tried to still the children's fears, tried to make a game of it. It was a timeless tableau, because there had always been women and children and flood water. He looked at the curve of Virginia's cheek in the yellow light, looked at the shape of her mouth, and loved her.

He put the boards down and went to the window and kicked the shutters loose, reached through, wrenched them off, pulled them into the room. The small amount of daylight left paled the flashlights. Dark water raced by.

As he started to look about to find something to lash the boards together, the house lurched again. It tilted at a greater angle, then seemed to stop. But Malden felt that it was still moving, very slowly, but moving. He knew it would go within moments.

He yelled at Flagan and took one of the doors and slid it through the window at an angle. He reached down over the sill and held it in the current. Flagan threw two boards onto it, but one of them was carried away.

Virginia came over quickly with the small girl, pushing Jean Dorn ahead of her. Jean hesitated. Steve thrust her through the window. She caught the door, held it as it tipped and nearly rolled her off. Virginia lowered the child to her and the woman managed to grasp the child. The buoyancy of the door would support no more. The strain on his hand was great. Jean screamed for the boy to be given to her. Steve released the door. It moved swiftly away on the current, the woman still staring at him, mouth open with her scream as the current turned the door, swirled it away, carried her off into the darkness.

The house tilted further, and Steve could feel the creaking and rending of the timbers of the frame. The new angle brought the water swirling into the room over the sill of the window. The small boy was yelling with terror. Flagan got the other door over to the window. Hollis thrust between Flagan and Malden, two heavy floor boards in his arms. One of the boards swung in the wind and hit Steve across the side of the head. He made an angry grasp for Hollis but the man was gone, moving quickly away into the night.

"Please!" the Hollis girl was screaming at him. "Please!"

He let her go. She slid into the current, holding a single board, and as she disappeared he saw that she held her head high, looking ahead for her husband.

Virginia went on the door, quickly and without protest, supporting the small boy, giving Steve Malden one long direct look just before he released the door, half smiling as she went, leaving him with the memory of that half smile, of her dark water-pasted hair, the small boy safely in the crook of her arm, her firm brown hand holding the edge of the door as she lay across it.

The house moved quickly. The board floated within the room, moving toward the window. The house had tipped until water filled almost the whole frame, leaving only the top right corner clear. Flagan held a clump of boards with panic grip. Malden thrust him through the window and as he turned to grasp the two remaining boards, the house went over. He took a deep breath and felt the wallowing, elephantine roll of the house. He thrust for the window, but in the turn of the house he had lost his sense of direction. His fingers touched rough solid wall. He felt along it. The house was moving, grinding, bumping. He felt in increasing panic for the window.

Then the house lost, all at once, the form and structure of a house. It was crushed and became broken flotsam. He was caught for a moment between unseen things that pressed against him from either side. Then he was free and he came to the surface. When he tried to swim something thudded against his shoulder from behind, threatening to push him under. He rolled and caught the edge of a huge section of roof, and pulled himself onto it. It was more than buoyant enough to support him. He crouched at the leading edge, staring forward, saw the dim shapes of tree tops coming toward him. The roof caught against the trees, swung slowly around and moved on.

It was now obvious that the wind was less violent. It was thinner, without the deep resonant notes. He moved to the center of the piece of roof and cautiously stood erect. He looked back toward the west. There was a low line of dark red fire across the horizon, the last glow of a moody sunset. In the slight path it made across the water he saw a struggling figure. He dived without hesitation, swam to the child, and by using all the power of his free arm managed to regain the section of roof.

He saw that it was the boy child, the one called Stevie, the one who had been with Virginia. He looked at the water. He could see nothing. He sat in the center of the piece of roof and held the trembling sobbing child. His raft wedged against something, moved, wedged itself more tightly. He did not investigate to see what had halted the raft. He sat and held the child. The roof piece shivered as the current touched it. The boy stopped sobbing. The red glow faded and it was night and he waited.

17

By dawn on the eighth of October, Thursday morning, Hurricane Hilda was blowing herself out in south central Georgia.

She had pushed great tides against the west coast of Florida. Never in the recorded history of the state had the sea come so far inland. The record was set in Hernando and Citrus counties where, due to the low level of the land, salt water came as far as seventeen miles inland.

It was estimated that the farthest highest point of the water was reached at approximately eleven o'clock on Wednesday night. By then the winds were gone. The water stood placid on the land for a time, and then began to move back toward the Gulf, slowly at first, and then with increasing speed and violence. It was augmented by the heavy runoff of hurricane rainfall. The night skies cleared and the stars came out, and the black water ran off the land into the Gulf.

Hurricane Hilda was gone, but it seemed as though the runoff was the final instance of her madness. Weakened structures collapsed into the current. Debris was swept far into the Gulf.

By eight o'clock in the morning a warm sun shone down on the steaming coast, on silted ruined buildings, on bodies half buried in sand, on bright automobiles tumbled together like forgotten toys. The earliest estimates were ninety to a hundred dead, two thousand homeless, damage in the hundred millions. The governor appealed immediately to have the area classified as a disaster area.

Weary people walked down streets no longer familiar to them, and looked at the places where they had lived. They reacted in many ways. With tears, with curses, with heavy silent dejection. And there were many who began at once to put things back together again, attacking the sand in the living room with a scoop shovel, tossing it out through the holes where windows had been.

179

Disaster teams moved into the area, searching for the bodies, making identification where possible, listing survivors, co-ordinating their efforts with jeep radios. Water trucks were brought in. Medical teams were flown in. Helicopters flapped slowly over the area, reporting their findings by radio.

This was morning after. This was hangover after debauch. As with the lesser variety of hangover, time was the only cure. And it would be a long time before the coast looked as it had before, with the white houses smiling in the sun above the blue Gulf, with the cool drinks on the terraces, the children playing in the sand.

The six cars marooned on the temporary detour were reported by a helicopter pilot at eight-thirty on Thursday morning. He said they were between two ruined bridges, and near the foundations where a house had been.

Two men in khakis walked in to the cars just before noon, a tall one and a short one, neither of them young. They had been at work since dawn, and they had lost, through fatigue, the capacity to be sickened at what they saw.

They stood and looked at the cars. The short one took out a sweat-damp pocket notebook and began copying the license numbers. "Be hell getting those cars out of here," the tall one said. "Have to fix one of the bridges first, and bring in a chain saw and get the timber out of the way."

The short one put the notebook away. A station wagon and a panel delivery truck were tilted on their sides. The other cars were erect, mud silted high against the wheels. "High water mark is about six feet over the car roofs. We better look around," he said.

They found the first body quickly. It was at the base of a tree, the body half curled around the trunk where the water had left it. The tall one turned her over with his foot. He examined the body.

"No identification."

The fat one wrote in his book. "Female, about sixteen," he said aloud. "Maybe five three. Heavy set. What color hair would you say, Andy?"

"I'd say brown."

"Let's put her over by the bridge. Get 'em out by boat will be the easiest way."

"If anybody can find a boat left," the tall one said.

A hundred yards downstream from where the house had

been they found two more, quite close together. A young one with a crushed leg. An old man with white hair.

"Look at here, Will! This old boy got himself knifed, I think."

They examined the wounds, talked it over, wrote down the description of the young man, the name and address of the old man. They carried the two bodies back and put them beside the body of the young girl. They ranged the area in widening circles and found one more body. The tall one turned it over, patted the sodden hip pocket, felt the wallet and took it out, read off the name on the smeared indentification card.

"How do you spell that last name?"

"F-L-A-G-A-N. Flagan."

"Okay, I got it. Jesus, he looks heavy."

They each took an ankle and dragged the body. It was a long distance. They looked down at the four of them.

"That isn't enough for six cars," the short one said.

"They could have been washed a long way from here, Will. We better go back and report and tell them about these four and the cars and all. We can come back with more people and cover a bigger area. Come on."

Andy looked back one time when they started out. He was too far away to see the bodies clearly. They could have been almost anything. Logs. Old bundles.

It was about a half hour after first light when the National Guard truck picked Steve Malden and Stevie Dorn up on Route 19 and drove them to Otter Creek where a rescue station had been set up.

A brisk young Red Cross woman worker whose kind eyes and sensitive mouth belied her officious manner interviewed Malden. He gave her his name and address.

"And this is your boy?"

Steve frowned at her and shook his head. The woman understood and called another worker to come and take the child. The boy hung back. "It's okay, Stevie," Malden said. "You go along with her. I'll see you in a few minutes."

When Stevie was gone he said to the woman, "That's a good kid. His name is Stevie Dorn. They were a family of four. They were headed north, moving out of Florida. I know the father is dead. I think his name was Harold. The wife's name was ... is Jean. And there's a little girl, younger than the boy, named Jan. Probably Janice."

"Were you traveling with them, Mr. Malden?"

"No. Could I have some of that coffee? I'll tell you how it happened."

The woman got him some coffee. He sipped it and said, "Are you keeping a list of the people who come through here?"

"Yes. It isn't alphabetical yet. I'm sorry, I'll have to finish this later. There's another truck load coming in."

He walked over to the truck. He knew no one who was on it. He saw a woman with a crudely splinted arm, tears running endlessly down her still remote face. He walked around the area and found a place where clothing was being doled out. He was issued khaki trousers and a clean faded blue work shirt. He changed in a dressing room for men made of blankets suspended from ropes between trees. He realized that he had never felt more weary in his life. The day had that glazed look that comes with exhaustion. A look of bright shimmering unreality. He did not permit himself to think about Virginia Sherrel.

The boy came racing over to him, too excited to be coherent. He tugged at Steve's hand. Steve went along with him. Army cots had been set up in the back of a garage. Jean Dorn was there with the little girl.

"Stevie says you brought him out, Mr. Malden."

He ruffled Stevie's hair. "We went floating on a roof together. We had a big time. Did you have any trouble?"

"Just at first. It was hard to hang on. Then the water was calmer. When we started to drift back it was shallow enough to wade. I carried Jan to the road and we waited there until daylight. Did ... did anyone else get out?"

He looked at her and looked away. "Not that I know of. I'm sorry about your husband, Mrs. Dorn."

She had her arm around the little girl. She looked up at him and said, "I am lucky, Mr. Malden. I'm still a lucky woman."

He went back and watched the trucks coming in. As more refugees arrived the area became a scene of confusion. Many were doing as he was doing, walking back and forth, looking for someone. Many were calling out the names of those they sought. When he listened he could hear the constant sound of those callings, all over the area, a mingling of sound like an atonal chant.

He shaped her name with his lips but did not say it aloud.

When he found the Hollis couple they were in the center of a small group. A sound truck was parked nearby. A man with a hand mike was interviewing them. They had been given fresh clothing. They looked surprisingly clean and rested. Steve, curious, moved closer.

"So you'd say it was pretty rough, Bunny?"

Bunny gave his athlete's grin. "Rough all right. I didn't think we were going to make it. The water really came up. We took shelter in an old house and watched it come right up over the top of our car. When it looked as though the house was going to go, we ripped up old floor boards. We floated out on them." He pitched his voice more deeply and said, "This is a terrible thing for these people living in this area. I want to say that I think the Red Cross is doing a marvelous job here."

"What are the plans for you and your bride, Bunny?"

"Well, I think we'll stay around a little while. Help out if we can. We're both going to volunteer to help. Then we'll see what can be done about getting our car out. Betty here lost her whole trousseau, you know. Every darn stitch."

"I guess it was a frightening experience for both of you."

Bunny shrugged. "I can tell you it made me pretty nervous." He put his arm around Betty and smiled down at her.

"Thank you, Bunny Hollis. The fans in the radio audience who followed you during your tennis career are, I'm sure, glad to know you came through this disaster in good shape. Thank you very much. Now, sir, if I could have your name."

Steve walked up to the Hollises as they left the group around the interviewer. Betty left Bunny and walked directly to him and held out her hand and said, "Thanks, Steve. Thanks for ... more than I can say."

"Have you seen Virginia Sherrel?"

She looked at him closely. "No, Steve. Not yet. We saw Mrs. Dorn and her little girl. They haven't found the little boy yet."

"I brought the boy out."

"But I thought Virginia was going to ..." She stopped as she began to understand.

Bunny said, in too palsy a fashion, "We really had ourselves a time in there, Malden. I figured on waiting outside the window to help the others out, but the current was too ..."

Betty said, with all the weariness in the world, "For goodness sake, Bunny, shut up. Just shut up. Don't talk. Good-by, Steve. I hope you find Virginia soon."

He watched them walk away. The man walked beside the woman. There was something servile in the way he walked, in the way he gesticulated as he talked to her, explaining something. She walked with her back straight and her head high, apparently paying no attention to what he was saying. He watched them walk and imagined that he could see all the rest of their marriage, see all their future history. And it would not be pretty. Because Betty had been there with him and had seen what had happened. Had Bunny been with strangers it would be only a matter of weeks before he would begin to believe, with all sincerity, that he had been the one who had held the group together, who had helped the others. But she had seen and her innate honesty would be the barrier he could never surmount.

He was given food at the field kitchen, but he had little appetite for it. The Red Cross woman found him and he listed the people who had been marooned with him. He gave the names, as well as he could remember them. He explained the death of Dorn, and then told about the knifing of Himbermark. She sent him to the field headquarters of the state police to tell them about Himbermark.

He identified himself, told his story, was questioned closely, and promised to phone in his local address as soon as he could find one.

At two in the afternoon the area was packed. People had come in from all directions, looking for the missing, maintaining a hope that grew more forlorn as the hours passed.

Though sodden and drugged with weariness, he kept moving, watching, hoping.

He stood for a time, big legs planted, fists on his hips, a strong man with a tired face, a dogged look, his eyes moving from face to face in the crowd. They had let him look at the lists. He could not find her name. Tomorrow he would go back and search the area, every square foot of it.

A hand caught convulsively at his elbow and spun him half around and he caught a glimpse of Virginia's face, close to his, a face twisted oddly with joy and tears. Then she was in his arms and he held her strongly, held the trembling

184

body, held in his arms the half coherent words. He stood with tears in his eyes, grinning like a fool, looking out over the heads of the crowd, and then he realized that this scene of reunion could very well be heartbreak to many of those who watched them. He turned her gently and led her away from the others, led her over to a motel that was serving as Red Cross headquarters, led her around the corner of the building and tilted her chin up and kissed her.

"Steve," she said. "Oh, Steve, I've been looking for you for so very long. Steve, the boy, I . . . I lost him. The door tipped over. I lost him. I'm sorry. I . . . just couldn't . . ."

"He's safe. I've seen him with his mother and his sister. I brought him in. The three of them are safe. And the Hollises."

"And Mr. Flagan?"

"I don't know."

They looked at each other, warmly, joyfully, intimately. She surprised him by blushing and looking away. He took her by the shoulders and made her look at him again.

"Virginia?"

"Yes, Steve?"

He shook her gently, impatiently. "There's no words."

She smiled. "There will be."

He shut his eyes and teetered a moment and caught himself. He smiled and said, "I'm bushed."

"Let's find a place where you can sleep. Then I'll go see what I can do to help Jean."

A tent had been put up for a men's dormitory. They found it and she took him to the door of the tent. "Don't let me sleep too long. Send somebody in to get me up in an hour. Promise."

"I promise," she lied. She kissed him lightly.

She watched him go into the tent. She walked toward the garage where he had told her she would find Jean and the kids. She thought of Steve and thought how dangerous and how convulsive a way it was to become so closely involved with another human being. This closeness achieved through danger seemed to have been achieved too readily. Yet when she tested it, tasted it, it seemed good. Valid. A relationship as sure and positive as though it had grown through months of intimacy. Maybe the thing was that they each knew what the other one was. Knew the things of the spirit. Saw the results of stress.

She paused in the early afternoon sunlight. The sky was a

bright clear blue. The air was washed clean. She thought of the woman who had driven north with the ashes. It seemed like quite another woman. A stranger, whose motives could not be understood.

She fought back her own weariness and went into the garage, into the plaintive sound of tired small children, the weary voices of many mothers, and the monotonous tin voice of a small radio that recounted, endlessly, the imposing statistics of disaster.

>>> If you've enjoyed this book and would like to discover more great vintage crime and thriller titles, as well as the most exciting crime and thriller authors writing today, visit: >>>

The Murder Room
Where Criminal Minds Meet

themurderroom.com